"Freeze, lady!"

The coarse male voice cut through the silence, and Lisa found herself pinned in the blinding glare of a flashlight. "Police! On your feet! Hands on the counter!"

A heavyset figure silhouetted in the light filtering through the living-room blinds lumbered toward her, and the ugly shape of a revolver emerged.

"Police? Thank God! I was just about to call you."

"Sure you were. You're under arrest."

"Me? For what?" She squinted into the darkness, astonished.

"Breaking and entering."

"What!" Sputtering, she scrambled to her feet.

A strong hand spun her around and shoved her against the counter, then patted the length of her slender frame.

I'm being frisked, she thought in amazement. Then anger exploded in her head, replaced by sheer panic when she felt the cuffs circling her wrists.

"Wait, please!" she cried. "This is a mistake, honest. This is my house. I live here! My name is Lisa Gillette!"

The response was a snort of derision. "Try again, lady. Lisa Gillette is dead."

Dear Reader,

For years, Silhouette Intimate Moments has worked to bring you the most exciting books available in category romance. We were the first to introduce mainstream elements, to make our books themselves something out of the ordinary for romance publishing. Next month we'll take another step in that direction when we introduce an extraordinary new cover design. At last our books will "look as big as they read." Our commitment to quality novels hasn't changed, but now we've come up with a package that we think does our stories justice. I'm hoping you'll think so, too, and that you'll share your thoughts on our new cover with me just as, all along, you've been sharing your thoughts on our books themselves.

But let's not forget the excitement this month in the middle of anticipating next month's big change. Veterans Jennifer Greene, Alexandra Sellers and Kate Bradley are in this month's lineup, along with talented newcomer Joyce McGill. Actually, Joyce has written young-adult novels before, but this is her first foray into adult fiction, and I know you'll be glad to hear that it won't be her last.

That's it for now, but keep your eyes open next month for the newest look in romance—only in Silhouette Intimate Moments.

Yours,

Leslie J. Wainger
Senior Editor and Editorial Coordinator

Through the Looking Glass

JOYCE McGILL

Silhouette Intimate Moments

Published by Silhouette Books New York

America's Publisher of Contemporary Romance

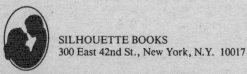

SILHOUETTE BOOKS
300 East 42nd St., New York, N.Y. 10017

ISBN: 0-373-07347-X

First Silhouette Books printing August 1990

Printed in the U.S.A.

JOYCE McGILL

began her writing career by writing for her high school newspaper, but soon became more involved with the theater. After winning several state awards for Best Actress, she went on to college to earn her B.A. in drama and literature. For some years, she acted in professional and community theaters and made some films and commercials before returning to writing. Ms. McGill previously published young adult romances under the name Tracy West.

ACKNOWLEDGMENT

To all the muses in my writing "class,"
especially Ruth Glick, Linda Hayes and Jean Favors,
who hung in there with me through several years
of revisions and labor pains,
my sincere appreciation.
To my long-suffering husband, Bob,
my gratitude and love.

Chapter 1

Come on, come *on!*"

Lisa Gillette, prisoner of a red light at Wisconsin and Western Avenues, waited impatiently for parole, clutch depressed, gearshift in first. The engine of her rented camper purred grumpily, as if it, too, were anxious for the moment it would breach the invisible line that separated Maryland and the District of Columbia. Yawning, Lisa scrubbed at her eyes, fighting fatigue. The dust of a thousand miles and countless antique shops seemed etched inside her nose, the promise of a sinus-clearing sneeze just beyond reach. Even her dark hair, splaying around her shoulders, felt heavier, as if permeated with dust. But after eight hundred miles of back roads and bed and breakfast inns, after dozens of attics and estate sales, she was almost home.

The traffic signal finally released her and Lisa accelerated gently, savoring familiar landmarks—Hamburger Haven, her favorite ground-beef haunt—Mazza Gallerie, the glitzy shopping mall housing an exclusive department store and other pricey shops. Funny, things looked exactly the same as when she'd left. A mere ten weeks had elapsed, yet it felt as if she'd been away for ages, she'd packed so much activity into each day. This one had been the worst, on the road for nearly sixteen hours. It was almost midnight now. By twelve-thirty, she promised herself, she'd be in the tub and by twelve thirty-one, dead to the world—unless Maria woke up. Lisa groaned. As much as she looked forward to seeing her best friend, she was in no shape for a reunion. Well, maybe she could stay awake for a little while tonight. Then she'd sleep until noon or die trying. Maria would understand.

Only a few blocks more to go. Past the car dealership, the video store, the automotive garage. This section of Wisconsin was commercial, but the narrow side streets were lined with single-family homes and row houses sheltered by sturdy maples and oaks. One of them was hers. She'd gone to settlement eight months before, and the role of home owner was still a novelty, a goal she had worked toward for ten long years. After a childhood spent hopping from city to city because of her mother's job, then ten years as a resident at St. Mary's Home for Girls, she had roots, a tree of her own. The next corner was her block, her neighborhood.

A wisp of ground fog writhed along the macadam, oozing free of a wooded lot on her right. Inexplicably a premonition of something amiss skittered across her subconscious as she flipped the turn signal to make a left onto Kelso Place. She checked the rear- and sideview mirrors. No traffic behind or approaching. A bag lady, shapeless under layers of clothing, scurried across Wisconsin towing a shopping cart, her presence a mute caveat against taking hearth and home for granted. Her bout of uneasiness waning, Lisa turned onto her street.

The row houses along Kelso—those few that were occupied—looked bedded down for the night, blinds and shades drawn against the amber glare of the streetlights. The remainder, still under rehab, were vacant, dusty windows peeking over piles of rubble on their porches. Giddy with fatigue, Lisa maneuvered past the few cars and pickup trucks parked along both sides of the narrow street. It had been a mistake to take the final three hundred miles back without a decent break, but she'd been anxious to keep going. Now, finally, she was home.

At the end of the thirty-nine-hundred block, Lisa eased to a stop, her hazel eyes aglow at the sight of her two-story house.

Other than being an end unit with the added perk of an L-shaped porch and a basement garage, it was much like the others on the block, except this one was hers—mortgaged, taxed, insured . . .

The smile on her lips faded. Something was different about the place. She couldn't say how, but it was, she was certain of it. Uneasiness came alive again. She cut the engine and got out, shivering in the chilly night air.

Nothing different on the front—the same hearty azaleas nestling along the base of the house, the same gangly forsythias at each corner. The door was barely visible, the whole of the porch in deep shadow, which meant Maria had changed her mind about coming.

Lisa sighed, juggling mixed emotions. She hadn't been surprised when her old friend had called to say she was leaving the convent.

"I don't belong," Maria Carlucci had complained. "I'm just not good at obedience. They've got me answering Superior's phone, for God's sake!"

Lisa had suppressed a giggle. An occasional stutterer, Maria hated using a phone.

"Mi casa, su casa, for ten weeks," she told Maria. "Having the place to yourself might even make the transition easier for you. I won't even call—you can ignore the damned phone."

"Oh, Lisa, that's so t-tempting."

"I'm renting a camper for the trip and leaving my car, so you're welcome to use it. I'll send you a set of keys and hit the road tomorrow."

"I'll be there as soon as I can. I'll take good care of your house, roomie," Maria had promised. "You'll be back when? I'll leave the porch lights burning after dark to welcome the weary t-traveler home."

The carriage lanterns beside the front door were unlit, however, the blinds at the windows closed tight. Maria had not come. I'll call her tomorrow to find out why, Lisa promised herself. But the question still remained—what was different about the house?

Unlocking the front door, she reached in and flipped the switch for the foyer lights. Nothing.

"Damn," she muttered. So much for the light bulbs' long-life guarantees. Easing the door closed behind her, she stepped in. Her nose twitched, teased by an elusive mix of aromas. It was a second before she identified them—fresh wax and lemon oil. Granted, she'd cleaned and polished like a woman possessed before she'd left, but would the smell have lasted so long? And she couldn't remember using anything with lemon scent in it.

Patting the wall, her fingers found the switch for the hall chandelier. Again, nothing except the matte-black darkness. A circuit breaker must have kicked off. A short somewhere? She added the electrician's name to the list of people to call in the morning.

Two paces toward the living room on her left, Lisa stopped, conscious of the unyielding surface beneath her feet. Where was the rug, the beige-and-scarlet four-by-six she'd bought at the auction? In fact, where was the skimpy welcome mat on the porch? Was Maria here after all? When they'd been roommates at St. Mary's, she had rearranged the furniture once a month.

"Carlucci!"

Her voice echoed hollowly, the sound flat and hard-edged.

"Hey, roomie, are you up there?"

No response. In fact, the house felt peculiarly empty, an aura of lifelessness about it. Uneasy again, Lisa rubbed the nape of her neck where her skin had begun to prickle.

The living room was pitch-dark, and rotating the dimmer for the ceiling light did nothing to change that. Moving cautiously, Lisa crossed to the front window to open the blinds. The golden glow from the street lamp at the corner scorched her sight for a second and she turned her back on it, blinking rapidly, urging her eyes to adjust. Once they had, a tiny sound escaped her lips, part gasp, part hiccup. The room was completely empty.

The twin love seats, the occasional chair, were gone. The Aubusson, the prints, the mahogany secretary, the plants, all gone. And the étagère housing her collection of miniatures, her beloved collection! "Oh, my God," she whispered.

Lisa ran through the dining room unimpeded by a single article of furniture. In the kitchen, the absence of the Shaker table and chairs transformed the room into a yawning, impersonal space. By the time she pelted up the stairs to the second floor, her heart thudding, she knew what she would find. Her workroom was empty, the built-in shelves and cubbyholes stripped of sample miniatures, brushes, solvents, swatches of fabric. The guest room, too, was bare. Stopping at the door of the master bedroom, she pushed it open. Cold, unfurnished. Except for the color of the walls—the slate-blue and warm beige it had taken her days to select—there was nothing of Lisa Gillette left. The whole damned house was empty.

Robbed, burglarized, ripped off. Lisa, in the sanctuary of the camper, struggled to regain the composure she'd lost as she'd fled the house on unsteady legs. Why hadn't Alec or Kitty tracked her down to let her know? They'd been in Europe when she'd left, due home on the twenty-ninth. They hadn't known about Maria coming, but since Alec had promised to check the house for her, she hadn't worried. Either way, she'd have been covered. He and Kitty had the itinerary and could have left a message that there'd been trouble. Her breath coming easier now, Lisa shook her head. A burglary didn't feel right. There had to be some other explanation.

"Think, Gillette," she said. She hadn't checked the basement. Retrieving the utility lamp from the back of the camper, Lisa approached the house again, this time from the garage, which took up one-half of the basement. The remaining storage space could never hold two floors of furnishings, her clothes, books and tools, but she had to keep hoping.

The garage door opened silently. No Toyota. "My car, too?" she whispered into the darkness. Unlocking the door at the rear of the garage, she stepped into the storage area. Not just empty. Sterile. Not a speck of dust in the corners. She'd been cleaned out. Literally.

"Just wait a minute, Lisa." Her voice bounced off the cinderblock walls. What kind of burglars ripped you off and played housemaid before they left? Remembering the aroma of lemon

oil and floor wax upstairs, she unlocked the basement door and
took the steps to the first floor quietly, as if someone might
hear. The utility room at the top of the stairs was spotless, her
laundry supplies gone from the shelf above the washer and
dryer. Edging into the kitchen, she played the searchlight across
counters, along glossy linoleum tile, into corners. The place was
immaculate. She opened an overhead cabinet. Even the shelf
paper had been removed. This made no sense!

Moving quickly around the room, Lisa yanked at drawers, no
longer caring how much noise she made. She stepped into the
pantry, felt painted wood under her fingers. The Contac paper
had been removed. "You couldn't have left my Contac paper,
for God's sake?" she bellowed, enraged.

Back in the kitchen, she checked the oven and broiler. The
speckled gray walls gleamed like new. She had been in Bur-
lington, Vermont, when she remembered that she'd forgotten
to clean the oven. This was no burglary. Burglars did not clean
ovens.

"Freeze, lady!" The coarse male voice cut through the silence like a cleaver and Lisa found herself pinned in the blinding glare of a flashlight. "Police! On your feet! Hands on the
counter!"

A heavyset figure, silhouetted in the light filtering through
the living room blinds, lumbered toward her, and the ugly shape
of a revolver emerged, its menace more potent than she could
have imagined.

"Police? Thank God! I was just about to call you."

"Sure you were. Assume the position, please. You're under
arrest."

"Me? For what?" She squinted into the darkness, astonished.

"Breaking and entering."

"What!" Spluttering, Lisa scrambled to her feet.

A strong hand spun her around and shoved her against the
counter, then patted the length of her slender frame, gently but
thoroughly.

I'm being *frisked*! The realization made Lisa gape with
amazement. Then anger exploded in her head, replaced by
sheer panic when she felt the cuffs circling her wrists.

"Read her her rights, Blaine."

"You have the right to remain silent," a voice droned from the door of the utility room. "You have—"

"Wait, please," Lisa interrupted. "This is a mistake, honest. This is my house! I live here! My name is Lisa Gillette!"

The response was a snort of derision. "Try again, lady. Lisa Gillette is dead."

Chapter 2

Jess Hampton opened his eyes, instantly awake, his senses at peak awareness, probing his surroundings like an animal in the wild testing the air to determine its status—hunter or prey. The soft glow of his bedside lights assured him that he was in the sanctuary of his apartment and not the suffocating humidity of a Vietcong tunnel. Other than that it did little to alleviate the tension that crackled through him like static electricity. He lay unmoving, his breathing rapid and shallow, coiled to respond to whatever had yanked him from a deep, dreamless sleep.

Something chirped in his ear, and he jerked toward the sound. The chirp trilled again. Jess chuckled, feeling foolish. Launched into a full-scale alert by a damned phone! Whatever happened to the kind that simply rang? Then he remembered the hour and sat up quickly, snatching the instrument to his ear.

"Hampton," he said tersely, his heart beating double-time again.

"Relax, home-boy. It's just me."

"Jesus!" Jess exhaled gustily, weak with relief. "I thought you were the hospital." Pete Owen. A friend, and a cop. D.C. Metropolitan Police, Homicide.

"How's our boy? Any change?" Owen asked.

"He's looking a little better. The coma's not as profound, and his brain activity has increased. He just keeps hanging in there, almost as if he's waiting for something." Jess glanced at the clock and swore. "Man, do you know what time it is?"

"I do indeed, but you have been bugging me every night for the past couple of months, so I couldn't pass up the chance to roust you off your virginal couch for a change."

"I'll ignore that snide remark, but consider us even, you bastard. What's up? A break in the case?"

"Just something unexpected enough for Blaine to get me out of bed. Considering the reason, I figured you might as well be awake, too."

"Let's hear it."

"There's a woman at the station awaiting the arrival of yours truly. It seems she's Lisa Gillette."

"What!" Jess was on his feet. "*Our* Lisa Gillette?"

"She may be yours, but she sure as hell ain't mine. Blaine found her prowling around the house on Kelso and brought her in on a B and E. He's pretty sure she checks out, though."

"Then who's the—?"

"You're wasting time, buddy. I'm on my way in to talk to her and no one's to tell her anything before I get there. I want to see her reaction for myself."

"Then you've changed your mind about her? You think she's involved?"

"No, I don't. I just thought you might want to sit in while we get her story. Keep your mouth shut, though, or I kick you out. Agreed?"

"Word of honor. See you shortly."

Jess slammed the phone down and went looking for something quick and easy to put on. Lisa Gillette? You bet he wanted to be there. If she was who she claimed to be, she'd better come across with answers to a lot of questions. Pete could think what he liked, but Jess Randall Hampton was convinced that Lisa Gillette had played a part in putting Mal in that hospital bed. She was . . . *is* . . . the key, he mused, shoving his long legs into a pair of jeans. Whatever her involvement, if his old pal wound up a vegetable the rest of his life because of her, he would see that she paid for it as long as she lived.

"That's a promise, buddy," he said under his breath, his lean face hardening. "I owe it to you. She'll pay."

The face of Detective Peter Owen, nutmeg-brown and moon-shaped under salt-and-pepper hair cut as severely as a marine recruit's, took on an expression Lisa couldn't read as he compared the tiny photo on the driver's license against the reality seated across from him.

"Exactly where have you been, Ms. Gillette?" There was more than a little exasperation in his tone.

The two-hour wait for the detective had left Lisa's nerves scraped and raw. She rubbed her fingertips against the fleshy pads of her thumbs. Even though she'd cleaned them thoroughly after she'd let them take her prints, her fingers retained the memory of the ink. She felt soiled, as though the whole process had branded her a criminal. Now, sitting before the battered desk of the man with cold, dark eyes, she was a centimeter away from collapse and determined not to.

"I've been traveling through New England," she explained. "I make miniatures of period furniture, then write how-to articles detailing their construction. I've been touring to gather shots and samples of certain kinds of pieces. Please, what's going on? Why would anyone think I was dead?"

"Bear with me, Ms. Gillette. When did you leave?"

"The twenty-sixth of January. I have receipts from everywhere I stayed, if you'd like to see them."

"I would indeed. You didn't use credit cards."

"No, but I have several." Lisa rooted around in the entrails of her capacious bag, found the envelope full of receipts and placed them on his desk. Then, retrieving a small leather card case, she unsnapped it and held it up, allowing the transparent sleeves to cascade in a foot-long proof of her credit worthiness. She had taken them just in case, but it was a source of pride to her that she didn't owe a penny on any of the treacherous plastic lures.

Owen removed the case from her hand and flipped through them. "If you had used these, you could have saved us a lot of trouble. You'd have been detained for possession of stolen credit cards and we'd have learned your whereabouts a lot sooner."

Lisa, outraged, let out a squawk. "I didn't steal them, and any number of people could have told you where I was! Look, my boss will vouch for me—Alec Joyner. He had my itinerary. I'll phone him. I'm entitled to one call, right?"

Owen didn't answer, apparently distracted by the arrival of yet another policeman. An undercover officer, Lisa assumed, given his casual dress—a navy turtleneck, well-worn jeans, running shoes. Tall and rangy, he folded himself into one of the chairs beside the door and laid his coat across his lap.

"Sorry," he said, addressing Owen. "Had a flat." Then his focus, laser sharp, locked onto her, and Lisa stopped breathing.

Eyes of obsidian dominated a face of fascinating angles and planes, his strength of character shouting from the cant of his jaw, the set of his lips. Perhaps under ordinary circumstances, the fine lines radiating from the corners of his eyes reflected a sense of humor; at the moment, they more closely resembled sprays of exclamation points underscoring the almost palpable dislike that emanated from the depths of his dark eyes.

Baffled by his enmity, Lisa met his gaze, wondering if he was someone she should know, someone with reason to dislike her so intensely. But she had never seen him before, she was certain of that, and even as she watched, his expression underwent a change. The hostility began to wane, replaced by guarded caution. He nodded a greeting, his brow puckered in a slight frown. She returned the gesture, then pivoted back to her interrogator, trying to recapture the thread of their conversation.

Leaning back in his chair, Owen linked his hands behind his neck. "Yes, Ms. Gillette, you would be entitled to a phone call, if we had reasonable cause for bringing charges."

The newcomer was forgotten as Lisa's temper flared like a Roman candle. "After cooling my heels in the company of pushers, prostitutes and God knows what else, I'd better be charged with something!"

Owen smiled. "Well, if you insist . . ."

Breathing deeply, she rubbed her eyes and counted to five. Ten was way out of reach. "I'm sorry. I'm very tired. I've been driving since nine this . . . no, yesterday morning, and this isn't quite the homecoming I had in mind."

"Just a minute." Owen raised a restraining hand as a shirt-sleeved detective passed him a slip of paper. Scanning it, he sighed, his face relaxing a bit. "Okay. Your prints match the others in the house, but we would still appreciate formal identification from someone. Mr. Joyner should be more than willing, considering the last time he offered to do it."

"The last time?" The elation Lisa felt at having won the skirmish was buried under the return of mushrooming dread. She'd been so intent on proving her identity that she'd lost sight of the real reason she was in this predicament. "Look, since I'm not dead, someone else must be."

"I'm afraid so, and I'm sorry to beat around the bush for so long, but . . ." Leaning back in his chair, he scanned her features. "The deceased was a woman, of course, Caucasian, twenty-five to thirty years old, five-seven, a hundred and twenty pounds. She was driving your car."

"Driving my—she stole my Toyota?"

"It was easy—she had the keys. When did you lose them?"

"I didn't. I . . ." Lisa's throat closed, silencing her voice. Her extra keys. She'd sent them to Chicago, overnight mail, in a small white box addressed to Sister Maria Julia Carlucci.

It became difficult to breathe. The ambient aromas seemed suddenly overwhelming—someone's cigar, a mélange of colognes and after-shaves, cigarettes, the perspiration of others and her own. And the piercing eyes of the plainclothes officer by the door were not helping.

She cleared her throat. "Your description of the woman . . . Is there anything else you could tell me about her?"

"Only that the two of you were the same general type and build." His gaze dropped to a form in the folder. "And she had flat feet."

The room tilted slightly. "No. Please, God, not Maria."

"You knew her?"

"Maria Carlucci. She was . . . my oldest friend."

He jotted down the name, requested a few other particulars. "And you left Miss Carlucci your car?"

Lisa hesitated, waiting for the world to right itself so she could regain her emotional footing. The pain could wait. There were questions to be answered, questions to be asked. Slowly she recounted her last conversation with Maria.

Surprise flared in Owen's eyes. "Ms. Carlucci was a nun?"

"For the past ten years, but she'd finally admitted it was a mistake. She was leaving the order and planned to start over. I . . . talked her into doing it here. Please," she said, weary of getting the information in measured doses. "What happened to her?"

The stocky man eyed her as if trying to gauge her reaction before the fact. "On January twenty-eighth, two days after you left, an '81 Toyota Corolla registered in your name blew up at Wisconsin and Western Avenues."

"The Toyota . . . exploded? How could it? Someone hit it?"

"In a matter of speaking." He paused. "There's no easy way to say this, Ms. Gillette. Someone fired at the gas tank of your car, using ammunition guaranteed to blow the tank sky-high."

Shock flooded every cell. "Someone shot at— Why? I don't understand."

"We're certain the target was the man with Ms. Carlucci."

"Man?" Lisa gaped at him. "What man?"

"His name is Clifford Mallory. Does that ring any bells?"

Lisa hesitated, distracted by a wisp of memory—small children in a circle, one in the middle chanting:

My last name is Mallory;
I live in Eden's Gallery . . .

The rest was gone.

She shook her head. "Clifford Mallory. No, it doesn't ring any bells."

"You're sure? White, early fifties, five-ten, stocky, brown eyes, gray hair."

Nothing came. "His name seems familiar, as if I might have heard it before, but I can't see a face for the name, and I'm usually good at that kind of thing." She sensed the plain-clothes officer stir restlessly in his chair.

"He wrote a best-seller a few years back—*The Roots of Crime*."

"Oh, of course. I remember. I never read it."

"Well, he was in the passenger seat, and the explosion blew him through the windshield. He landed sixty feet away and his injuries were pretty extensive. There's still some question whether he'll ever fully recuperate."

"He's alive?" Lisa demanded, nearing overload. "Someone was trying to kill *him* and Maria's the one who died? This is crazy! Why were they after him?"

Owen's eyes locked with those of the officer in plain clothes. He seemed to choose his words with care. "Mallory was working on a sequel of his first book. We suspect he stumbled on to something he shouldn't have, because this was a professional job."

"Professional— Wait, please." Lisa's mind whirled, trying to mold the incredible into something that made sense. Hit men. Executions. That was for television scripts, movies, not real life. "You're saying that Maria was in the car with a man who had a contract on his head? And it was so important that he die that it didn't matter he wasn't alone? My God! What kind of animals are these?"

"There's no polite answer for that. All I can say is that your friend didn't suffer. She died instantly."

I should have called, Lisa thought, unaware that she'd said it aloud. "But I promised her I wouldn't! I'd promised!"

"Why, Ms. Gillette?"

Lisa shook her head tightly, past answering as her emotions, a howling, shrieking anger and grief, catapulted beyond the point of containment. In self-defense, something inside her, acting on its own, began to shut down, drawing a soft blanket over her head as protection against the bitter cold of reality. It's a dream, she told herself. All she had to do was wake up and find that nothing had happened. She could forget it, pack it away...

A voice harsh with alarm penetrated the buffering around her. "Pete, she's checking out!"

Something hard slammed against her cheek, snapping her head to one side.

"Ms. Gillette? Hey, are you all right?" Owen's voice pierced the rapidly thinning miasma.

Hand to her face, Lisa blinked, startled to find him standing over her with genuine concern. The officer in the turtleneck was on his knees in front of her, his hands gripping her shoulders. His fingers were strong, viselike.

"She's back," he said, watching her intently. "Talk to me, Lisa." It was an order.

"Talk..." His features swam into focus and she noted with odd detachment that his eyes were not black at all, but a very dark walnut, like his hair. There was something else she'd missed before—faint vertical creases between his thick brows and around his mouth—souvenirs of some distant pain.

He regarded her silently, then nodded and stood. "Sorry about slapping you," he said, "but... well, you were about to pass out."

Lisa frowned. Pass out? But there had been none of the distortions of sight and sound that accompanied fainting, only a slow, gentle fading of both. And he had stopped it, as if he'd known, known what? Lisa rubbed her eyes, baffled, unnerved.

For a fraction of a second, his expression softened as he looked down at her, and Lisa felt a sudden longing to reach up and smooth the troubled lines from his forehead. Appalled at the intensity of the urge, she tucked her hands under her thighs. This man was a stranger. How could she be thinking of anyone but Maria?

"Maybe we should get Doc Wiener," Owen was saying.

Lisa stopped woolgathering. "No, please, I'm fine. Just give me a minute." Rallying, she began to rein in the disparate parts of herself, binding them together with a skein of pure strength of will.

Owen retreated behind his scarred government-issue desk. "I think you've had enough for one night. Drop by tomorrow with Mr. Joyner so we can dispense with the formal identification. We'll take your statement then and get more information on Ms. Carlucci."

"Wait, please. There are things I need to ask." Encouraged at the strength of her voice, Lisa stood. It was a small test of her legs and she passed it, moving around behind the chair so that the dark-haired officer was out of her line of vision. "Do you know who did it?"

"Not yet, but we lucked out on a witness who spotted the shooter making tracks after the explosion, so we have a pretty fair description of him. We've traced him to National Airport where he boarded a shuttle to Newark. We're working with the police force there to get a line on him."

"Newark." She'd never been to Newark, didn't know anyone from Newark. "I still don't understand how Maria could be mistaken for me. She was an inch shorter, her hair was lighter and she had no birthmark."

"You do?"

Leaning forward, Lisa flipped her long hair off the nape of her neck to show him the port-wine blemish marring the smooth, creamy skin. "See? This alone should have..." Her voice trailed away as the implications of the erroneous identification hit home. "She was that badly burned?"

The expression on the detective's face said clearly he wasn't sure she could handle it. "Her body was unrecognizable. We couldn't find a dentist with your records on file, so we had to go with the obvious—height, weight. And she wore a ring like that one." He pointed at the band of meshed silver.

"She still had hers?" Lisa's gaze dropped to her right hand. Tears stung and she blinked them away. "We bought them at the same time, after graduation from high school. Sisters forever, that kind of thing."

"I see. Well, Mr. and Mrs. Joyner identified the ring as yours."

"Oh, Lord, what have I done to them? They didn't know I'd gone. Originally I'd planned to wait for them to get back from Europe, because Alec had volunteered to check the house for me. Then Maria said she would come right away, so I left."

"I'm surprised you didn't hang around until she got there."

"I wish I had, but she was so anxious to be alone. I thought I was doing her a favor. Now..."

"Hindsight is cheap, Ms. Gillette. You couldn't have known. Neither could we. There was no reason to suspect that the bod—the woman was anyone but you, and Mallory's in no shape to tell us otherwise."

Lisa had had enough. "Thank you. I...think I'll leave now."

Owen nodded crisply. "No problem, but we would appreciate the name of Ms. Carlucci's next of kin before you go."

"There isn't anyone. We grew up in a home for orphaned girls."

"Ah, yes." He sighed. "Well, I'll contact the convent in Chicago for a line on her dental records. We don't want to make the same mistake twice."

Lisa whirled. "She hasn't been buried yet?"

"Yes, the Joyners took care of that, but the case is still open, so all the paperwork on her is still here. Where can we reach you? At the Joyners'?"

The prospect of a reunion with Alec and Kitty was more than Lisa could bear. "I'll check into a motel for tonight. If someone could give me a ride back to my camper..."

"Of course," Owen said as the officer in plain clothes came to his feet abruptly. "We'll be looking to hear from you. Get some rest."

"Rest," she repeated and stuffed her belongings back into her purse. Easy to say. It was past three. In a few hours the sun would be up, time to start another day. Another life, since the old one seemed to have been yanked out from under her. At least she had one, unlike Maria.

Jess waited until she had stepped out into the squad room before he made his move. Even then, he found himself at a loss. Lisa Gillette had not fit the profile he'd constructed of the mystery woman who was supposed to have died in that car. She was neither siren nor slut, nor any of the decidedly uncomplimentary pictures he'd drawn of her over the past two months. In fact, he'd been disoriented from the moment she'd turned to look at him.

He knew her, knew those eyes, had seen them somewhere before, he was sure. But where? He was certain they had never met. He wouldn't have forgotten that hair—lustrous, dark and heavy, longer than was fashionable by today's standards.

Probably wouldn't have forgotten the face, either, even though it wasn't all that—

He gave himself a mental shake. To hell with her looks, she couldn't possibly be the innocent she seemed. He'd had plenty of time to think during the past couple of months, to probe the accepted motive attributed to the attack on Mal. He hadn't been able to convince Pete of his theory before, but surely now...

"Excuse me," he said, touching her elbow lightly.

"Yes?" A facade of control slipped into place, but the ravages of the evening showed clearly in her eyes.

"I'm Jess Hampton. I'll be glad to give you a lift, if you don't mind riding in a broken-down pickup."

"At this point, I'd accept a ride on a dog sled," she said with a game attempt at a smile. "Where are you parked?"

"Around back. Hang on for just a moment." He eased a chair under her and hurried away to corner Pete Owen. "Look, give me a call before you question her in the morning. I want to be here."

"Question her?" Owen asked, shrugging into his coat. "What's to ask? She didn't know Mal and Carlucci did, or they wouldn't have wound up in the car together." Owen squinted at him. "You aren't still hung up on that theory of yours, are you?"

"You bet I am, even more than I was before. The fact that her friend was the one who died, not her, proves I'm right."

Owen sighed. "Give up, Jess. We checked for any connection between her, Mallory, the syndicate, the Girl Scouts even, when we thought she was dead. She's precisely what she seems. She's never even gotten a parking ticket."

"Didn't you see the way she hesitated when you asked her if she knew Mal?" Jess persisted. "I may be off the force, but I still have the instincts of a cop. Something's fishy about her."

"As far as we're concerned, she's clean. If you dig up information to the contrary, let me know. Meanwhile, leave the woman alone, Jess. We gave her a bellyfull of grief tonight.

Take her back to her camper and say good-night. I'll be talkin' at ya." He gave Jess a conciliatory pat on the arm and left.

Jess stared after him, fuming, and pivoted to watch Lisa surreptitiously. She sat, eyes closed, her face a tragic mask. All right, so the news about her friend had hit her hard, harder than she realized, considering the way she had reacted to the pain. But he felt the same brand of pain every time he stood beside Mal's bed and saw the IVs and tubes and incessantly beeping monitors. Mal was there because of Lisa Gillette and no one could tell him otherwise. She may have told the truth tonight, but not enough of it to satisfy him. Not by a long shot.

"Where to?" he asked as he climbed under the wheel of the pickup and started the engine.

"Thirty-ninth and Kelso. Head toward Sears on Wisconsin. I'll direct you from there."

"I'm familiar with the area. Which hotel are you going to?"

"Motel," she corrected him. "The Beecher."

"Why there? It's not exactly a triple-A accommodation."

"Perhaps not, but it's close to home. Plus my camper's full of stuff and I'll feel better if I can park it right outside my room."

This was a development Jess had not anticipated. He had assumed she would be stopping at her camper to get her bags before going on to one of the ritzier hotels farther downtown. Taking her that distance would have given him more time to feel her out, whereas Kelso was a ten-minute ride, if that, and ten minutes were too little for his purposes.

She rubbed the back of her neck, her hair swirling in a sable mass around her shoulders. "I'm sorry, I've forgotten your name."

"Jess Hampton."

"I really appreciate the ride, Mr. Hampton."

"It's Jess. No problem. By the way, I'm sorry about your friend. I really do know a little of what you're feeling. Clifford Mallory is a very special friend. He and Pete—Detective Owen—and I served together in Vietnam. I'd have died there, too, if it hadn't been for Mal. That man saved my bacon."

"Oh." Her eyes widened. He couldn't quite decide their color—green, brown, gray or all three. And the dark ring around her irises was unusual. He had seen those eyes before. *Where?* "I can see why he'd be so special to you," she was saying.

"Right. He walks away from Vietnam in one piece and gets messed up for life a mere three blocks from my place."

"Yes. I'm sorry."

He heard the wary undertone, sensed a pulling away. Backing off a little, Jess decided to clear up the obvious first. "Had he known Maria long?"

Lisa answered after a lengthy silence. "Maria lived at St. Mary's for eighteen years and went into the convent from high school. A sheltered order, Mr. Hampton—no visitors, other than family, which she didn't have." Her voice broke. She cleared her throat and went on. "Maria must have met your friend after she got here."

The story wasn't quite what he'd expected, but the point was that Mal hadn't known Maria before. That left Lisa. It was time to get down to business. He checked his speed. They weren't that far from Kelso and he needed time.

"I guess that's what makes this so incredible," she said softly, gazing blindly into the night. "She'd just met him. Maria was shy. It took her a long time to relax around people, partly because she was a stutterer. Yet in less than two days she was comfortable enough with this man to let him get in a car with her. He must have been a real charmer."

Jess's hackles rose—he resented the implication. The gloves were off. "Oh, so you have met him."

"Pardon?"

"You must have met him to know he could talk an oyster out of its shell."

"No. You were there when I told Detective Owen that."

"I was there, all right. He didn't ask if you'd met him. His exact words were, 'His name is Clifford Mallory. Does that ring any bells?' You repeated his name, and said, 'No, it doesn't.' And between his question and your answer, there was an interesting little pause."

"Oh?" She didn't move, but he was certain he'd captured her attention, that she remembered the moment.

He slowed to let a light catch him. "I got the impression you were being very careful how you responded."

"Because I stopped to consider the question?"

"Sorry, I don't buy that. You see, a person who has nothing to hide, you ask him a direct question and he answers immediately, then backs up to be sure what he said was accurate. He speaks first, thinks second. You did the reverse."

Lisa shifted sideways to face him, turning as far as the shoulder harness would allow her. "Are you accusing me of lying?"

"If the shoe fits . . ."

She stiffened. "I have never met Clifford Mallory and I resent being called a liar."

"Have you ever been to Baltimore?"

As he'd hoped, the change of subject seemed to throw her. "Sure, lots of times. Why?"

"That's where Mal lives. You're a writer, he's a writer. Perhaps you ran into him there at a conference or something."

"Does Mr. Mallory hang out in craft stores?" she demanded. "Because those are the only places I've been to in Baltimore, besides the Inner Harbor. Why do you insist we've—" She stopped, her lips parting as the eight ball dropped into the pocket. "Are you suggesting I was involved with what happened to him?"

"It's certainly crossed my mind."

"My oldest friend is dead because of *your* friend, and you're accusing me of being an accomplice to her murder?"

"You may not have—"

Fury suffused her features. "If that's what you think, stop beating around the bush and arrest me."

She had him. "I can't. I'm not a cop."

"You're not? Then why were you there?"

"Because Clifford Mallory is my friend. I used to be on the force and when Pete heard you'd turned up, he knew I'd be interested."

They'd arrived at Wisconsin and Kelso. "Let me out. I'll walk," she said, struggling with the seat belt.

"Stop that!" Jess clamped his hand over the buckle. "Keep your shirt on."

"I ... want ... to ... get ... out." She spoke softly, deliberately, color high in her cheeks.

God, she's lovely, Jess thought, surprising himself. "I'll let you out when we get to your camper and not before. It's late. A woman alone this time of night is asking for trouble."

"I'm grateful you don't think I'm a streetwalker, too. Right there, end of the block. Thank you very much for the ride, *Mr.* Hampton. How much do I owe you?"

Jess stood on his brakes, bringing the pickup to a shuddering halt. "Don't get on your high horse with me, lady. I've got a good buddy lying in a hospital bed, two breaths short of being a vegetable. Pete may be right about the motive for the hit on him, but it seems damned funny to me that it wasn't until he started researching a mysterious Ms. X that he became secretive about what he was doing for the first time since I've known him. From what you say, there's no reason to believe that he was looking into the background of a woman who'd been a nun for the past ten years. That leaves you. He winds up in D.C. in *your* car and somebody tries to blow him to hell and gone. Make sense of that!"

Releasing the seat belt, she let it retract with a snap, unlocked the door and got out. "You may have a good friend in the hospital," she said, anger coarsening her voice, "but I've got one in the cemetery. I'm sorry he was so badly injured, but as far as I'm concerned, if it hadn't been for him, Maria would not be dead. Good night." She slammed the door, making the pickup rock, and strode toward a VW camper at the corner.

Jess watched her get in, start the engine and pull around the corner onto Thirty-ninth. He was tempted to follow her, but what would be the point? He'd blown it, fooled by the wholesome aura of the girl next door, the wide, startlingly beautiful eyes. And that fraction of a moment when she'd started to tune out....

Had he misread the situation? He wasn't sure, but he'd seen enough bizarre reactions to stress in 'Nam to take any chances. She had bounced back immediately, he'd give her that. Perhaps she was stronger than he thought. Under other circumstances, he might even like her.

The taillights of her camper disappeared and Jess roused from his musings. He might as well go home. He'd have to figure another way to find out what he needed to know about her. If Lisa Gillette thought he was giving up, she had a lot to learn about Jess Hampton.

Lisa managed to check in and lock the door of her motel room before she broke, tears gushing, her sobs so violent that her stomach rebelled, leaving her weakened and shaken. After rinsing the foul taste from her mouth, she washed her face and brushed her teeth. Her image met her gaze blearily, eyes red and swollen, her face pinched with tension. Oddly enough, she was struck by how much she looked like her mother, what little she remembered of Eloise Gillette. *I haven't thought about Mom in a long time,* she realized with a guilty start. *But tonight had brought it all back.*

Thank God she'd been strong enough to hold everything in until now, wanting no witnesses to her tears, especially Jess Hampton. How dare he suggest she'd had anything to do with Maria's murder! And she had let him get away with slapping her!

Lisa tried to recapture the moments before he had hit her, but they were gone, her patchwork memory being a peculiarity she'd learned to live with. The auto accident, which she had survived and her mother had not twenty years before, had left bizarre blanks in her childhood—a severe concussion, the doctors had said. But to have forgotten her thoughts of an hour before was a little frightening. She had lost several seconds of awareness.

I seem to keep losing things, and people I love, she thought bitterly, her eyes filling again. First her father, of whom she had no memory at all, then her mother, now Maria. Overwhelmed with a sense of isolation and loneliness, the tears began again, but by the time she'd disrobed and slipped into bed, Lisa had burrowed her way to the truth. She had cried for Maria tonight and the brutal way her friend had died, but not all those

tears had been for Carlucci. Most of them had been for Lisa
Gillette.

She and Maria had become connected at the soul back at St.
Mary's, fighting the knowledge that they were eight—no, nine,
alone and unwanted, past the age most couples would prefer to
adopt a child. Even after Maria had closed herself off behind
that blasted gate at the convent, the connection had remained.
Now it was gone, irrevocably severed. She was alone again,
because of Clifford Mallory.

She had to see him. She had to look into the face of the man
who had robbed her of her dearest friend and had, for all
practical purposes, wiped every trace of Lisa Gillette from the
map. There was nothing to be gained from seeing him except
the satisfaction of having exorcised a bogeyman and proving to
Jess Hampton that the man was a stranger. Then she could
forget him and his friend and get on with rebuilding her life.

Chapter 3

Angie Sarnof woke with a start, rheumy eyes scrutinizing her surroundings. Pushing aside the layer of newspapers and plastic spread over her, she sat up and peered beyond the doorway in which she'd spent the night, to see the clock outside the bank. Five-thirty. Good. Old Dawkins wouldn't show up until six to heat up the grill and get stuff ready for the breakfast crowd. That would give her time to gather her belongings, wash up a little in the rest room of the gas station—if Tommy was in a good mood and would give her the key—and make herself presentable.

Old Dawkins was a puzzle. He would chase you away if he found you sleeping in the doorway of his snack shop. But if you rapped at his back door around six-thirty, quarter of seven, and you looked halfway decent, he'd pass you a little piece of sausage and a bit of scrambled egg on a biscuit. A cup of coffee, too, but she always paid for that. Angie knew coffee was more than the dime she gave him, but it was important for her to show she wasn't nobody's charity case. She could take care of herself.

Things like that were important so you never forgot you were somebody. There were other things to remember, too, like who

your people were and where you came up. It was also important to have things of your own, like a grocery cart and belongings to put in it.

Angie would not steal. What she had she'd come by honestly, either given to her or she'd found it. Poppa would be
proud, she thought later as she scrubbed her face with paper
towels in the rest room. His little Angie was getting by just fine.

She used the last sliver of the stick deodorant she'd found in
a trash can, buttoned the front of her tattered dress, pulled on
her baseball cap and threadbare coat. Then she took a few
minutes to sort her things and repack her shopping cart.

The gray box went in first, the one with Poppa's big Bible in
it, her fading snapshots of Baby Girl tucked securely inside the
front cover. Then her only other dress, socks and underwear.
She reached for the dried flowers—a person needed beauty in
her life—then stopped to reconsider. The briefcase had to go
back in, well covered so that it couldn't be seen by some nosey
parker.

Setting it on the edge of the sink, she plucked at the lock.
Damned thing just wouldn't give. She ran her fingers across its
scarred sides and the letters stamped under the handle. A *J* and
a *C* and an *M*. Out of the sky, practically, this thing had come,
the day the car blew up.

Angie had missed seeing it—her back had been turned, but
she'd heard it sure enough. The next second this old briefcase
came sailing across the street and almost took her head off.

Wheezy Whisnant, he saw it all, said that poor fellow flew
through the air like he'd been shot out of a circus cannon. It
occurred to her a day later—"Angie, this satchel here mighta
been his."

She took a paper towel and brushed at the scarred leather.
She had to keep it in decent condition, just in case. She'd
thought about giving it to the police, except they might think
she'd stolen it and put her in jail. Wheezy said the man was still
breathing when the helicopter came. If he was still alive and this
belonged to him, maybe he'd pay a little something to get it
back. A reward, that's what they called it. Next time she got
some extra change, she'd call around to the hospitals, find out

where he was so she could take it to him. Course now, if he was dead, finders, keepers. That's what Poppa used to say.

Wrapping the briefcase in newspaper, she crammed it into the cart, then topped it off with her dried flowers, followed by the cheese from the shelter. Carefully she covered it all with plastic bags.

It was a good start on the day. Tommy, the manager of the gas station, gave her two whole dollars—he was nice like that—and she was in plenty time to get breakfast at Dawkins's place. Gave him a quarter for it, too. Head held high, Angie started walking, mulling over places to go and things to do. But first she had to find a newspaper.

It was important to read the paper every day, because it proved something. She might miss some of the big words, but she got the little ones. She could read. And everybody always saying she was retarded.

"Retarded, my Aunt Fanny," she muttered to a lady approaching. The woman gave her a wide berth, increasing her pace. Angie didn't care. Angie Sarnof knew she was as smart as a lot of people and a whole lot smarter than some others.

"Mornin'," she said to the next man coming in her direction. She gave him her best smile, her lip tucked tightly over her bottom teeth so the gap in front wouldn't show. "Nice mornin', ain't it?"

"It certainly is," the man responded solemnly. "Have a good day."

Angie straightened her shoulders and patted the collar of her coat into place. Tommy had paid her, she had something in her stomach and a well-dressed gentleman had spoken to her just as polite as pie. Shoot, her day was already good.

"It's coming up on seven a-yem, Capital City! Rise and shine! We'll take a five-minute break for headline news and a few commercials—hey, they foot the bills, folks. Then it's time for the top twenty to get your blood stirring and—"

"Spare me, please," Lisa growled and reached over to slap the off button on the clock radio. She'd been awake since six, but hadn't gotten up immediately, taking what time she needed to put things into perspective.

Maria would always be with her. God, she'd known her twenty-one years, almost three times longer than she'd known her own mother. But the truth was that Maria's stay in the convent would help mute the pain of losing her now. It was small comfort, but it was all she had. Then she'd gotten up, ready to face the first day of her new life.

A steam-filled shower had soothed stiff muscles. Lisa sat on the side of the bed, brushing her hair into submission. She lifted the heavy mane off her neck, wondering why she still wore it so long. She was twenty-nine. Surely a child's promise to her mother never to cut it was null and void after all this time.

Every now and then she imagined herself with a smooth, face-hugging cut, almost boyish, except, of course, she could never wear it that short; it had to be long enough to hide the ugly birthmark on her neck. Wishful thinking, she surmised, and checked the clock again.

Fifteen past seven. Time was up. She had calls to make, and she couldn't put it off any longer. For three-quarters of a second in the shower, she'd considered calling Jess Hampton to ask which hospital Mallory was in, until his accusations reverberated through her mind. She could find out at the police station. Someone there was sure to know. Reaching for the phone, she dialed the Joyners', holding the receiver in a white-knuckled vise as she counted rings at the other end. It was answered within four, lifted from its cradle with an ear-stinging clatter.

"Yeah," her friend, supervisor and Dutch uncle growled, his whiskey voice at its worse. He was not a morning person.

"Alec..."

"Yeah. Who's this?"

"It's me. Lisa." She hesitated, stumbling over the words she had rehearsed in the shower.

"Lisa who?"

"Gillette. I'm alive, Alec."

Silence. Then, "Why don't you check into St. Elizabeth's, lady? You are very sick!" Click. The dial tone hummed in her ear.

Fingers trembling, she punched the numbers again. He answered after a single ring this time.

"Please, Alec, don't hang up," she said quickly. "Honestly, it's me. I just got back and found out what happened. It wasn't me, Alec, it was my friend, Maria. She was coming to house-sit for me, so I left on the twenty-sixth. Maria was in the car, not me."

There was a confusion of sounds—the mattress creaking, the clink of a glass or, more likely, an ashtray.

"Gillette?" He was hoarse with incredulity. "No games, please. Is it really you?"

Her promises to herself dissolved at the hope in his voice. Tears cascaded down her cheeks. "Oh, Alec, it's so god-awful. I talked her into coming and now she's dead."

"Lisa." His whisper spoke volumes. "It is you! Jesus, do you know how often I've dreamed of something like this?" His voice broke. "Wait. Don't go 'way."

She heard the click of the phone as he set it down, then a monumental honk. The tales of how loudly Alec Joyner could blow his nose held the editorial staff of his magazines together on rough days.

"Let's start this again," he said. "This is Lisa No-Middle-Name Gillette, the snot-nose kid who whacked me with the electric stapler over a harmless pat on the fanny?"

"It was seven years ago at my first Christmas party with you guys. You were stinking drunk from Kitty's spiked eggnog or I'd have stapled you to the bulletin board." She sat up straight, feeling better.

"This is incredible! Damn it, Gillette, where have you been?"

"You know where I've been, Alec. You had my itinerary."

"You mean, all this time you've been gallivanting around New England? You couldn't have called, for Pete's sake?"

"Who was it who told me to forget the office, don't even bother to check in? Who was the smart aleck, pardon the pun, who said it would be a relief to have me out from underfoot?"

She heard his sigh. "You can't imagine how often I've regretted saying that. So it was the nun from Chicago? What was she doing here?"

"Getting acclimated. She had just left the order."

"Geez, honey, what a helluva thing to come home to. I can't tell you how sorry I am it was her, and how glad I am it wasn't you. Boy, I wish Kitty was here. She's in New York. I'd better call her, get her used to the idea. Where are you?"

"At the Beecher, and before you blow a gasket that I didn't come to your house, I needed to be alone, okay? Now I have a favor to ask."

"Name it."

"I need someone to swear to the boys in blue that I'm me. Formal identification."

"When?"

"Meet me at the station at ten." She swallowed, in a cold sweat about the possible answer to her next question. "Alec, has the house been sold yet?" She had named him executor of her estate, with instructions to sell the house and donate the money to St. Mary's.

"Your house! My God! We've got to move fast. A couple has signed a contract on it, but they haven't gotten financing yet. We'll probably have to do some fancy footwork to get out of this. We'd best talk to Spalding today."

"I plan to call him next. What about my things?"

"They're in storage. Kitty took inventory and packed everything, but hasn't been able to face picking what she wanted to keep. Whenever you want them, you've got them. What else?"

"Do I still have a job?"

"You figure miniaturists who can design a Louis XVI table and then write a decent article about putting the thing together are a dime a dozen? Your desk hasn't even been dusted."

Lisa chuckled and wiped her eyes. "How nice to know some things never change. One last thing—don't be hurt, but I need time alone to sort things out. Can I bunk in the loft above Kitty's studio until I can get back into the house?"

"It's yours. It's also full of junk."

"I love junk. That's it for now, I've got a million things to take care of. By the way, do you know which hospital Mr. Mallory's in?"

"Mallory. No, but check the phone book for a Jess Hampton—he should know. Seems he and Mallory were pretty tight."

"Oh, you've met him?"

"Several times. A nice guy."

"You couldn't prove it by me. I'll see you at ten. Thanks, Alec."

She hung up before he could question the reason for her remark and began dialing her lawyer's home number. Next would be Maria's convent in Chicago. She dreaded explaining the details of Sister Maria Julia's death, but it was what a surviving member of a family was supposed to do, and she was Maria's family. St. Mary's would be last. They would want to know about Maria, too.

Half an hour later, her duty done and her appointment with Spalding scheduled for noon, Lisa consulted her list of things to do. The only one of the morning's tasks still hanging was finding Mallory's whereabouts and Detective Owen could tell her that. So she had no explanation when, moments later, she flipped through the residential section of the phone directory until she found the listing for Jess R. Hampton in Chevy Chase, Maryland. His line was busy. Okay, she would give him five minutes and try again. Who knows, he might even be civil this morning and apologize. "Dream on, Lisa," she muttered and sat back, one eye on the clock.

"Thanks for subbing for me, Lem. I'll check in with you later." His skin still beaded with water from the shower, Jess replaced the receiver and tightened the towel around his hips. As part owner of Security Specialists, he was obligated to give his trainees, and the firms for which they would work, the best he had, but after the sleepless night he'd spent, he was in no condition to teach anything, much less a course in honing one's powers of observation. More than one security guard had survived a treacherous situation, thanks to six weeks of intensive training with Jess and his partner, Lem Silas. If he couldn't give them a hundred percent, one of them might pay for it on the job with his life some dark night. Barefoot, he headed for the kitchen to get more coffee, and hesitated as he passed the open door of the guest room.

The bed was made but other than that, the room was precisely as Mal had left it the day after Thanksgiving, his shaving kit, deodorant and cologne on the dresser, a tie draped on the closet doorknob. This was where the mystery had begun that day. He had been making coffee. Mal, lazing away the morning, was reading in bed, the day's papers strewn all over the covers. He'd heard Mal's startled exclamation, "My God, it's her! It's got to be!" just as the toast popped up, but he'd waited to butter it and to pour the coffee before stopping to see what all the fuss was about.

By the time he'd stuck his head into the guest room, Mal was half-dressed, tossing his belongings into his weekender, his hands trembling with excitement. Ten minutes later he was on his way out the door, saying only that he'd just gotten the lead of his life. Jess had perused the papers after he'd left, but hadn't found a clue to what had sent his buddy scurrying into the frigid November morning.

Mal had called several days later, no more informative than he'd been before. He would not be around for Christmas, which they were to have spent at Jess's cabin in the mountains.

"I can't talk about it, Jess," he'd claimed, "or I'll jinx the whole thing. All I can tell you is that it's deep background stuff, intensive research, more important than anything I've ever done. Bear with me, buddy. When this is over, you'll be the first to know. No, second. She'll be first. I'll be in touch, okay?" And that was it.

For Jess, everything hinged on the identity of the woman in question. The problem was, Pete had nothing to go on but his word. They'd found no evidence of the research, and Pete's willingness to believe him was due solely to fifteen years of friendship.

The phone chirped, startling him, and Jess crossed to the nightstand to snatch the receiver to his ear. "Hampton."

"Mr. Hampton, this is Lisa Gillette."

Jess almost choked on his surprise. "What can I do for you, Ms. Gillette?"

"I'm sorry to disturb you so early, but would you give me the name of the hospital Mr. Mallory's in, and his room number?"

Jess stiffened. "Why?"

"I'd...just like to see him. Where is he?"

"You aren't serious."

"It's eight-fifteen, Mr. Hampton. I've had about an hour and a half of sleep. I would not call you at this time of morning if I weren't serious."

Jess shook his head. "No. Thanks, anyhow, but you're one visitor he can do without."

"I won't disturb him, I'll just look at him, okay? Two minutes, that's all I'm asking. Considering what's happened, I think I'm entitled to see him once."

Her voice, exuding the kind of patience one used with a cranky toddler, set him off.

"Not okay, lady. You are trouble. He had something on you and it almost got him killed. Stay away from him, understand?"

He slammed down the phone, his hand shaking. See Mal? After the lengths he'd gone to to lessen the chance that some sleaze ball might get to him again? As soon as Mal could be moved, he'd had him taken to a small private hospital in the suburbs. Mal was now registered under an alias and no one visited James Hampton unless his or her name was on the list Jess had left with the receptionist. Lisa Gillette's would not be added under any circumstances.

Jess glared at the phone, his temper subsiding. He'd spent months in therapy to overcome such flare-ups, but if he had talked to her one second longer, he'd have blasted her. His response had been completely visceral, stemming from his conviction that had it not been for Lisa Gillette, Mal would be at home in Baltimore, pecking away at the keyboard of his computer. Opening the blinds, Jess peered out, wondering if he was being irrational. Why, with all the evidence to the contrary, this gut instinct that Gillette sat dead center of the whole business?

He poured himself a glass of orange juice and took it to the window. Seven floors below, rush-hour traffic streamed toward the District line. Had he been looking out of the window on January twenty-eighth, he might have seen the smoke from Gillette's car. He flinched, reacting to the pinprick of pain that inevitably accompanied his guess that Mal might have been en route to his apartment that day. A demon on a freeway, he refused to drive in the District, professing outright cowardice when faced with circumnavigating the Capital's infamous

traffic circles. He had hopped a commuter bus from Baltimore to Washington that morning and, they assumed, the
subway to the stop closest to Gillette's home. Since she had not
been there, Maria Carlucci may very well have offered to drive
him to Chevy Chase.

Jess swore. He was back at the starting gate, still operating
under the assumption that Cliff Mallory had gone to Kelso
Place to see Lisa Gillette. Like Mal and D.C.'s traffic circles,
he kept going around and around, only to wind up at the very
spot from which he'd started.

Pete Owen's argument against Lisa Gillette as a subject of
interest to Mal was based on routine legwork; his men had
found nothing on her that remotely touched the general topic
of Mal's next book—prostitution—and her name had not appeared in any of his notes and work papers. There was, in fact,
no indication that he'd been researching anyone at all over the
previous couple of months and it was this glaring omission that
Jess found most difficult to swallow. Where were the results of
the deep background stuff he'd mentioned on the phone?

They must have been in Mal's attaché, which no longer existed. But that, he realized, giving himself a mental kick in the
behind, was an assumption, and one of the cardinal rules of
investigation was never to assume anything. He grabbed the
phone and dialed Pete Owen's number.

"Look, pal." Pete sounded much put-upon. "This is my day
off. Unlike your bed, mine is not empty and my wife is looking bullets at me. What do you want?"

"Think back—Waco's report on what was left of Gillette's
car and its contents. Was there any mention of metal fittings—
a lock, hinges, anything that might have been the remains of a
briefcase?"

He heard a mattress squeak. "No. Why?"

"That beat-up old embarrassment Mal carried everywhere.
I'll bet you a rib dinner those missing research notes were in it.
I'll double-check but I'd swear it's not in his apartment."

"Well, it wasn't in the car, either, or Waco would have found
traces of it in the debris. He's sharper than an ice pick. He
wouldn't have missed it."

"Maybe Mal left it at Gillette's house."

"You're back to that again?"

"It's one of the foundations of my argument."

"Which one? All I remember is the bottom line, which is way off base."

"Look, Pete, Mal called me two days before his birthday—"

"January twenty-sixth. The call I mean."

"Right. He was following up on his promise to let me know when he'd finished his hush-hush project. He said that now that he had, he wasn't sure what to do. Bringing it out into the open might cause her grief she didn't deserve. He couldn't decide whether the end result would be worth it."

"So?"

"So he phones the night of the twenty-seventh, leaves a message on my machine that he'll be in town to celebrate his birthday with me, and will be coming by with a lady or a gun to blow his brains out, one or the other. To me that says he'd made up his mind to tell her, and to hell with the consequences—"

"Maybe, but aside from the fact that he was in Gillette's car, there isn't a shred of evidence linking her or the ex-nun to him. We've gone through reams of his notes on prostitution. A few touched on the new sex-by-phone fad, and there were dozens of interviews with call girls up and down the East Coast—their backgrounds, motivation, all sorts of seamy stuff. Gillette's no hooker. She's as clean as Ivory soap."

"Nobody's that clean."

"Oh, for . . . Wait a minute, I'm gonna change phones."

Jess, sensing a turning point in his debate with Pete, reached across the counter and grabbed a mug. The coffee was ready. The least he could do was reward himself with a cup of French roast. Before he could pour it, Pete was back on the line.

"You there? Now listen, hardhead," he said without waiting for a response, "because I'm only going to run through this once. I called in a favor from a young woman I knew long before she began pulling in four figures a night for the pleasure of her company. According to her, all the high-priced pro's in town had been warned not to talk to Mal, especially the ones whose regular customers pull the strings of this nation. There were a lot of high-powered careers on the line, so the word was out—stay away from Cliff Mallory or neither of you will live to regret it. They thought it was a lot of hot air until they read what had happened to our pal."

Jess felt his jaw loosen with shock. "You shut me out! You had that information and you shut me out!"

"You are still out, buddy, but if it makes you feel any better, so are we. The feds are on to this ring of local ladies and their clients, and we've been ordered to tippy-toe around their investigation like ballet dancers."

"The hell you say!"

"Don't interrupt. I have it on good authority that Gillette is not and never has been connected with any of these ladies or their bosses. If Mal was on to something after Thanksgiving, it was hot enough to warrant a contract on his head, so it looks like you were right about part of it and you'll have to be satisfied with that. If we find the briefcase and get the gritty on what almost got the man killed, that'll be icing on the cake. Until then, we wait to hear from Newark."

"But what about Gil—"

"We may never know how Gillette and Carlucci wound up in the middle of this," Pete cut him off brusquely. "As for Gillette, consider her as pure as Snow White. Forget her *and* this conversation. That's it, Jess. Case closed. I am hanging up." He did.

Jess replaced the receiver and stared morosely into his empty mug, a scowl etched deeply across his forehead. Pete's argument had been strong enough before and this new information reinforced it. Mal had wandered too close to men with a great deal to lose—careers, reputations, families. People had been killed to protect a lot less.

But in his book, that did not eliminate Lisa Gillette. So she wasn't a hooker. She could be a friend of a hooker. Or a close friend, perhaps even the lover, of one of the men with a reputation to protect. He'd been a damned good cop because his instincts were always sound. His instinct put Gillette in the loop somewhere. All he had to do was find out where she fit in.

He turned off the coffee maker and headed for his bedroom to dress. He might as well go on to the job. Perhaps he'd suit up for Brody's morning workout in the gym, expend some energy, sweat a little. He had to do something. Forget Gillette? Not on Mal's life. The notion of Lisa Gillette as innocent bystander was a leaden weight in his gut, like a five-course meal eaten far too late in the evening. It was time he took something for it.

Alec Joyner was waiting outside the police station, his iron-gray hair bristling with impatience when Lisa finally arrived, ten minutes late. Dubbed Little Hitler by the editorial staff of his magazines, Alec was five feet five, weedy as a dandelion stalk and had been known to set off mass palpitations if a deadline were missed. Under normal circumstances, he nurtured his tough-guy reputation, playing the role to the hilt, but he took one look at Lisa and lost it. Laughing and crying on alternate breaths, he grabbed her in a hug that would have incapacitated a bear, lifted her completely off her feet and planted his lips against her cheek in a kiss that left her ears ringing.

"By God, Gillette, I was beginning to think I'd dreamed your call this morning! Don't you *ever* put me through something like this again!"

"But I didn't do anything."

"The hell you didn't. My parents are still alive, you know, so this was my first experience losing someone I loved."

Lisa was more than a little stunned. "Alec, that's the nicest thing you've ever said to me."

"Yeah, well, don't let it go to your head. And if you ever tell a soul I said it, you're fired." Sniffling, he rooted in his pocket for a handkerchief and wiped his eyes.

Touched by this gruff show of affection, she bussed him on the nose. "I love you, too, you big bully. And I swear I'll never tell a soul the boss has tear ducts just like everybody else."

Trying to hide a sheepish grin, Alec crammed his ubiquitous meerschaum between his teeth. "You look like hell, but I've never seen a more beautiful sight in my life. How're you doing, kiddo?"

"All things considered, just fine. Did you get Kitty?"

He chuckled around the pipe. "Oh, yes. You know Kitty, hysterics come as natural to her as breathing. She threw a hissy fit when I gave her the news. She's catching the Metroliner home, so be prepared. I tried to get Brad, too, but he didn't answer. He's been going to Mass every morning since you died."

Lisa groaned around a tired smile. "Heaven help me." Brad, Kitty's assistant, was also her male counterpart when it came to shows of emotion. Between the two of them, Lisa knew she was in for two very soggy reunions.

Alec eyed her mistily. "Come on, let's get this over with. This time, it's a pleasure." Taking her arm, he escorted her into Second District Headquarters.

He stuck to her like rubber cement, swore to her identity, witnessed her deposition, then unsuccessfully tried to run interference for her with a *Washington Post* reporter who'd gotten wind of her resurrection and recognized a good human-interest story when he saw one.

Seeing a chance to spread the word, which might lessen the chance that she'd cause a coronary coming upon someone who hadn't heard, Lisa agreed to a ten-minute interview and to having a picture taken. As a result, it was almost noon before she managed an escape from the station and, with Alec tailing her in his car, played havoc with the speed limit to get to Duncan Spalding's office on time. Another hour and a half elapsed before, drained, her spirits flagging, she and Alec stepped out into the sunlight on K Street again.

For once, Alec, too, seemed at a loss for words as they walked to the parking lot behind it. "What an all-fired mess," he muttered, his pipe belching smoke.

Lisa nodded, in a daze. "I'm a nonperson, Alec. I don't exist! It'll take weeks to get this straightened out. No bank accounts, no money, no credit, no home, no car. What am I supposed to do?"

"Count your blessings, that's what. You're alive, aren't you? You've got Kitty and me, and a rent-free roof over your head—at the loft or with us, take your choice. I can float you a loan for as much as you need to get by. I know you'll be good for it."

"Oh, Alec..."

"Your job's waiting, but don't worry about it for the time being. With all the running around you'll have to do, you won't have time to work." He fished in his jacket pocket as they arrived at their vehicles. "Here's the key to the loft and this one's for the storage bin at the warehouse. You can take back all your things, if you want. What else will you need?"

Meeting his worried gaze, she managed a wan smile. "You're right, I shouldn't complain. What hurts is knowing the house won't be mine until all the red tape's unsnarled. I can't even go home. The things in storage probably aren't legally mine, either."

"Maybe, maybe not. The way I figure, what Spalding doesn't know won't hurt him. Take what you want and let him squawk about it later. Where are you going now?"

Lisa reviewed her options and found them limited. "To the studio, I guess. I might as well check the loft, see what needs doing to make it livable."

"Strategically placed sticks of dynamite, if I remember correctly. You go on. I'd better get to the bank. You figure you can get by on a couple of thousand, to start with?"

"Alec! That's probably twice what I'll need."

"Two thousand it is, then."

Lisa hugged him. "I don't know what I'd do without you, and I'm not talking about the money."

"Bull," he growled. "You're tough, Gillette. I saw it two minutes into your interview with me. You weren't afraid of me and that's why I hired you. Another thing," he added solemnly, "not once did you undress me with your eyes."

It was a second before that registered. When it had, Lisa erupted, her peals of laughter reverberating against the walls of nearby buildings.

Alec's sober expression dissolved, his bottom lip bowing into a smile. One never knew about the top lip, camouflaged as it was with his thick, bushy mustache. "That's better," he said, taking her arms. "You've got a great laugh, kiddo. One of the hardest things to accept was that I'd never hear it again. Keep laughing and you'll get through this mess just fine. If you don't come by the office this afternoon, I'll bring you the money when I stop to pick up Kitty at the studio. She had tea or something silly scheduled with that Sheffield woman this evening, but with you here, she'll probably cancel."

He stood smiling up at her for a moment longer, as if he still couldn't quite believe she was there, then got into his car and headed up the alley to K Street. Lisa heard the squeal of brakes and a second later, the nasal whine of an engine in reverse gear being pushed to its limits. The rear of Alec's Chrysler appeared as he zoomed backward into the parking lot, screeching to a halt at her side.

He stuck an arm out of the window. "Here! I forgot this."

She removed the slip of paper from his hand. "What is it?"

"You wanted to know where that Mallory is, didn't you? I asked—you were in the john—and one of the guys copied it off Owen's blotter. See you later." Leaving a streak of rubber on the rough cement, he took off and this time disappeared.

She had forgotten to ask for it herself. Lisa unfolded the slip of paper and read, Greenhaven, room 426. Underneath was the telephone number of the hospital. Her spirits lifting a notch, she tucked the information into the pocket of her blouse. Considering how much she had to do, it would be days before she'd have time to get out to Greenhaven. Perhaps she'd make time on the weekend. Clifford Mallory wouldn't be going anywhere. She would visit the hospital just to satisfy herself that she was not mistaken about knowing him, and take great joy in calling Jess Hampton to let him know she had been there.

Slipping into the snarl of traffic on K Street, Lisa felt a tug of regret that the present situation had made them adversaries, the image of his lean, angular features rising to haunt her. Still, he had no reason to hold her responsible for his friend's condition and she doubted she could ever get past that. It was time to begin rebuilding her future, of which Clifford Mallory and Jess Hampton would have no part. As much as she detested the expression, in this instance it was more than apropos—it was time to look out for number one. And that's me, she thought. I. Whichever.

Jess Hampton, winded, was flat on his back staring up into the amused face of Chip Brody, who stood over him, hands on his hips. In the eleven months they'd been working out together in the gym at Security Specialists, this was the first time Chip had managed to get the better of Jess.

"Who is she?" Chip asked, squatting beside him.

"She who?" Jess rolled over and sat up, shaking his head to clear it. He'd landed hard.

"Don't play dumb with me. On your worst days when you were in therapy, even after Mal got blown to hell and gone, every morning you came in here, you kicked my butt. But you weren't here today, and that means there's a woman. Who is she, how'd you meet her and when do I get to?"

Jess punched him lightly on the shoulder and got to his feet. "Give yourself a little credit. You threw me fair and square. It was bound to happen some time. Enjoy it, because it won't happen again soon." He snapped a salute at Chip and strolled toward the showers, refusing to limp.

Half an hour later, he was dressed and in his office but in no better frame of mind for work than he'd been when he'd arrived. He opened the window behind his desk, breathing in the scents of early spring. Chip was right. Lisa Gillette had really gotten under his skin. She was mixed up in this somehow and sooner or later he'd work it out. He had to do something. Her image kept tugging at him, interfering when he least expected it. Lisa Gillette had managed to stir the part of himself he'd placed in hibernation. She was a threat in more ways than one.

Spotting his attache beside the desk reminded him that he should double-check to be certain Mal's old faithful wasn't crammed in a closet somewhere. He envisioned the Baltimore condo as he'd last seen it the week before when he'd gone to check on it. The briefcase had not been out in the open, he was sure of that. Mal must have had it with him the day he'd come to D.C. If it hadn't been destroyed in the explosion, there was every chance he'd left it at Gillette's. Was finding it worth a faked apology? Hell, finding it was worth anything he had to do.

Grabbing the Washington phone book from a bottom drawer of his desk, Jess found the number for the Beecher. Sorry, but Ms. Gillette was no longer registered.

He flipped to the *G*'s. There were a surprising number of Gillettes, one L. E. Gillette, but none on Kelso Place. Annoyed, he dialed Information, and hung up before anyone answered. What was wrong with him? They wouldn't be able to help him; her phone would have been disconnected, and her house was vacant. The dead had no need for either, and the contents of her house may have been sold already.

He pawed through his memory for the name of the couple who'd identified the body. It began with a *J*, or perhaps a *G*, and that was as far as he got. The name hovered just out of reach, torturing him. Swearing colorfully, Jess dropped the directory into the drawer, kicked it shut and slammed out of the office. Here he was with a perfectly legitimate reason for calling Lisa Gillette and no idea how to reach her. Perhaps it was just as well. She was poison and he was in no mood for suicide.

Chapter 4

Kitty's studio, Joyner Interiors, occupied the first floor of a narrow brick building squeezed between a unisex haircutting salon called the Clip Joint and a travel agency that changed names and ownership every six months. Whenever possible, Kitty scheduled buying trips for Fridays through Mondays, so the studio was still closed, another small blessing for Lisa to add to the list. She wouldn't have to face Brad, Kitty's second-in-command. There was no telling how he would react to seeing her without having been warned first. As for her impending reunion with Kitty, she could only hope the woman had gotten all her hysteria out of her system. The waterworks would flow—Katherine Joyner could cry at the drop of a hat—but if that's all she did, Lisa considered that she'd have gotten off light.

She parked behind the building and let herself in the back door, moving along the narrow hallway to the front. The main room basked in tones of muted beiges and white, while Kitty's collection of oriental rugs supplied a carnival of colors underfoot. It was restful and welcoming and Lisa stood for a moment, gathering the atmosphere around her, letting it still her anxieties.

If she had a second home, this was it. Alec had brought her here a week after hiring her, knowing she'd taken several courses in accounting. Kitty had just joined the ranks of the self-employed and had a satisfying working relationship with color, texture and line, but had known next to nothing about running a small business, the proof in the mincemeat she'd made of her checkbook. She had welcomed Lisa with open arms, taking her on part-time, and gradually Lisa's employers had become her friends. She'd spent as many hours here as she had in her tiny apartment, before she'd bought her house, so there was a great deal of comfort in taking up temporary residency on the floor above. Fingering her keys, she returned to the rear hall and climbed the stairs to the loft.

The chaos on the second floor made her give serious consideration to checking back into the Beecher. The three big spaces were, in effect, Kitty's Dumpster, crammed with all the things for which she had no further use or had nowhere else to put. The two largest rooms contained everything from furniture, remnants of carpeting and upholstery fabric to empty picture frames. The bathroom defied description, and the smallest room in the rear was a rat's nest of lamps, planters, vases and a motley collection of bric-a-brac.

The ghosts of commissions past, these bits and pieces of Kitty's career as an interior designer cluttered the whole loft. Lisa, overwhelmed at the massive effort it would take to make any one of the rooms habitable, picked her way back toward the stairs. She didn't have the energy to tackle it without a decent meal under her belt. Breakfast had been a Danish and a cup of the embarrassing excuse for coffee the Beecher served in its dining room, and hunger gnawed at her middle with sharp little teeth.

As she secured the door at the top of the stairs, Lisa, hearing movement below, froze, the key still in the lock. Kitty stepped into the opening at the bottom of the stairwell and looked up at her, eyes wide, her lips parted. "Lisa," she said, her voice a hoarse whisper.

"Kitty! My God!"

Kitty Joyner was a dumpling of a woman, described as pleasingly plump within earshot and chubby beyond it. She could, if pressed, hit the sixty-one-inch mark, and carried a good twenty pounds more than she should. Her gently rounded face, sweet expression and the judicious application of smoky ash brown to her hair once a month made her look far younger than the fifty-one years she admitted to. All in all, she was a woman who'd once been very pretty and wasn't that far from it still. At least that had been true the last time Lisa had seen her.

Kitty, for whom trying the latest fad diet was an avocation—to no avail—was considerably thinner than she'd been ten weeks before, and the skin of her face and neck appeared a trifle slack, as if it hadn't had time to shrink and catch up. Most distressing were the blue-gray shadows under her eyes. Grief had clearly wreaked havoc on her, rendering her a pale imitation of the pretty, ebullient woman she had been.

Lisa, knowing her friend's penchant for histrionics, had been dreading this moment, but seeing the change in her, knew that Kitty no longer had the emotional stamina for that kind of performance. She looked drained, on the edge of collapse. Remembering how close she herself had been to it the night before, Lisa ran down the steps, her arms extended.

Kitty came into them and began to cry, but even these weren't the kind of tears Lisa had expected. Her chest heaving, Kitty sobbed quietly, her face pressed into Lisa's shoulder, her body trembling. Lisa made shushing sounds, smoothing her friend's silky curls, trying to offer comfort while fighting back her own tears.

Leading her into the studio, she sat down with Kitty on the Queen Anne sofa in the rear corner of the room, dug into her purse to free several tissues from their wrapper and pressed them into Kitty's hand. Sniffles subsiding, Kitty wiped her eyes and blew, finally settling back against the white-on-white brocade to peer at Lisa from beneath swollen lids.

"I'm sorry," she said, shaking her head. "It's just that . . . Oh, Lisa, I can't tell you how awful it's been. I just never realized how…how important you were to us until I thought we'd lost you."

"I should have called," Lisa said, remembering the number of times she'd considered and rejected it.

"Alec told me he'd ordered you not to. I'm just so glad you're back, so glad. But your friend, Maria . . ."

She dabbed at her eyes, her head lowered, silent for so long that Lisa suspected there was something else to come, something she did not want to hear. Alec had told her that while the police had been willing to rely on their identification of the ring to spare them the pain of viewing Maria's body, Kitty had insisted on seeing it. Lisa suspected that she needed to talk about it, and considering what she'd been through, was probably owed an audience.

"I know Maria was very special to you," she said softly.

"Oh, Lisa, I'm ashamed of myself. I've always been a little jealous of her. You were the daughter I never had, and I wanted you all for myself. I thought I was being punished for being so possessive."

Kitty's admission rocked Lisa. Not that she'd taken the Joyners for granted—it simply never occurred to her they felt as deeply about her as she did about them. She took a fresh tissue and dabbed at Kitty's cheeks. "Kitty, listen to me. Maria had a very special place in my life, but you and Alec are every bit as dear to me. I adore you both. And I'm not dead, so you see how wrong you were about being punished?"

Kitty lifted her head to meet Lisa's gaze. "I have something to tell you, and you'll hate me when I finish. That'll be even worse punishment. Just promise that you won't tell Alec. Let him think we had an argument or something. If he knew, he'd hate me, too, and then I wouldn't have anyone."

"Kitty, what—?"

"Promise first. I know you, you won't go back on your word."

Seeing the desperation in her eyes, Lisa nodded. "I promise. Cross my heart. Now what is it?"

Kitty pulled in a deep, shuddering breath, her shoulders hunched as if anticipating blows. "Lisa, what happened to your friend . . . what I thought had happened to you . . . it's my fault. I'm responsible and I'll never forgive myself."

This was the last thing Lisa had expected and she wasn't sure how to react. It wouldn't be the first time Kitty had blown her bit part in some unusual event into a leading role, but, Lisa reminded herself, this was not the old Kitty. She was deadly serious and the haunted look in her eyes was genuine.

"How are you responsible?" Lisa asked, prepared for anything.

"We got back from Europe a day early and...well, you know Alec, he insisted on going to the office. Things were a mess. The staff was trying to put the *Journal* to bed, and Flo wasn't there to filter the calls for everyone. I knew his blood pressure would be sky-high if they didn't get some help, so I went over to play receptionist."

Lisa listened patiently, reading between the lines. *Miniature Mania* was issued quarterly, but the *Collector's Journal* hit the stands every other month and was due out in early February. Flo, who lost periodic bouts with arthritis, was an excellent receptionist, primarily because she'd been trained by Kitty, who'd had the job prior to marrying the boss. With a deadline looming, Flo kept interferences to a minimum and would have been sorely missed.

"I'd been there about an hour," Kitty went on with obvious reluctance, "when . . . this man came in asking to see you."

"Mr. Kroner? He's been testing the directions for my Shaker models."

"No, it wasn't Mr. Kroner. I've met him."

"Then who was it? A salesman?"

Kitty bristled, showing the first signs of life. "I can smell a salesman at a hundred yards. He was not a salesman. I explained that you were on leave and that he should check back in April. He looked so stricken, Lisa. He asked if there was any way he could get in touch with you. I told him no, you'd be leaving town in a few days and were busy taking care of last-minute things."

She paused and Lisa, uneasy, rubbed the back of her neck and forced herself to wait it out.

"He just stood there hugging his briefcase. He said it was vital that he talk to you before you left, that if he missed you, it might be late spring before he'd have a chance to try again. I asked what it was about, and he said it was a personal matter. He'd come to the office because your home phone was unlisted and he didn't have your address. You know me, Lisa, I'm a good judge of character. He was genuine, and heartsick that he might miss you. So I tried to call you, but your line was busy—"

"It was?" Lisa was surprised, knowing Maria's attitude about telephones.

"—and stayed busy for a long time. He looked so anxious, Lisa, as if his life depended on seeing you before you left. So I did the unforgivable."

A cold, hard lump moved into Lisa's heart. "You gave him my address."

"I *know* I shouldn't have. It's against office protocol and plain old common sense, but he...he seemed almost desperate. I gave him directions to the Metro and told him how to get to your house from the subway, and he left. We didn't know about the explosion until we saw it in the paper the next day. So it's my fault. If I hadn't given him your address, he'd have gotten himself killed somewhere else and Maria would still be alive."

"For the record," Lisa said, her throat constricted, "his name was Clifford Mallory?"

Kitty nodded. "He gave me his card, but after the... accident, I tore it up."

"You didn't tell the police?"

"I couldn't! If I had, Alec would know it was my fault you were dead and...I don't know what he might have done. It's been eating away at me ever since. Lisa, can you ever forgive me?"

The question barely registered. She couldn't imagine why Clifford Mallory had wanted to see her. For the moment the fact that he had left far less impact than the knowledge that if she hadn't skipped town early, if she'd been at home when he'd arrived, Maria would be alive today. That she herself might now be dead was another matter. She wasn't. Maria had died in her place.

Lisa had not yet responded to Kitty's plea for forgiveness and looked at the silly, self-indulgent woman who had taken her in so long ago. Kitty had a good many faults, but she'd been generous with her time and talents, and was largely responsible for the miniaturist Lisa had become. All things considered, the scales tipped heavily in Kitty's favor.

Lisa embraced her. "There's nothing to forgive, Kitty. I'm as guilty as you are—I'm the one who talked Maria into coming in the first place. All we can do is hope there's some purpose in everything that's happened."

Kitty began to cry again and Lisa held her until the newest flood had subsided, her mind a thousand miles away. Maria's death had taken on additional weight and meaning. So had Clifford Mallory's life. What could he have wanted? Had she inadvertently lied to Jess Hampton? Was Mallory someone she'd met, someone she simply didn't remember?

Releasing Kitty, Lisa patted the pocket of her blouse and heard the crackle of the slip of paper she'd put there. "Do you feel better?" she asked.

Kitty bobbed her head. "I'm all cried out. I must look a mess."

"You do." Lisa smiled, relieved at seeing a resurgence of the old Katherine Joyner. "I've got an errand to run. Go home and get some rest. I'll call you later. And don't worry."

"Oh, Lisa..."

"And eat something! You're thin as a rail!"

Leaving Kitty to her own devices, Lisa found a directory for suburban Maryland and scribbled down the address for Greenhaven Hospital. A minute later she was backing out of her spot behind the studio. She knew Mallory would not be able to tell her anything, but that didn't matter. She had to see him anyway.

It didn't occur to her that he was in such an out-of-the-way hospital until she'd gotten lost twice and found it by accident, almost bypassing it because of its resemblance to a members-only country club. Her first impression was borne out as soon as she stepped into the lobby of the low-slung T-shaped building and found herself surrounded by gleaming Italian marble, baroque wall hangings and waiting room furniture upholstered in butter-soft cinnamon-colored leather. She was in alien territory. Greenhaven was the kind of exclusive facility millionaires checked into to dry out or to be coddled back to health. Either Clifford Mallory belonged to one dynamite medical plan or best-sellers pulled in far more money than she'd ever imagined.

A brushed brass sign mounted on the wall behind the reception desk announced that visitors' badges were required. "Mr. Clifford Mallory in 426," she said to the gray-haired woman waiting to help her. The name tag on her ample bosom identified her as Mrs. Rose Wolcott.

"Mallory. I don't remember . . . let me check." She swiveled to the computer and pecked at the keys, raising her head to peer at the monitor through the bottom half of her glasses. Her eyes flickered ever so slightly before she turned back to Lisa. "I'm sorry, we have no patient by that name."

"Pardon?" Lisa checked the slip Alec had given her. "Clifford Mallory. Room 426. He was badly wounded back in January. He may be in your critical care unit, instead of—"

Mrs. Wolcott shook her head. "I'm sorry, we have no patient by that name. Now, if you'll excuse me . . ." She gave a tight smile of dismissal and began to sort through a stack of mail.

Lisa was determined not to be disposed of so easily. "He must be here. This information came from a friend of his, someone in a position to know."

"There is no Mallory here," Mrs. Wolcott repeated, blinking rapidly. It gave her away. The woman was lying.

"Did Jess Hampton leave orders not to admit me?" Lisa asked.

The response was a stolid silence, but a telltale flush rose in Mrs. Wolcott's cheeks. Lisa clenched her fists, holding her temper on a very tight lead. It would not be fair to vent her anger on the receptionist who, after all, was only doing her job. Anyone who could afford medical care in this place had every right to expect anonymity, if that's what he preferred, but she was not about to give up yet.

"Mrs. Wolcott, would you please check a D.C. directory— I'm sure you must have one—and look for the number of a Peter Owen? He's a detective with the D.C. Metropolitan Police. Call him and tell him that Lisa Gillette is here asking to see Mr. Mallory."

"Oh. You're a policewoman?" She seemed relieved.

Lisa hesitated, but saw no point in lying simply because Mrs. Wolcott was required to. "No, but he'll vouch for me. Please?" she added, seeing the woman's hesitation. "I'll take a seat and wait." She left the desk and moved purposefully to an easy chair in sniffing distance of the coffee service set out on a marble-topped sideboard near the window. She could see the information desk from the corner of her eye. Mrs. Wolcott was already on the phone, but there was no way she could have found Detective Owen's number that fast. She was probably calling a security guard. So be it, Lisa decided. But I'm not leaving until they kick me out.

Ten minutes later, she was still waiting. Traffic flowed around her, visitors coming and going, but no guard had appeared. Lisa got up and helped herself to a cup of coffee. Her stomach had begun to announce its displeasure at being empty, and smelling the rich aroma was sheer torture. If something didn't happen soon, she would go in search of their cafeteria, eat, come back and call Detective Owen herself.

She was engrossed in an article about antiques in a popular magazine when she became aware of the subtle scent of a fresh, woodsy cologne. She looked up into a face in which several strong features warred for dominance—the angled sweep of cheekbones, the dark, blazing eyes, the firm jawline—and resigned herself to a fight. Jess Hampton had arrived and he was furious.

Jess had been standing over her for a full minute before she felt his presence, a minute he put to good use banking his anger. He'd been on his way to Baltimore to search for Mal's briefcase when the receptionist had reached him on his car phone. Thank God he'd had the foresight to request he be notified if anyone not on his list of approved visitors appeared, especially if that person used Mal's name instead of the fake one under which he was registered.

He got right to the point. "Who told you where to find him?"

"So he is here." She closed the magazine, wedged it in the rack beside her chair, then focused on him again. Her eyes, in the softly tinted light filtering through the wall of windows, were a clear amber, the dark rim around the irises magnifying the contrast between the two colors. "I don't know his name, and I wouldn't tell you if I did. Now that I'm here, may I see Mr. Mallory?"

"Shall I call security, Mr. Hampton?" Mrs. Wolcott stood behind him, her voice a whisper. She glanced nervously at a couple who sat not far away, watching them curiously.

"I don't think that will be necessary. Is there somewhere I can speak to Ms. Gillette privately? Just for a minute."

"Oh, yes. Of course. The conference room, just past the public phones." She seemed more than happy to get them out of sight.

"Thank you. Ms. Gillette?"

Lisa rose to her feet with silken, effortless grace. "After you."

She was cool, he'd give her that, Jess thought as he led the way into a short corridor to the left of the spacious waiting room. She would not be easily intimidated, but there were things he had to know. Opening a door marked Private, he steered her into the room. It was simply furnished, five occasional chairs positioned around an elegant rosewood table. He gestured toward the nearest seat as he closed the door, but she shook her head, placed her purse on the table and stood, waiting.

Her implacability played havoc with his temper. "You've got a lot of nerve coming here. Is it time to change your story about having met him?"

She took a deep breath. "Look, let's be civil about this. As far as I know, Clifford Mallory is a stranger to me. I'd like to see him to prove to you that he is."

"Oh, was that your intent?" Jess folded his arms and smiled sardonically. "How'd you plan to do that without me here?"

She flushed, which added much-needed color to her cheeks. She wasn't as pale as the night before, but fatigue had left indelible shadows beneath her eyes, lending her an air of fragility. "I was going to see Mr. Mallory and call you afterward," she admitted.

"To let me know you'd been smart enough to find out where he was?" Her color rose even higher and he felt a surge of satisfaction that he'd been right. Miss Sweetness and Light was human after all. But he refused to be diverted. If a rank amateur could ferret out the name of this place, anyone could. He had to know her source.

"Who told you? Don't play with me, lady," he said, moving closer, trapping her against the conference table. "I want to know how you got the information and who you've told."

"It's whom," she said, eyes narrowing. "I haven't told anyone, and I don't appreciate the implication."

"I don't need a grammar lesson from you," he snapped, "and it's not an implication, it's an accusation, the same one I made last night."

She lifted her chin, not giving an inch. "Obviously the police don't agree with you or I wouldn't be here, I'd be in jail."

She'd hit home and it rankled, nudging him dangerously close to the limits of his control. "As far as I'm concerned, a few days in jail might jog your memory. You're pressing your luck, Ms. Gillette. Go home."

"Home? *Home?*"

Jess watched, fascinated as her eyes changed color from the clear bright amber of a moment before to a hard, dark mahogany flecked with a green that flared into tiny bolts of emerald lightning.

"I *have* no home! My earthly possessions consist of two suitcases of clothes I can no longer hang in a closet because I no longer have a closet. I have been expunged from a host of computer memory banks, Mr. Hampton—Lisa Gillette, deceased, all because a man I've never met made enemies of people who snuff out human lives the way other people step on cockroaches! I am a zero, thanks to the patient in room 426, and I think that gives me the right to see him."

"I don't. When it comes to Mal, you have no rights. I wouldn't trust you within fifty yards of him."

"Why? Do you think I've come for revenge, that I'm packing a gun?" She emptied her coat pockets, tossing several sets of keys onto the table, then turned the pockets inside out. "If you think I'm such a danger to him, frisk me. In fact, I'll go you one better!" Shrugging out of her trenchcoat, she hurled it to the floor, her gaze fixed on him. "It's called a strip search, isn't it? Then by all means, do it, if that's what it'll take to convince you!''

They were barely an inch apart, fury crackling around them like static electricity. She held out her arms, as if she expected him to begin undressing her, and a soft floral bouquet escaped from the open neck of her blouse, its essence so overwhelmingly feminine that it became his undoing. She was so near, so inviting, her mouth barely inches below his, her lips parted, her warm breath caressing his face. To capture the enticing fullness of her lips was only a matter of lowering his head. Her eyes, that marvelous palette of earth and grass and stormy sky, were fixed on his mouth, as if she, too, anticipated their joining.

"Dr. Martinez, please call 704. Dr. Martinez, please call 704."

The tinny voice of the intercom broke the spell and Jess jerked backward. What the hell was he doing?

"Just . . . cool it, okay?'' he said, more for his benefit than hers. "All right, you've made your point, you can see him. I'll take you up."

The chameleon phenomenon began again, her eyes lightening by degrees, her cheeks a rosy pink. "Thank you."

She stooped to pick up her coat from the floor and her hair parted under its own weight, exposing the birthmark on the nape of her neck. Cascading in a shimmering sable tide around her face, her long tresses brushed across the swell of her breasts, generating a reaction in Jess's nether regions, which startled him, spurring him to move away from her. She picked up her purse and keys, her face a blank mask, and dropped them into her pockets, then looked at him expectantly.

He opened the door for her and was rewarded with a nod of gratitude and a second dose of her cologne as she stepped past him. Cursing her silently for having reminded him how long it had been since he'd been intimate with a woman, Jess marched out, working hard to revive the gut-deep hatred he'd harbored for her until last night. He had to get it back. It was the only effective shield to use against her, like a crucifix thrust in the face of Dracula. Drastic measures were called for, because in the space of a little more than twelve hours, Lisa Gillette had begun to nibble away at his soul.

Jess was silent in the elevator, for which Lisa was grateful. She might be tempted to apologize for her behavior, but since it had evoked the desired result, she would keep quiet. The anger she'd felt in his pickup last night was nothing to the utter fury she'd experienced when he'd told her to go home. And if it had taken an offer to submit to a strip search to convince him she wasn't armed, what would it take to convince him she'd had nothing to do with the murderous assault on his friend?

Certainly the news that Mallory had gone to her house hoping to talk to her would not help. If anything, it would confirm Jess's suspicions of some mysterious link between them, even though she was still positive there was none. She was a miniaturist, with a growing reputation. Mallory might well have wanted to commission her to construct a particular miniature or the model of a room. Perhaps he had come to request her help in acquiring something specific from the London exhibit she was scheduled to attend this summer—several people had asked that she represent them at the auction, which was to follow.

Jess Hampton would probably dismiss all of those possibilities. Perhaps as a former policeman, suspicion was an element of his makeup. He would believe what he wanted. Since he was so single-mindedly hardheaded, it would make more sense not to tell him anything at all. He was antagonistic enough toward her already. Yet there was a moment back in the conference room, when she had the distinct impression he was about to kiss her—which proved just how tired she was. Either that or she was going bonkers. This man hated her guts.

The elevator doors opened. They stepped out and crossed to the nurses' station at the hub of the T-shaped unit. A petite blond nurse watched a bank of monitors embedded in the surface of a large circular desk. She glanced up.

"Hi, Mr. Hampton. You're early."

"Played hookey from work," Jess said. "How's he doing today?"

She flashed him a quick professional smile, her eyes darting to Lisa with open curiosity. "No better, no worse. Dr. Trent's on the floor, if you'd like to talk to him."

"No, don't bother him. We won't be long," he said, with a pointed look at Lisa.

"If I see him, I'll let him know you're here."

"Thanks. This way." He tilted his head toward a wing to their left and set off at a brisk, loose-limbed pace, leaving Lisa to catch up.

Annoyed, she trailed him, refusing to hurry. Now that she was here, she wasn't looking forward to facing someone in Clifford Mallory's condition. She took her time, bolstering her courage, reminding herself that she needn't stay any longer than it would take to get a good look at him, inform Jess Hampton that she'd never seen the man before and leave.

Each of the rooms they passed had a large window, affording the staff a clear view of the patient inside, and preparing her for what waited in 426. The patients on this floor were obviously in need of critical care and all that implied. Steeling herself, Lisa followed Jess to the open door at the end of the hall. The blinds over this window were down.

Jess went into a room deep with shadows. "Damn it, Mal, have you been in the dark all day?" He moved to the window opposite the door and opened the curtains, flooding the room with afternoon light.

Lisa, hanging back, could hear the steady, rhythmic voice of a heart monitor. The sound chilled her. Perhaps it was just as well the patient in 426 couldn't hear it.

"Excuse me," someone said from behind her.

Lisa jumped, startled to find a nurse practically on her heels. She was a tall, thin woman, her cap perched like a fluted cupcake container atop her wispy brown hair.

"I'm so sorry, Mr. Hampton," she blurted, bustling into the room. "I just remembered the curtains. We closed them when the sun came around to this side of the building and I just hadn't had a chance to get back."

His scowl melted. "No problem. I thought they'd been closed all day. It's important that he be able to feel the sun on his face. If he has any awareness at all, it'll help him distinguish day from night." Seeing that Lisa had not yet entered, he waved her in. "What's the problem? Considering the lengths you went to get here, I'd have thought you'd beat me through the door."

"You have company, Mr. Mallory," the nurse sang out cheerfully as Lisa stepped into the room. "Mr. Hampton's here and he's brought a beautiful young lady to see you. Isn't that nice?" She became very busy, arranging covers, patting pillows.

Lisa walked to the foot of the bed and tried to ignore the bottles, tubes, wires and assorted gadgets she couldn't identify. Mounted on the wall above the patient's head were several monitors, one with a tiny red light that blinked periodically, others with the ubiquitous screens, jagged lines dancing across their faces. It was a second before she could identify the one that beeped and she watched it, a hostage to its one-note song.

"I'll leave you to your visitors now, Mr. Mallory," the nurse announced loudly. "I'll be back to look in on you in a while." She checked an IV drip, took one last look at the screens above the bed, smiled vacuously and left.

With her departure, the room seemed less crowded, the monitors and other paraphernalia a bit less threatening. Lisa lowered her eyes and looked into the face of Clifford Mallory, understanding immediately why Kitty had reacted as she had. There was an open, boyish quality about the broad forehead and rounded chin, and the thick, curly hair contributed to the impression of youth despite its color, a beautiful steel gray.

A faint stubble protruded from his cheeks. His skin was pale, with a lifeless quality, and it was obvious that he'd lost considerable weight. Despite that, she had a sense of a dynamic individual whose vitality was in stasis. And he was a stranger, his face completely unfamiliar. If she had ever seen or met him before, she'd had no reason to remember him.

Jess's scrutiny of her was a palpable force. "Well?" he demanded truculently.

Lisa shook her head. Oddly she felt a curious absence of rancor toward Mallory. She'd expected to be filled with something—anger, hostility, soaring satisfaction that fate had dealt his man such a crushing blow. But she had no such emotions.

She knew intellectually that this was the man who had left her life in shambles but the animus she'd anticipated was not there. Instead there was only an overwhelming compassion for someone suffering death of another kind.

He was so still, breathing without help of a respirator, but other than the rise and fall of his chest under the sheet, he was absolutely motionless. The thought that he'd lain like this for ten weeks made her heart squeeze with sympathy, for him and for Jess and the long, lonely vigil he'd been keeping.

Lisa moved to the side of the bed, careful to avoid the tube that snaked its way up to one of two IV bottles suspended from a pole anchored to the headboard. Jess stirred uneasily, but she ignored him, her attention riveted on Mallory.

"I should give him a shave." Jess sounded defensive. "They give him one every morning, but—" he raised his voice a little "—you're a hairy brute, aren't you, old man?"

"Go ahead," Lisa said, startled at the hoarseness of her voice. Clearing her throat, she sat in the easy chair beside the window, wondering why she felt a need to stay.

She watched in silence as Jess progressed through the ritual—wetting Mallory's face with a damp cloth, spreading the thick white foam, wetting the disposable razor in the lavatory tucked in an alcove beside the window. Then he began to shave him with smooth, even strokes and launched into a lively monologue, which consisted of the day's events—the news in capsule to the accompaniment of the slow, persistent beeps of the monitor. It had not fluctuated at all since they'd arrived. Lisa found that her attitude about it had changed. There was something reassuring about the slow, even chirp, proof that despite whatever else might be amiss with him, Mallory's heart tended to its business, keeping him alive.

Lisa was also trying to come to grips with a Jess she hadn't seen before, a warm, caring man whose tender ministrations to his friend betrayed an aspect of his character she would have never dreamed existed. He had expressed his feelings for Clifford Mallory last night, but Lisa, seeing the open, gentle affection Jess was displaying, realized that the bond ran far deeper than he'd indicated. Father and son, or brother and brother, she wasn't sure which, but it went a long way toward increasing her understanding of Jess's concern for Mallory's safety.

"Oh, I forgot," he was saying. He'd finished with the right side of Mallory's face and moved around to the left. "The Orioles won yesterday. Three in a row. How about that? They play again tonight. The Bullets aren't doing so badly, either. Mal's a rabid basketball fan," he said in an aside to her.

Lisa forced a smile. If he could be civil, so could she. "He and Alec would make a matched set, only with Alec, it's baseball, football, basketball and hockey. Unless there's a deadline looming, he goes to all the—" Her sentence went unfinished, interrupted by a gasp.

Jess stopped on an upstroke, his head whipping back to look up at the machines above the bed. The pace of the monitor had increased.

Lisa jumped to her feet, her eyes darting from the luminous green square to Mallory's face. "What's wrong? What's happening?" He looked no different than before, except that the rise and fall of his chest was considerably faster.

The silence between soundings lessened even more, and the jagged line danced rapidly across the center screen. Jess, his lips pinched in a hard, straight line, reached for the call button, unnecessarily, since the muted hiss of crepe soles on resilient tile were already hurrying in their direction.

A short, compact man, a stethoscope dangling from his pocket, dashed into the room. "Out!" he snapped, bending over the bed. "*Now,* please!"

Jess tossed the razor into the sink, took Lisa's arm and bustled her out into the hall. The petite blond nurse came at a trot, entered the room and closed the door behind her.

"Does he have a bad heart?" Lisa asked, her throat dry with fright.

"No. I don't know what happened. I didn't nick him. Even if I had, it wouldn't have mattered. He hasn't been responding to pain. Damn it, he can't die now. He's come too far to die now."

Lisa turned away from the raw anguish in his eyes, unable to think of anything to say. She suspected it wouldn't be well received at any rate, and took refuge at the window, which looked out over a rolling green lawn. Head lowered, Jess paced like a caged tiger, hands buried deep in his pockets.

Ten minutes elapsed before the door opened and the doctor stuck his head out. "You can come in," he said and stepped back to let them pass. Lisa moved into the room but remained near the door, not wanting to be in the way.

"Is he all right?" Jess positioned himself at Mallory's side.

"He's fine."

"Really, Doc? He's out of danger?"

"Calm down, Hampton. He's fine. What happened in here anyway? What were you doing?"

"Shaving him. I've done it before. You can see I didn't cut him. I was talking to him about the Orioles' game when the monitor started going crazy."

"Is this the first time you've mentioned the team to him?"

"Hell, no. Your orders were to talk about subjects that interested him and that's what I've done."

"Odd. Did he look any different to you while you were shaving him?"

Jess shrugged helplessly. "Not to me."

The doctor turned to Lisa. "What about you? I'm Dr. Trent, by the way. Were you watching?"

"I couldn't see his face while Jess was shaving his right side, but when he moved around the bed I—"

Lisa stopped, her eyes widening. The beep-beep-beep had speeded up and the red light on the second monitor blinked faster.

"Oh, God." Jess groaned. "Not again."

Lisa stepped out of the door as the doctor peeled back the sheet and pressed the stethoscope to Mallory's chest. "Check his BP," he ordered. The nurse grabbed the cuff, wound it around the free arm and inflated it, the squish-squish of the bulb in breathy counterpoint to the persistent call of the monitor. There were a few seconds of silence while she watched the gauge.

"Same as before, Doctor. One-fifty over eighty-five."

He straightened, removing the stethoscope, and eyed the screens overhead, frowning.

"What's happening to him?" Jess demanded.

Dr. Trent waved a hand for silence, watching the indicators gradually slow to their former speed. After several interminable minutes, he replaced the sheet and stood gazing thoughtfully at Mallory. "Interesting. Let's go over this again. You were talking about the Orioles at the exact moment it started before?"

Jess nodded. "Yes. I was telling Lis . . . Ms. Gillette what a fan he was. And she said—"

Dr. Trent, his attention still riveted on Mallory, held up a hand again. Jess broke off in midsentence, his expression a blend of annoyance and confusion. "You said what, Ms. Gillette?" the doctor asked, his back to her.

Lisa moved one step into the room. "Something to the effect that Mr. Mallory and my boss would get along fine because—"

The monitors accelerated. Dr. Trent swiveled in Lisa's direction and stared at her. "I'll be damned. It's her."

"Pardon?"

"You're the culprit who's setting him off. He's responding to your voice. When I asked before, Hampton gave me the impression that he was speaking when this happened the first time, but he wasn't, was he? You were. The last time you were responding to my question about whether you could see his face, and just now, when it happened again, you were speaking. He's reacting to your voice."

"He couldn't be," Lisa protested.

"Want to see a printout? His respiration, heartbeat and blood pressure increase considerably—not to the point there's anything to be concerned about, but it scared the bejabbers out of us because it's the first time it's happened since he was admitted and we couldn't tell whether it would escalate into a life-threatening condition." He grinned, and ten years dropped from his face. "You speak, the monitors go yah-ha. You shut up and they slow down. Don't you realize what that means, Hampton?" He spun around to Jess, his eyes sparkling, and patted the top of his thinning hair. "He's *in* there! He's reacting, man! Why aren't you kicking up your heels? This is what we've been waiting for!"

Jess smiled, took a deep breath and ran his fingers through his hair. "I guess I'm in shock. One second I think he's about to check out on me and the next... Give me a minute to adjust."

"Take two minutes—you deserve it. Wysocki, get somebody to run an EEG. I want to compare yesterday's brain activity with today's."

"Yes, sir!" She dimpled prettily and trotted out.

"Now, Ms. Gillette. Tell me about yourself. What are you to our friend here?"

"A man after my own heart," Jess said dryly. "Gets right to the point." He strolled around the end of the bed and collapsed in the chair, leaning back to look up at her lazily. "I'm as interested in her answer as you are, Dr. Trent. Wouldn't you deduce that if Mal is reacting to her voice, it's one he recognizes, one he knows particularly well?"

Dr. Trent stared at him curiously. "Of course."

"Of course. That's what makes this so bizarre," Jess said in a conversational tone. "Because my old buddy there is responding to the voice of a woman who says she doesn't know him. According to Ms. Gillette, until today, she'd never seen him before in her life."

Lisa felt trapped. If she spoke, tried to defend herself, the monitors would be off to the races again, blinking and beeping, putting the lie to anything she said. But she could not tolerate the smug smile on Jess's face or ignore the dare in his eyes.

"I am telling you for the last time," she said, her teeth clenched, "I have never met Clifford Mallory. Considering his choice of friends, I'd just as soon leave it that way. I'm sorry he was so badly injured, but I had nothing to do with it. I sincerely hope he recovers. As for you, Jess Hampton, you and your blasted suspicions and your nasty disposition, you can go to hell." Nodding a terse goodbye to Dr. Trent, she turned and marched out.

Chapter 5

Lisa trudged up the stairs to the loft, balancing a bag of groceries, her attaché case, several library books and the day's *Washington Post*. Unlocking the door, she nudged it open and went in, dropping the books and letting the attaché case slide off her arm to the floor. The loft was now a model of "after," with little resemblance to the riot of clutter that had comprised the "before."

She'd come back from the fiasco at Greenhaven to find that Kitty, having learned that she'd be using it for a while, had started getting it ready for her with the same manic energy with which she approached her design projects. "This was where Alec and I spent our honeymoon," she bubbled. "Our first, sweet little home. It'll be perfect for you. You'll see."

It had taken the better part of an afternoon and evening's hard labor, with Brad supplying the muscle for the heavier lifting, to make a dent in the loft. It now contained a sitting area, a screened-off bed- and dressing room and a kitchenette Lisa hadn't realized was there. She had rejoiced at the prospect of cooking her own meals for the first time since she'd left for New England.

Spotting something new, a big bag from Sears, she opened it. Dishes, a twenty-piece set, a contribution Brad had promised. She put the perishables away, her nose twitching; the faint aroma of an unfamiliar cologne lingered in the air. Musk? It had to be Brad's. Kitty swore that the smell of musk made her queasy, in which case he would not be using it for very long.

Rescuing her briefcase from behind the door, Lisa sat down in the rocking chair she had discovered behind a highboy in the next room. After a breather, she would run over to the warehouse and start ferrying what she'd need to exist for a while, especially clothes. The heavy things she'd worn against the New England winter were beginning to suffocate her—the April temperatures were in the sixties. But first came her daily ritual—checking her list of things to do before Kitty bustled in from her shopping trip with the client who lived in Virginia hunt country.

Kicking her shoes off, Lisa sent a silent thank-you to Sara what's-her-name. She had picked Kitty to redo the living and dining room of her new home just before Christmas and the two had been thick as thieves ever since, chatting on the phone daily like teenagers. It was Sara, Kitty maintained, whose moral support had helped her survive the previous two-plus months. Now, with things back to normal, they were planning to remodel Sara's kitchen.

Lisa scratched a line through the errands she'd tackled today, before her gaze snagged on the fourth item on the list—"Check on C.M." She was still surprised that she'd had the nerve to call and talk to Dr. Trent the day before. He had surprised her by being far more forthcoming than she'd anticipated, making it clear that concern for his patient overrode all other factors.

"There's definite improvement, Ms. Gillette. My impression—and I'll admit it's as unscientific as hell—is that he's been biding his time, waiting for something—or somebody. I think that someone was you, which is the only reason I'm talking to you. I'm not interested in whether you knew him before or didn't. All I care about is that he responded to you, and needs the stimulation you provided. I think you can make the difference between his pulling out of that coma in the very near future."

This startling opinion might prove to be a godsend, Lisa mused. "Have you told Jess . . . Mr. Hampton that?"

"No, I wanted to talk to you first. He's not very rational about you. I'd sure appreciate it if you two made peace with each other for Mr. Mallory's sake."

And for her sake as well, Lisa thought, after their conversation had ended. If Clifford Mallory was able to talk when he regained consciousness, she wanted to be there. The sooner she found out what he'd had to tell her, the sooner she'd be able to sleep nights. But to see him she'd have to work around Jess, which seemed impossible now, or make him an ally, which seemed unlikely. Still, the unlikely left more room for her to work with than the impossible, if she could just figure out . . .

"Yoo-hoo! Lisa, you up there?" Kitty was back.

Sighing, she put aside her list. "Hi, Kitty!"

"Are you decent?"

Please, let her be alone, Lisa thought to herself, shoving her feet into her shoes. If she dragged Sara whatsis up here . . . But the only footsteps on the stairs were Kitty's high heels, and a second later she poked her head in the door, her eyes gleaming with mischievousness.

"You're dressed. Good." She eased the door closed behind her like a conspirator arriving at a meeting of a cabal. "You've got company. Tall, dark and dangerously intriguing."

"Who?"

"Josh Hamilton." Kitty slaughtered names on a regular basis.

"Jess Hampton! Downstairs?"

"He was parked outside in the most gorgeous Porsche. It's lucky Sara let me out in front or he'd have left. He saw me unlock the door and asked if he could leave a message for you. I told him you might be back already. Are you here or not?"

"He knows I am now. You yelled up at me, remember? And I answered."

"Oops. I wasn't thinking. It's just that he's so...intense and brooding, like Heathcliff."

"Make that Bluebeard and you've hit the nail on the head. Send him up."

"All right, but do something with yourself. Good grief, you aren't even wearing makeup." She hurried out.

Lisa scooped up the coat she'd draped over a kitchen chair and tossed it on the bed, hidden from view by a pair of folding screens. There wasn't time to deal with lipstick if she'd wanted to—Kitty was chirping for him to go on up. She smoothed the pleats of her blue-and-green plaid skirt and tugged at the bottom of her sweater. She missed having a full-length mirror. There was one downstairs, but no way for her to get to it.

"Oh, stop it," she said aloud. It didn't matter how she looked. Jess wouldn't notice one way or the other.

He was halfway up the stairs when she remembered the copies of Mallory's books from the library. Snatching them from the floor, she slid them under the sofa and nudged them out of sight just as he tapped lightly at the door.

"Come in," she said, ready for the next round of her running battle with Jess Hampton.

The door was slightly ajar. Jess pushed it open, stepped in and for the space of several seconds forgot what he'd planned to say. Lisa must have slept well the night before. The shadows under her eyes were gone. Her skin, clear but China-doll pale before, now had a healthy outdoors glow, and her eyes were more green today, reflecting the rich avocado of her cowl-neck sweater, angora or perhaps lambswool, fluffy and begging to be stroked. In spite of its loose fit, Jess had no problem imagining what was under it, and the memory of how close he'd been to making a fool of himself in the conference room was jarring enough to remind him why he'd come. He needed her. More accurately, Mal needed her. And he had come up with the only logical conclusion for his buddy's reaction to her voice.

Mal had been researching the sex scene. His emphasis had been on call girls, but he had also investigated the most recent variation of the world's oldest profession, call girls of quite another type, the ones on the other end of a telephone line, whose steamy conversations could evoke in some the same re-action as that of a face-to-face encounter.

Jess had been astonished to learn that the sister of a friend was paying her way through graduate school by fulfilling the erotic fantasies of gentlemen callers three evenings a week. According to her, all it took was a bit of imagination and the ability to listen and surmise what the party on the line wanted to hear. It was harmless, she maintained, safe sex in the most literal sense, and the longer the call lasted, the bigger her cut. She had chuckled, remarking that he would be surprised how many perfectly respectable women, quite a few of them housewives, saw no harm in supplementing their regular paychecks and budgets in this manner. Considering Mal's reaction to Lisa's voice, she had to have been one of the telephone titillators he had interviewed. Even Pete had to admit it was possible, but from his point of view, it made no difference.

"You may be right," Pete conceded grudgingly, "but even if she's been stupid enough to get involved in that kind of thing, it still doesn't put her under suspicion for murder." Pete saw no point in wasting manpower in an attempt to prove that Lisa had an unorthodox part-time job.

Jess realized that his supposition was based on more "ifs" than there were in Kipling's poem, but damn it, it made sense. If he could establish that Lisa had been one of the women Mal had interviewed by phone, he had a jumping-off place. If Mal had stumbled on to her identity and had used her to get more information about the entrepreneurs who'd set up the system in Washington, the contract on his life was a foregone conclusion.

And now that the news of her return had made the morning paper, Mal's head would be on the chopping block again to prevent any possibility of his continuing what he'd started. The fact that they'd put the hit on him rather than Lisa meant that he was important to somebody. Relieved at having a focus for his suspicions, Jess had decided on a plan, and this visit played a part in it. Now if he could just get her out of the room for thirty seconds ...

"How'd you find me?" she asked.

"Process of elimination. You have lots of casual friends, but only two you'd feel comfortable enough to bunk with for any length of time—the Joyners."

A trace of irritation flashed in her eyes. "You've been busy. Only I'm not bunking with them, I'm staying here. Have you come to make a citizen's arrest or what?"

"Sorry to disappoint you," he said, forcing a light tone. "Not enough evidence."

"That's good to know. How is Mr. Mallory?"

"Improving. You really started something. He'll squeeze your finger lightly or move his toes if you keep asking him and wait long enough for something to happen."

"Really? That's marvelous!"

Good, he thought. Her response seemed sincere. "It looks like he's fighting to come out of it for the first time. I'm sorry, I should have asked—are you free? If you have a moment, I'd like to talk to you." She tensed. "It won't take long, I promise."

"I was just about to leave but I can spare five minutes. Would you like to sit down?"

Jess found himself breathing a little easier. She hadn't kicked him out. He lowered himself onto a spindle-backed chair, and she took the rocker, but sat forward on it, her elbows on her knees. The message was clear—she would not be there long.

"How're things going with you?" he asked. "I imagine you've had a lot of things to do."

"Yes. It's scary to find out how much of your life depends on the space you take up in various computer banks. I spent the morning at Social Security, thinking I'd be able to use my driver's license as proof of identity, until someone pointed out that under the circumstances, my license is probably void. So now that's on the list of things to straighten out, too."

"I have a few contacts at Motor Vehicles, from my days on the force. I may be able to speed things up a little, if that would help."

"Would you?" He could see he'd surprised her. She hadn't expected that. "It terrifies me to think I've been driving around with a license that isn't any good. Not that it'll matter after tomorrow."

"Why not?" He settled back. Perhaps he'd have ten or fifteen minutes, rather than just five.

"My lease on the camper runs out. I kept wondering why it hadn't been listed as stolen, especially after all my credit cards were canceled. The answer's simple. I paid for it in advance with a check, which must have cleared the bank before my accounts were frozen. It goes back tomorrow because I can't afford to keep it any longer."

"How will you get around?"

"Like everybody else—by subway or bus." She checked her watch. "You said you wanted to talk to me about something? I'm about out of time. I've got to get to the warehouse before dark."

"The warehouse?" Jess echoed blankly.

"All my things are in storage. I'm hoping a copy of my birth certificate arrived before the post office stopped delivering my mail. I had sent for it to use with a passport application, but Social Security will accept it as proof of identity, too. If it didn't come, I can use my school records as proof, if I can lay my hands on them."

"Oh, that's right. Someone else packed for you."

"Yes, Kitty, and according to the inventory she made, there are over eighty cartons to paw through. I have to cram whatever I can into the camper tonight, since I won't have it after tomorrow."

Jess's lowered eyes masked a gleam of triumph. Opportunity seemed to be shoving things into his lap. Here was a chance to see if there was a stray briefcase on that inventory. "You may not be aware of it, but those boxes will be stacked to the ceiling. You'll never be able to move them by yourself. I have a suggestion. I'll go trade the Porsche for my pickup, take you to the warehouse and we'll load it with everything you'll need."

"I could bring my collection, my tools?" Her voice became husky, her expression wistful. "It's been so long since I've had a pin vise in my hand." She looked down at her open palm, then up at him. In that fraction of a second, her eyes had hardened. "What do I have to do in exchange for your generous offer of help? Write a full confession? Name names?"

Jess let several heartbeats go by. It was important that he say this right. "Look, Lisa, you may not know Mal, but you have to admit that he must know you."

She looked away, reinforcing his initial impression. She knew something—she was holding out on him and the police. He hurried to get the rest said before it was too late. "We got off on the wrong foot and I'm sorry about that. Pete says I'm too close to the situation and shooting at anything that moves. If you want an apology, you've got it. Just don't take your anger at me out on Mal."

"How do you mean?"

"I have a favor to ask. Would you mind visiting him, say, every couple of days?" Her eyes widened and Jess pressed his case. "For whatever reason, you're good for him. He'll work for you, fight harder if you're there, I don't care why. You can pull him out of this. I'll pick you up, take you there and bring you right back to your door."

"Does this mean you've dropped the idiotic notion that I'll try to kill him?"

"I overreacted. That's how much he means to me. Please, Lisa. I . . . *he* needs you. What do you say? Truce?"

She took her time about responding and Jess forced himself to be patient. There was too much at stake. If she thought she was making him sweat, she was right. He wasn't sure what he'd do if she said no—he was willing to mangle his principles only so far and no farther. Up to this point in his conversation, he had not lied to her. He didn't think she would try anything. But she was still under suspicion—way under.

She extended her hand. "All right, Jess Hampton. Truce." They shook on it. "Now if you'll excuse me, I'd better go slip into something more comfortable—for crawling around a warehouse, that is," she added hurriedly. She blushed, then laughed with genuine mirth for the first time since they'd met. Even her skin seemed to smile, and Jess's breath stopped somewhere in the vicinity of his epiglottis. Still chuckling, she disappeared behind a pair of folding screens and he pulled himself together. He wasn't over the hump yet.

"Mind if I use the phone?" he called.

"Help yourself. Just make sure Kitty isn't on the line first."

Picking up the receiver, he dialed his own number and turned his back to shield her view of his activities if she should look around the screens. Working quickly, he unscrewed the cap of the receiver and wedged a listening device into its interior. "No answer," he said, replacing the cap. "Thanks anyway."

"Sure. Can I get you anything? Coffee? Tea?"

Jess plopped back down, supplying the finish of her question—"Or me?"—in his mind. "No, thanks." Was she deliberately being suggestive? Whether she was or not, he could not afford to lose sight of his goal—Mal's rehabilitation, and proving once and for all her link with his buddy. He must not allow her to bewitch him any more than she had already for another reason as well.

Two years before he'd faced the fact that a part of his mind was still in a hot, stinking VC tunnel in Vietnam, that he'd brought home all the anger, pain and terror he'd suffered as a prisoner of that hole, trapped underground for several days. He had turned in his badge and gun, afraid of the intensity of the maelstrom should he ever fail to control it.

The flare-ups and, for the most part, the nightmares, were now history. Only one souvenir of his experience hung on, a minor problem, all things considered, but a problem of which he was deeply ashamed. He had promised himself that until he was able to sleep at night like every other adult he knew, in a darkened room, no lamps burning, no night-light, he would avoid even the possibility of a serious relationship with a woman. Celibacy was vastly overrated but it was simpler.

He'd been helped by the fact that he hadn't met anyone who threatened his resolve—until Lisa Gillette. He'd tried his damnedest to hate her and had failed. Hell, two days ago, he'd been a breath away from kissing her. Now the thought that she might be half-dressed behind those folding screens was playing havoc with his body. It had been so long since he'd held a woman in his arms.

But he didn't dare touch her. She was under suspicion, if only his suspicion, and that meant he had to keep his distance. Even if he hadn't been out to prove she wasn't the innocent bystander Pete considered her, he'd be in the same boat. He would never share his bed with any woman until he no longer broke out in a sweat at the thought that she might reach over and turn out the light. That day—or night—had yet to come, so no matter how he felt, it was hands off.

Lisa came around from behind the screen in form-fitting jeans and a long-sleeved boat-neck T-shirt. Pushing her hair back from her face, she looped a rubber band around the long, shimmering mane. The action pulled the fabric of her shirt taut across her uptilted breasts, emphasizing their fullness.

Hands off? Jess thought. God help me.

Finding what she needed wasn't as simple as Lisa had thought it would be, primarily because of the method Kitty had used to mark the cartons—an indication of the room from which the contents had come but with no other clues. A container labeled master bedroom might hold linens, draperies, books or clothes. As a result, by the next evening, the loft bore a disheartening resemblance to the "before" picture again, with stacks of boxes substituting for the clutter it had taken so long to remove.

"This is ridiculous," Lisa declared when Jess came in with the last of the load from his pickup truck. "Jess, I'm sorry. It never occurred to me that I'd have to move half my worldly possessions just to find a few papers and a change of wardrobe. I can't imagine why Kitty labeled them this way."

Jess eased his burden to the floor and eyed the row of cartons he had shuttled to an out-of-the-way spot behind the door. "It's understandable. She was packing for storage, not for a move from one house to another. At least you'll have what you need. When you've finished, I'll reseal them and take them back."

"Jess! I couldn't ask you to do that."

"You don't have to," he said, folding his arms. "I'm volunteering. I'm just sorry we couldn't start this process yesterday."

Lisa still wasn't sure why Jess had voted to wait and begin this morning. Granted, rather than the storage cage they had anticipated, they'd been confronted with a trailer-sized packing crate, complete with interior work lights and ventilation system. Unfortunately the bulb at the end where the boxes were stacked had burned out, leaving the area in deep shadow. Despite the problem, Kitty's fat, round letters were large enough to be seen fairly easily. Jess, however, had balked at working in such poor visibility. Seeing that he felt so strongly about it, she had bowed to his wish to wait and get an early start this morning. The delay meant a revision of the schedule she'd mapped out for herself—there was no point in returning to Social Security without the documents she needed—but the notion of having her belongings, if not her house, seemed a fair enough trade-off.

Taking a visual count of the cartons, Lisa frowned as she reached the ones pushed into the corner. "Jess, these are from my workroom."

"Right. You wanted your tools, didn't you?"

"Yes, but that was before I saw what a monumental job this would be. I never dreamed there'd be so many from my bedroom."

"Then what's a few more?" He perched on a windowsill, his long legs extended, ankles crossed. "The loft looks very comfortable, Lisa, but without the special things that will make it yours, you'll always feel like a transient."

Lisa was nonplussed by this show of sensitivity, especially since he'd struck a nerve. As hard as Kitty had worked to make the place livable, it still had the impersonal air of a rental unit, reinforcing her status as a refugee. She missed her home and the atmosphere she'd worked so hard to create.

"Now," he said, pushing up his sleeves to bare, lean, muscular forearms. "I'll arrange them so you can get to them easily. While I'm at it, I'll separate the ones from your workroom and the front hall. I have a utility knife, so I might as well open them, too."

"Jess, that's not necessary. You've done enough. I can..." The sentence and the thought that had propelled it lost steam under the piercing quality of his gaze. He seemed focused on her with intense concentration.

"Do you always have this much trouble accepting an offer of help?" he asked gently.

The question brought her up short. "Yes, I guess I do."

"Used to doing things for yourself? Or are you afraid I'll think you're taking advantage of my good nature?" His lips twitched.

"A little of both," Lisa admitted, preferring to take the question seriously. "I do appreciate everything you've done. You've been terrific. I guess I'm just accustomed to tackling things on my own. My mother drummed that into me pretty early. I keep hearing her voice. 'Be sure you can depend on yourself before you depend on anyone else.'"

"She sounds like a very independent lady."

"She was. My father died when I was three and she raised me alone. It couldn't have been easy."

"Did she work?"

"Oh, yes. She was into computer systems, an unusual job for a woman back in the late sixties. She must have been good at it because as soon as she'd gotten one company up and running, another would be waiting to hire her. We were constantly on the move, from one town to another, one boarding house to the next. Between the first and fourth grades, I went to more schools than a substitute teacher."

"That's a lot of moving," Jess said, his laser-sharp gaze turned up to full intensity.

"We traveled fairly light and that made a difference. By the time I started elementary school, I had learned to pack everything I owned in an hour. We used to make a game of it...." She paused, a puzzled expression slipping across her features.

"What's wrong?" Jess asked.

"Nothing. One of those memories that sneaks in and out of your head before you've had a chance to grab it."

Jess pushed himself to his feet. "Change of plans. You are looking at a very hungry man. Why don't I run out and get a couple of pizzas?"

Lisa gave that half a second's thought, came up with an alternative, but wasn't certain how it would be received. "I've got a better idea. I'm cooking."

Despite his smile of delight, Jess held up his hands. "You don't have to do that. It's been a long day. You must be beat."

Her head tilted to one side, Lisa asked, "Do you always have this much trouble accepting a home-cooked meal?"

He blinked, then his rich, full laughter filled the loft, sending a strange little quiver down Lisa's spine. "Touché, mademoiselle. I would love a home-cooked meal."

"Is spaghetti okay?"

"Spaghetti sounds great. I'll help. I'm very good at twist-off lids and pop-top cans, and I have more than a nodding acquaintance with ready-made tomato sauce."

Lisa assumed an expression of lofty indignation. "I make my own sauce, thank you very much. Consider it payment for all the lifting and hauling."

"Which is in exchange for your visits to Mal, so we're square. Why don't I go get a bottle of wine?"

"Chianti," she amended.

"Chianti, it is. Back in a jiffy." He shrugged into a denim jacket and was gone.

Lisa gazed at the closed door in thought. It had taken her a while to relax around Jess. They had had so few civil exchanges before yesterday that she had difficulty adjusting to him in the role of Dr. Jekyll. She kept expecting a metamorphosis, certain that Mr. Hyde would surface at any moment. So far, that hadn't happened. Perhaps it was time to lower her guard a little. When he wasn't waging a witch-hunt, Lisa decided, Jess Hampton could be very pleasant company.

What a stroke of luck that he'd unwittingly solved the problem she'd faced yesterday, making it unnecessary to use subterfuge to visit Mallory. He'd thrown the door wide open for her, which as far as Lisa was concerned, meant that a hidden agenda lurked somewhere out of sight. Truce or no, she wasn't quite ready to take the declaration of his change of attitude about her at face value. A leopard couldn't alter its spots, no matter how much bleach he used. His suspicion of her would always linger in a shadowy corner of his mind and once Mallory was awake and able to talk, he'd know that his reservations were justified. But what game was he playing with her in the interim?

Her battery of questions continued as she began the makings for the spaghetti sauce, browning, chopping, dicing, mincing, her hands on automatic pilot while her mind wandered through a maze of possibilities, running up against one dead end after another. By the time the sauce began to simmer, Lisa had concluded that whether or not Jess was up to something, she was in no position to point a finger and shout, "J'accuse!"

She had yet to tell him that Mal had come to her house to see her, and wouldn't, for the time being, no matter how hard her conscience bucked and kicked. She didn't want to rock the boat. This new, unfamiliar Jess had a number of unsettling but affecting qualities, among them the low-key manner and quiet masculinity that combined to give him a presence she found difficult to ignore. Something about Jess heightened her awareness of herself, her body, her senses, the physical and emotional needs she kept locked behind closed doors.

Furthermore her intuition told her that he understood things about her that she had yet to understand. It unnerved her. She felt vulnerable and at his mercy, a singularly precarious position, under the circumstances. Their truce was as fragile as a spider's web. Once it ended, as it was bound to sooner or later, mercy would be the farthest thing from Jess's mind. She dreaded that day because, in spite of everything, she liked him. Still, there was no point in getting used to him. They were on borrowed time and she would be wise not to forget that.

Jess came back with the Chianti, two long-stemmed plastic wineglasses, a loaf of Italian bread, a basket of strawberries and a half-pint of heavy cream. Lisa put him to work making the salad while she mixed the dressing, prepared garlic butter and hulled the berries. The mood was relaxed and they worked well together, moving in tandem as they performed their respective chores in a smoothly choreographed culinary pas de deux.

The meal, too, was relaxed and unhurried. Jess complimented her efforts by having seconds and scraping the pot and his plate clean. But Lisa was determined to make the most of the moment. Baiting her hook with carefully posed questions, she cast her line, fishing for information about Clifford Mallory. Jess lounged in his chair, sipping at his Chianti, his attitude a mellow blend of nostalgia and pensiveness.

"My parents died when I was in Vietnam," he began, in response to her query about how he and Mallory had become such good friends, "killed by an idiot driving under the influence."

"I'm sorry. How old were you?"

"Eighteen. It's funny, I went off to 'Nam knowing there was a distinct possibility I'd never see them again," he said, as if expressing the thought for the first time. "Only it never occurred to me they'd be the ones to die instead of me. At any rate, Mal was my superior, a major. He was the one who had to tell me about my folks. When I got back from emergency leave, he was the one who saw me through the grief and guilt and bitterness."

"Guilt?"

"That I was alive. Mal sort of adopted me and played daddy for a while. Once I was past needing a father, he became a friend."

"You said he saved your life."

Jess nodded. "He and I and a kid named Cherry walked into an ambush about a month before troop withdrawal began in earnest. Cherry was killed. I caught a bullet in my hip. Mal wouldn't leave me and we were captured."

"You were a POW?" Lisa asked, uncertain how far to pursue this. Jess's face had tightened and his eyes were narrowed with remembered pain.

"Yes, but not for long. They played imaginative games with us for a couple of days, but they lowered their guard the second night and Mal managed to free himself. I was only half-conscious, so a lot of it is hazy, but the next thing I knew, Mal had me draped over his shoulder carrying me through the jungle."

"How far did he have to travel?" She hadn't meant to draw things out, but it seemed important to see the patient in 426 as a fully fleshed-out person.

"Mal guesses he walked roughly four miles, but four miles in a jungle is like twenty anywhere else. With a bullet in your hip, multiply that by a hundred."

"You weren't given medical treatment?"

His laugh was hollow and humorless. "Treatment, yes. Medical, no. At any rate, we almost bought it when Mal ran right up behind a VC scouting party. He spotted them just in time, and we played possum until dark. He found a place for us to lie low, since it looked like the VC weren't going anywhere, and came back to get me. I was in pretty bad shape by that time, burning up with fever, really out of it."

"So you were lucky to survive."

Jess sat up and folded his hands above his empty plate. "I survived because that pigheaded SOB cut out the bullet and fed and nursed me for a week, right under the noses of the VC. When they finally left, he carried me to the nearest road and we were picked up by our guys. I owe him. He practically butchered my hip, but if he hadn't, I wouldn't be here."

"I can see why he means so much to you," Lisa said solemnly.

"I think we'd have been good friends even if that hadn't happened. I get such a kick out of hearing him talk. He talked the whole time we were hiding, to take my mind off the pain, gave me his autobiography from his childhood on up, his marriage, his career, the books he wanted to write." His lips formed a warm smile. "He still does it. We see each other every couple of months and I get the next chapters of his life story."

"If he's that open with you, you must be very special to him."

Jess thought it over for a second. "Well, there's open and there's open. Every spring he goes into an emotional black hole. It's not so much a depression as a . . . a silent rage. When he's like that, I might as well be talking to a cement wall. He's promised to explain some day. So far that day hasn't come."

Lisa sensed that Jess was hurt by this omission. "I guess everyone has their secrets. Do we ever tell anyone absolutely everything about ourselves?"

He raised his eyes, paralyzing her with a look that seemed to burrow into her core. "Perhaps not." The moment seemed to last for aeons.

Lisa didn't move, waiting for the resurgence of Mr. Hyde. She had inadvertently supplied a blatant reminder that he'd accused her of hiding something, which she was. To her relief, he pushed himself away from the table and stood abruptly.

"We'd better tackle the dishes and get back to work. Those boxes won't open by themselves." The moment was over and what passed for normalcy resumed.

Jess stuck to his guns, insisting on arranging and opening boxes for her, teasing her about having had the most crowded bedroom in the District. "How many pages did the inventory run?" he asked. "Five hundred?"

Lisa extracted it from a pile of documents and shoved it under his nose. "Eleven, thank you, and that's because Kitty counted every sheet of sandpaper and drill bit I own."

He took it and flipped through it, scanning each page, and paused at the next to the last. "Only four attaché cases? You're slipping. There are five working days in a week."

"They're all gifts. I have a custom-made case for my miniatures and tools, so I don't use the attachés that often."

He returned the inventory, but seemed distracted, as if his thoughts were somewhere else.

They exchanged histories as they worked, the native Washingtonian and the orphan who had adopted his hometown. Lisa found him easy to talk to and was almost sorry when the cartons had been opened and there was no further reason for him to stay. She agreed to go with him to the hospital the next day and Saturday, leaving Sunday free for relaxing.

After Lisa outlined her schedule for Monday, they settled on a time he would pick her up at the subway station, the agenda to include ferrying a few cartons back to her storage unit before the trip out to Greenhaven. Jess was still adamant about doing whatever needed to be done before dark.

He was about to leave when Brad came up the steps. "Kitty asked me to dig this out for you," he said, placing a space heater just inside the door. "It's still pretty chilly at night."

"Bless her. I've been freezing. By the way," Lisa said, stopping him as he turned to go, "Kitty would never mention it, but she has sort of an allergic reaction to musk cologne."

Brad's high forehead creased with a puzzled frown. "Why are you telling me?"

"You don't wear musk?"

"God, no. My sister used to bathe in the stuff. Turned me against it for life. If what I'm wearing even hints of it, I'm throwing it out."

Lisa assuaged his doubts and he trotted down the steps, mumbling about cologne.

"What was that all about?" Jess asked.

"Oh, nothing. Thanks again, for everything," she said, steering him toward the door. "I'll see you tomorrow."

He took the hint. "Tomorrow it is. And thanks for dinner." After one last puzzled glance, he left and closed the door behind him.

Lisa remained where she was, only vaguely aware that Jess was gone. As a clerk behind a perfume counter at Garfinkles to pay for art classes years before, she had discovered she had a good nose for scents. Musk especially had a very distinctive note, whether combined with floral or spice, or alone.

She was positive she'd detected the fading aroma the day before. Kitty didn't wear it. If Brad didn't, either, and she had little reason to doubt his word, who did?

Lisa gazed around the cluttered loft, trying to talk herself into believing she had imagined it. The windows had been closed, so it could not have wafted up from the street. Perhaps the clerk who'd handled the bags in which the dishes were wrapped had been wearing it. One of the free-lance writers for the *Journal* wore a very distinctive fragrance—"Pink Jasmine"—and her manuscripts were always permeated with it. That had to be the answer, because the only other conclusion would be that a stranger, more accurately an intruder, had been in the loft yesterday. And that was patently ridiculous.

Chapter 6

Angie Sarnof shuffled along Connecticut Avenue, pushing her grocery cart with one hand, clutching the lapels of her coat with the other. The doctor at the free clinic had fussed at her about keeping warm and dry so her cold wouldn't get any worse. Easy for him to say. Her favorite doorway for sleeping sat back a little ways from the building, so it wasn't like she was right out on the sidewalk with nothing to cut the wind, but it was still outdoors and this was April and April nights could be just as chilly as February days.

She trudged along slowly, hugging the curb. She'd missed breakfast. It was a right far piece to the nearest shelter where she could get some hot soup or something filling, and it'd be Christmas before she got there. This was Saturday so people walked slower. They hogged the sidewalk and took their time, making it hard for a body with a grocery cart to go around them.

Stopping in front of a coffee shop to catch her breath, Angie parked her cart beside a trash can and watched the crowds go by. A young woman in a bright red sweater caught her eye because she liked red, and the way the lady walked, tall and proud, with all that pretty hair spread out around her shoulders like shiny brown sateen. Baby Girl's hair had been that color. At the thought of the toddler the judge said she wasn't smart enough to take care of, Angie hugged herself and rocked a little. Somehow rocking always helped the hurt.

The lady slowed at the vendor near the corner to look at his flowers, and Angie watched her choose a bunch of sunny yellow tulips. Someone else was watching, too, Angie noted, a man in a brown raincoat and tan cap. He had crossed the street behind the lady and now he stood at the corner, looking around like he wasn't sure where he was, but mostly looking at the pretty lady.

The lady paid the vendor and came in Angie's direction. Seems to me I seen her before, she thought. Angie's memory could be sometimey, but she was a demon about faces. Could see you once, meet you again a hundred years later and before long she would place you. She was proud of that. And she knew that pretty face from somewheres.

The lady noticed Angie and smiled. Angie stopped rocking and smiled back. The lady went into the coffee shop and took a seat at a table right in the window. Then Angie stopped smiling. The man in the raincoat moved to a spot between the sewing machine store and the coffee shop, and looked around, casual-like. Then his eyes slid to the side and he leaned forward to peek in the window at the lady. He tugged his cap lower and after a minute, strolled into the shop. A masher, Angie decided. Ought to be ashamed of himself, old as he was.

But he didn't speak to the pretty lady. He moved past her to a booth at the end and sat down. He pulled a magazine out of a pocket and began to read, his elbows on the table big as you please, which to Angie meant he'd had no raising at all. Even she knew that folks with breeding ate with their mouths closed and their elbows off the table. Called himself being sneaky, too, but the rascal didn't fool her a tap, making like he was reading when he wasn't. He was watching her pretty lady like a beady-eyed hawk.

Angie moved around to the other side of the trash can so she could see better. The waitress had poured coffee for the lady, and she pulled a pack of mail out of her pocketbook and began to slit open the envelopes. The beady-eyed rascal watched her and Angie watched him.

The lady was on her second cup of coffee when she picked up one of her envelopes, looking right surprised to see it. But when she read what was inside, it made her frown. She read it again, her mouth tight. Must be bad news, Angie decided. That was the trouble with mail. Sooner or later it brought bad news. The lady looked at her watch, put money on the table and got up quickly, waving goodbye to the waitress. She picked up her tulips and hurried to the door.

Angie cackled. Raincoat just about fell over himself, scrambling out of his booth. He threw some money onto his table and walked to the door. The pretty lady stopped just outside, had to, to let a bunch of gigglers go past. High-school girls, Angie reckoned, spread out all over the sidewalk, talking loud, using language that would have got her knocked on her butt if her ma had heard such filth come out of her mouth. The pretty lady moved in behind them, walking slowly.

Suddenly Angie's eyes narrowed. Raincoat had come out. Seeing the lady stuck at the back of all the gigglers, he crammed his hand into his pocket, and his eyes went flat and hard. Angie, who had been on the streets long enough to know when somebody was up to no good, acted without thinking. He was fixing to rob her pretty lady!

Gathering all her strength, she gave the grocery cart a mighty shove, sending it hurtling across the sidewalk into the man's path, then muttered the kind of word she wasn't supposed to say. She'd hoped the cart would catch him in the family jewels, but it had clipped his shins instead, which was almost as good. He howled, grabbed the cart and flung it on its side, spilling her precious things onto the cement.

Angie scurried over. "I'm sorry, mister, the blamed thing just got away from me," she said, making it good and whiny. "It's so heavy and I've got the arthritis in my hands something terrible. Can't always keep a hold of it. Did it hurt you bad?"

He glared at her, then glanced up to see how far the lady had gone. She had stopped at the curb and was looking over her shoulder at them. "Get out of my way," he snarled, and hurried off in the other direction.

Bless Paddy, the pretty lady was coming back.

"Here, let me help you," she said, righting the cart. She gathered the clothes and the briefcase, then the dried flowers, the stems bent like straws now, and placed them in the cart, gently, as if they were as special to her as they were to their owner.

Angie looked up into the biggest, prettiest eyes she had ever seen. She *knew* that face. "Thank you, ma'am, but I hit that rascal on purpose. He was following you, was fixin' to rob you. He had a gun or something."

Pretty Lady looked in the direction the man had gone, but he was out of sight. "Did you see it? The gun, I mean?"

"No'm, but he had his hand in his pocket like I seen the holdup men do and he was trying to catch up with you. I had to stop him."

The lady—a tall one, she was—gazed down at Angie, her face sober as a judge. Finally she gave that sweet smile. "That was very brave of you. Would you let me treat you to lunch—to show my appreciation? I'd join you but I'm meeting someone in a few minutes."

Angie felt her face warm with pleasure. "You would eat with me?"

"Of course, if I didn't have to worry about keeping my friend waiting. Stay here a minute."

Now, ain't she the nicest thing? Angie thought. She watched while her pretty lady went back into the coffee shop and spoke to the waitress, pulling her out of sight. Must have talked up a storm, because it was five minutes before she came out again.

"You can go in. Beverly has a booth for you near the back. She'll even park your cart right behind it so it'll be safe. Order whatever you like—it's already paid for. Get something to take with you, too. I don't know about you, but I get hungry in the middle of the afternoon."

"Me, too," Angie admitted. "This is awful nice of you. I been wondering, do I know you?"

"I think I saw you one night about a week ago, but we've never met. My name is Lisa. And yours?"

"Folks call me Angie."

"I'm pleased to meet you, Angie. You have a good lunch. And thank you again." Reaching into the green paper around her flowers, she pulled out a tulip and handed it to Angie. Then, with a parting smile, she hurried toward the corner, just as a shiny black car stopped at the traffic signal. She got in, the light turned green and the shiny car slid into traffic and was gone.

Angie deposited the tulip on top of the cart where it wouldn't get crushed, smoothed her coat, patted her hair and opened the door of the coffee shop. Sure enough, the waitress came and led her to a nice booth big enough for herself and three more. She wedged the cart in a space by the kitchen door, poured her a cup of coffee and handed her a menu.

Angie opened it, her mouth flooding with saliva at the long list of sandwiches—hot *and* cold—and buns and muffins and breakfast food even! This is what heaven will be like, Angie decided. Warm, smelling like coffee, with all the food a body could ever eat.

She ordered breakfast. "That's to start off with," she said shyly to the waitress. After that, she'd have a slice of that pie, maybe with ice cream melting all over it. And a sandwich to take with her, and potato chips. That would be enough. She didn't want to be a pig.

Angie was halfway through her bacon and scrambled eggs when she dropped her fork, her rheumy eyes wide with shock. It had taken a while but she'd finally remembered where she had seen her pretty Lisa before.

"By gum, Angie," she said, forgetting that her mouth was full, "you may not be r'tarded, but you sure are slow. That was the lady in the newspaper, the one everybody thought got blowed up in that car. You coulda asked her what to do with that satchel."

Angie sat back and wiped her mouth. Fact was, this gave her something to do, somewhere to go. All she had to do was find Wheezy Whisnant. Wheezy would have the paper. He collected them and sold them to a fellow at a 'cycling center. She'd buy it off him if she had to, find out what Lisa's last name was and whereabouts she lived. Then she'd go explain how she came to have the satchel and ask if the man it belonged to was still alive.

Picking up the menu, she began considering her takeout order. She had better get a couple of sandwiches. Lord knows how far she'd have to go to find Wheezy and a body with a cold needed her strength. "Waitress?" she called shyly.

List in hand, Lisa sat on a bench in Metro Center, the multi-leveled hub at which Washington's subway lines intersected. Of the five places she'd hoped to get to today, she'd managed only three, perhaps because it was the warmest Friday so far and people seemed to move in slow motion, as if they wished they were somewhere else.

The city teemed with tourists. The cherry trees were in bloom down on the Potomac Basin, an event guaranteed to double the usual amount of traffic, aboveground and below. Rush hour would begin shortly, at which point the fare would increase. Perhaps those factors accounted for the crowd waiting for the Red Line train.

Lisa eyed the errands yet to be run and crossed them off the list. Even if she weren't meeting Jess to go to the hospital, she probably wouldn't have gotten everything done today. Not that she minded the time it took to get out there—Jess knew the back roads and the ride was soothing. The azaleas had bloomed early in a blaze of reds, pinks and purples, and the dogwoods were flowering, adding a touch of white lace to the palette of greens.

That Jess invariably noticed such things and could point out the progress of buds to blossoms at a given site never ceased to amaze her, but his demeanor toward his friend went farther toward canceling out those first violently negative impressions than anything else could. His affection for Clifford Mallory softened him, exposed him as a person who cared deeply and had no qualms about showing it. Lisa found herself envying the way he grasped Mal's arm as he talked to him, the warmth in his voice, the concern in his eyes.

This would be her fifth trip to see him since the truce, as she'd come to think of it, and although Mal had yet to regain consciousness, the range of his reactions had increased. He responded more readily to her voice, to the extent that he now turned his head to follow her as she moved around the bed and spoke. As for the reason, she still had no idea. And that frightened her.

With each new sign of improvement, Lisa's apprehension grew. Once Mal awoke, the truce would dissolve as fast as an ice cube on a barbecue grill and Jess's attitude toward her would undergo an abrupt about-face. She was less concerned about his learning that Mal had been trying to see her than she was about the most recent complication, introduced in the guise of a bottle of imported cologne.

It was, according to Jess, Mal's signature scent—he'd left it following his last visit. Jess had brought it to provide another source of stimulus, and the moment he'd opened it, Lisa had faked an excuse to leave the room. Its clean scent, reminiscent of freshly cut grass, had opened a door in her mind—just a crack, much too narrow a space to expose what lay beyond, but Lisa knew without a doubt she had smelled that bouquet before. Jess had already mentioned that it was a custom blend mixed specifically for Mal. It was also an aroma from her past, in this instance, the years before her mother's death.

Lisa had poked and probed her memory ever since, with little to show for her efforts. She and her mother had moved so many times that it was possible she had encountered Mal in any one of a dozen places. And Eloise Gillette had been a very attractive woman, rarely lacking for male companionship. One of the few memories she could call up at will was a picture of herself sitting in various boarding-house windows, when they were lucky enough to have a room overlooking the street, watching for her mother to come home from a date.

The men in question were now phantoms, faceless characters. Only one stood out at all, but so far out that she couldn't envision his features. He was in shadow, very tall, slender, and made her extremely uneasy. Lisa doubted it was Mal. He wasn't that tall, and Jess said that prior to the accident, he'd been stocky.

Still, this would have been at least twenty years ago or longer. Anyone of average height might seem tall to a child, and he may have gained weight in the intervening years. Whether or not

Mal was the man in the shadows, she trusted her nose. But if she was a little girl when she'd met him, why would he react to her voice two decades later? She knew she didn't sound the same as she had then, and she did not sound like her mother. Not that she remembered her mother's voice so much as she did its quality—deep, for a woman, and slightly hoarse.

Lisa stirred, pulled into the present by a departing train on the opposite track. Hers was due any minute. She slipped her notepad into her purse and joined the crowd, her focus on the recessed lights along the edge of the platform, which began to blink softly signaling the approach of a train. A youngster, obviously new to the subway system, yelped. "I didn't do it, Ma, honest! It came on by itself!" Laughter rose toward the vaulted ceiling, the response of those in the know.

Lisa was wedged between the mother of the protesting youngster and a man in a U.S. postman's uniform. Despite the impatient jiggling, pushing and shoving were rare in Metro's clean, brightly lit stations, so Lisa felt little concern at sensing someone on her heels. The ensuing events seemed to occur in parallel universes, one in which things happened in slow motion and in the other like a videotape in fast forward.

Something nestled in the middle of her back, followed by a sudden pressure, and she lurched forward, off balance, propelled over the edge of the platform. She reached out to break her fall and landed on all fours, collapsing onto her side, her purse a whisker away from the electrically charged rail.

The tracks hummed under her, vibrating with the weight of the oncoming cars. Dazed, Lisa turned her head and saw the lights of the lead car approaching the mouth of the tunnel. A cacophony of sounds battered her senses—gasps, shouts, screams, the high-pitched squeal of metal against metal as the train's brakes engaged. Lisa levered herself into a sitting position, but her knees were numb from the impact of her fall. Her legs wouldn't seem to work properly.

"C'mon, miss, you gotta help me."

The man in the postal service uniform bent over her, his mocha face twisted in fear and determination as he pulled her to her feet and shoved her toward the platform. Helping hands reached for hers and his. The postman rolled onto the plat-

orm on his stomach, grabbed her under the arms and pulled
her up, and a second later, the lead car squealed past, gliding
to a stop several yards ahead of the point where she had fallen.

Someone guided her to a bench, and the next half hour became a blur of solicitous faces. There were paramedics who,
having failed to talk her into letting them take her to the nearest emergency room, advised her that she should at least take a
cab home. There were policemen and a Metro representative,
reports to make, dotted lines on which to sign, attesting that she
had not been drinking or dizzy, had not been attempting suicide and had no plans to sue the transport system. The platform had been crowded, she explained, and as everyone
jockeyed for position, she had been jostled from behind, had
lost her balance and had fallen.

Through it all, Lisa's calm demeanor masked her inner turmoil. Even after the tragedy that had greeted her return from
New England, death had retained a certain remoteness. No
longer. She had witnessed its approach today, had escaped it in
the space between one breath and the next. Until now, she had
avoided going to the cemetery, unable to face seeing her name
on the marker above Maria's grave. She would go tomorrow.
If nothing else, she'd come face-to-face with the folly of pro-
crastination. And perhaps seeing her name on the marker
would drive home how fortunate she'd been today.

The Metro representative hailed a cab for her and she used
the long ride to the Friendship Heights station, where Jess
would be coming to meet her, to pull herself together and repair what damage she could. There was little she could do.
Abrasions stung her hands and knees, and her slacks were
ripped. She felt dirty and clumsy and embarrassed, and dreaded
having to explain what had happened. She was getting out of
the taxi when she realized that in the confusion following her
rescue, her knight in blue had disappeared and she hadn't had
a chance to thank him. It was the proverbial straw. Tears lurked
behind her lids, and she dashed them away. She could not cry,
not now. Maybe later. Definitely later.

Jess had begun to worry. He'd been waiting for forty-five
minutes and there'd been no sign of Lisa. He was sure he had

the time right, so where was she? Picking up the car phone, he dialed Security Specialists and asked if Sinclair, the trainee he'd assigned to follow her, had gotten back yet. He had.

"You wanted me, Mr. Hampton?" Sinclair asked, sounding out of breath.

"I'm at the Friendship Heights station. The subject hasn't shown."

"She hasn't? She couldn't have missed it. She must have gotten off at another stop."

Jess smelled a rat. "But you did see her board?"

There was a second of silence. "Not actually, sir. I waited until she went to the edge of the platform with everyone else, and when the lights started blinking, I left. You said I could so I wouldn't miss my class," he added hurriedly, "and I thought it was all right, since you'd be picking her up at the other end."

Jess ground his teeth and counted to ten. The fault was his. He should have known better than to use someone with as little fieldwork as Sinclair had had, but the co-worker who'd been tailing Lisa was having his first baby, and Jess had packed him off to be in the delivery room with his wife.

"Lesson number one, Sinclair, never assume anything. You should have waited until you saw her board the train and it left. I'd have covered for you with Boxleitner if you'd been late."

"No excuses, sir. I'm sorry I let you down."

Then he saw her. "Damn it, she did pull a fast one. She's getting out of a cab. Did you see her speak to anyone?"

"No, sir." Sinclair sounded relieved and puppy-eager to please. "Never said a word to anyone."

"All right. Get to class. Thanks for your help."

Jess disconnected, slipped the phone back into its niche and leaned over to open the door for her. All of his speculations to account for the forty-five minute delay evaporated once he'd gotten a look at her close up. There were snags and smudges on her white blazer and rips in the knees of her slacks. "Lisa! What happened?"

She secured her seat belt and sighed. "I feel so stupid. I fell. One minute I was up, the next down."

"It must have been a pretty bad tumble. Your knees are bleeding."

She peered through the rips in her slacks. "More like seeping. I can't go to Greenhaven looking like this. Do you mind if we stop at the loft so I can clean myself up? It shouldn't take long."

"Let's skip the visit, Lisa."

"No, I want to go. I just need to get out of these things."

He hesitated. "Okay, but if you change your mind about it, fine. Now sit back and relax. We've got plenty of time."

The fact that she did, without argument, closing her eyes in the bargain, convinced Jess that the fall must have shaken her badly. He watched her as he headed back toward Connecticut Avenue. Her cheeks were pale, almost translucent, and it was all he could do to keep his hands on the wheel. All wasn't enough.

Slowing for a light, he reached over and brushed a finger over her brow. "Are you sure you're all right?"

Her eyes opened. "I'm fine, just a little down. All the running around, that idiotic letter from Pennsylvania, which has really been bugging me, then this. I—"

"Hold it. What letter from Pennsylvania?"

"Remember I mentioned that I'd sent for my birth certificate? Well, it had arrived, but Kitty had packed it with the invitation to London, so I didn't find it until last Saturday. The good state of Pennsylvania says I wasn't born there. I called and they've double-checked but I'm not in their computers. As if I didn't already feel like a nonperson...."

"Any chance you've got the wrong state?"

She shot him the ghost of a smile. "That's not the sort of information you forget. I was born in Scranton, June 24, 1961. I admit that every now and then I find myself thinking I'm twenty-eight instead of twenty-nine, but otherwise I do remember my vital statistics."

"Did you ask them to check '60 and '62? I've known a few cases where a mother fudged about the year her child was born."

She nodded. "They checked every which way from Sunday. I don't understand it. I remember Mom going through the whole routine, how much agony she went through in labor—

God, I hated that! And how she'd wanted to have me at the hospital in her hometown instead of Scranton.''

"Why do mothers do that? Where was she from?"

"Charlotte, North Carolina. My father, too. That's where he died."

"What will you do about your birth certificate now?"

She shrugged. "Go through the few things of hers that survived the fire, and hope I'll find something that—"

"Wait, wait, wait. What fire?"

"The accident in which Mom was killed." She made a face. "That's another reason the thing with Maria and Mal hit me so hard. It was history repeating itself, only in Mom's case the car skidded off the road in the rain. It rolled down an embankment, hit a tree and burst into flames. I don't remember it, but the assumption is that I was thrown out because I wasn't wearing a seat belt."

Jess digested that bit of news in silence. No wonder she had started to tune out that first night. The parallels were eerie.

"I'll stop at the warehouse when I have a chance," she said. "There's no hurry. At the rate I'm going, I can forget the trip to London this summer." Jess, pulling up behind the studio, set the brake. "And if I'm sounding sorry for myself, that's exactly how I'm feeling. Don't worry," she added with a genuine smile. "It never lasts more than a couple of minutes. Why don't you come in? I'll try not to be long." She opened the door and got out, moving gingerly. "Have a beer while I try to undo the damage."

Jess followed willingly, thinking she might have trouble with the stairs. She took them slowly and with her usual fluid grace, but he suspected that her pride wouldn't allow her to reveal how painful her injuries truly were.

He made himself comfortable while she vanished into the bathroom, reflecting on the predicament he was in. Lisa Gillette had come to mean one hell of a lot more to him than he could afford. He had known it before, but the panic he'd felt when he'd realized that something had happened to her had driven home the point with the ease of an ice pick through warm butter.

Initially he'd lain his feelings for her squarely at lust's door. He wanted her. He couldn't look at her mouth without succumbing to two-second daydreams about kissing her. What wouldn't he give to bury his nose in the valley between her breasts, to drown in her scent.... The daydreams exploded like flashbulbs in his head more and more often. As usual, his body reacted with a will of its own, just thinking about it, an embarrassing rigidity growing between his legs even now, straining against the fabric of his clothing. He shifted on the sofa, knowing there was little he could do about his discomfort. He could only hope it would diminish before Lisa came out again. Even then, his discomfort would be no less acute. His emotions were in as much turmoil as his body.

He had learned many things this week in Lisa's company, not the least of which was that the woman after whom he lusted was a bright, giving person, fiercely independent while trying to learn how to receive, vulnerable yet with an inner strength he admired for its tenacity. He liked her and more, and so far he hadn't come up with a thing to link her to his dial-a-porn idea. Frankly he was relieved, and ashamed that he was.

Jess refused to consider that he might be falling in love with her. You didn't fall in love with someone you'd known less than two weeks—at least he didn't, sidestepping the issue by concluding that what he really wanted was not so much Lisa as someone, anyone, to love. She was simply the agent who had made him face that conclusion. And that was too bad, because he couldn't have any of it, or her. He wasn't whole, not with this one last fear to conquer, and even if he were, he'd be a fool to fall in love with Lisa Gillette.

He still maintained that somehow she was the catalyst that had caused Mal's world to blow up in his face. And he might almost believe that she was involved without knowing how or why, were it not for his continuing conviction—which grew stronger every day—that she wasn't being completely honest with him. He'd seen it in her eyes, read it in the language of her nubile body. It obviously hounded her, sneaking up on her when she least expected it. Her features would tighten, her pupils dilating like the lens of a camera. She was probably a lousy poker player. Her face would give her away every time.

And if she was hiding something, well, hell, so was he, the fact that he was using her for Mal's benefit *and* prying into moments she assumed were private. Guilt rode him with the intensity of a physical addiction now. The more he knew of Lisa, the heavier his rider became. But sooner or later she would meet or speak to someone who would give him the lead he needed. He had the tail on her and the tap on her phone, illegal as hell, but he was desperate. It wasn't enough to catch Mal's assailant, he had to nab the person who'd hired him. As for his feelings for Lisa, there was nothing he could do beside accept the necessity of using her now and forgetting her later. His consolation? Mal would be safe.

"My knees weren't as bad as I thought," Lisa said, coming back from the bathroom. "Just scratched, and not that deep." She had changed into a blouse and skirt, and lifted the hem of a periwinkle-blue wraparound to show him. Her knees were pink with a few angry-looking places. He wasn't fooled. They were the kind of abrasions that stung like fire.

"I recommend a long hot bath tonight, or you'll regret it tomorrow," Jess advised her. "These things have a way of sneaking up on you, after a certain age."

She made a face at him. "Thanks a lot. That's what I get for telling you when I was born. I'll be right with you. I dropped an earring this morning—of course, the only ones I can wear with this color. I've got to find it." She disappeared behind the folding screens and Jess heard the scrape of furniture being moved.

"Need help?" he asked.

Her answer was an expletive, issued with considerable heat. She stepped into view, glaring at a streak of brown smeared from shoulder to elbow of her long-sleeved white blouse. It had not been there a few moments before.

"How'd you do that?" he asked. "What is it?"

"I'm not sure. Come look at this." She led him around her bed, which she had pulled out on one side so that it stood with the left post of the headboard abutting the wall. A cluster of blue and white stones lay on the floor behind it.

"Isn't that your earring?" He started to reach for it, but Lisa grabbed his arm.

"Careful." She pointed to the rear of the mahogany head-board. Dead center on its back was what looked like a blob of dark brown putty. It almost, but not quite, concealed a tiny metal cylinder about the size of a battery for a watch.

Jess stood perfectly still, astonished. Apparently he wasn't the only one eavesdropping on Lisa Gillette. Stooping, he examined it closely. This was a model he'd never seen before and in his line of business, he was supposed to know them all.

Evidently the feds had handed Pete a line. Lisa's name was on their list. Damn it, had he stumbled into the middle of an FBI investigation? He wished he had more time to figure out how to handle this. The last thing he needed was to get in hot water with the FBI for exposing their surveillance of her. At least he knew he was on the right track after all. Now if he could only mask his disappointment that he was.

"Here's your earring," he said, picking it up. It was important that he sound as normal as possible. He touched the blob, scratched it and it flaked off in his hand. It was supposed to camouflage the bug it should have covered. Whoever had put it there had done a sloppy job, perhaps thinking there'd be no need to go overboard to hide it, considering its location. The question now became, had Lisa guessed what it was? He soon had his answer.

She beckoned him into the bathroom and closed the door. "Is that thing what I think it is? A bug—as in listening device?"

He tried to stall. "Probably, but there's no way to tell how long its been there."

"It wasn't there when we moved the bed from the other room. We went over everything, checking for insects. Jess, did you put it there?"

"No." He was taken aback that she had thought of him and relieved at being able to respond truthfully. "What reason would I have to stick a bug behind your bed?"

"I'd rather not answer that." Pushing past him, she went out, dug two suitcases from under the bed and became a flurry of motion, tossing clothes into her luggage.

"What are you doing?"

She shot him an impatient look and shoved him back into the bathroom, closing the door behind them. "I won't stay here. I'm leaving."

"Where will you go?"

"I don't know yet. I don't even care, but I won't stay here. You finally convinced him, didn't you?"

"Convinced who?" Jess asked, completely stumped.

"Detective Owen. You finally got him to listen to you and now he's listening to *me*! I won't live like this, Jess. I've been stripped of everything. All I had left was my privacy and now that's gone. I haven't done anything to deserve this!"

"Shh! Keep your voice down." Jess reached behind her and turned on the water full blast. "Lisa, think about your... activities in the months before your trip. Are you certain everything you've done has been completely aboveboard, as far as ethics and morality are concerned?"

"Ethics? Morality? Jess, what *are* you talking about? I design miniature reproductions of period furniture. Then I write articles on how to make them. That's my life. It may sound offbeat to you, but that's what I do. As for ethics, I never steal a design someone else has done. I don't plagiarize from articles that might serve perfectly well for something I've designed. Morality? There I can't help you, except to say I've yet to come across a piece of furniture I'd consider immoral."

The problem, Jess decided, was that it sounded like the truth. He gazed down into her hazel eyes, waiting for a telltale sign to give her away. Granted, he didn't know her that well, but he simply couldn't imagine her spelling out erotic fantasies for the benefit of a faceless caller. A perverse ventriloquist lurking in a corner of his subconscious reminded him he had felt the same way about Kent's sister.

"I'm getting out of here," Lisa said, at the end of her patience. "With or without you."

"I'll take you, but we need to do something to cover the time we've spent in here. It's been awfully quiet out there for the past few minutes. That's bound to have raised their suspicions."

"Their suspicions have already been raised, remember?" She turned off the water, opened the door and walked out, saying,

"Okay, Jess, it's a deal. I'll take the hot bath you suggested, under one condition."

It was a moment before he realized she was playing to the microphones. "What condition?"

"That you take it with me," she said, going back to her packing. "But not here. Kitty pops in unannounced day or night. Is your tub big enough for two?"

Her hands were busy folding, arranging quickly. Her voice, however, might have belonged to someone else. It was languid, husky, erotic. He could almost imagine how she would sound "on the job."

"My tub's a whopper."

"Terrific. I'll take some bubble bath and we can wallow in decadence."

Jess was extremely uncomfortable. Her schizophrenic performance was unnerving enough and the thought of sharing a bath with her was playing havoc with his glands.

She finished, closed the bags and wrestled the larger one off the bed. He moved quickly to her side and took it from her, and picked up the other one, stepping out of her way as she grabbed her trench coat from the wardrobe, her purse from the table, and walked quickly toward the door.

Jess hustled to catch her and almost ran over her when she stopped suddenly, whirled around and darted back toward the bedroom. She returned immediately with the sturdy leather case that contained her tools.

"Sorry. Forgot the bubble bath." She opened the door for him with a watery smile.

He went through, waited until she had closed and locked it and started down the steps, unaware that he was alone until he reached the bottom. Lisa stood at the top landing, her forehead against the wall.

"Hey." Dropping the bags, he took the steps two at a time. Her cheeks were wet with tears. "Come on, don't cry."

She brushed them away. "Sorry. This just doesn't seem to be my day. I'm okay."

"Are you sure?" He took her free hand and squeezed it.

She winced. "Careful, Jess."

"What . . . ?" Her palms were as scratched up as her knees, and a wide purple stripe had begun to swell just above her wrist. "My God, Lisa, did you fall against one of the benches?"

"Jess, don't make a big deal of it, okay? I fell off the platform onto the tracks."

"Onto the tracks." Jess felt goose bumps stand to attention along his arms. There was hazard enough in the drop from the platform to the track bed—she could have broken a bone. And if she had touched the power rail . . .

For the first time he knew how close he had come to losing her. Taking her hand, he pressed his lips gently against the wounded flesh. Lisa gasped, in pain, Jess thought, until he looked into her face and saw his own hunger mirrored in her eyes.

His arms slipped around her and she came into them without resistance, her breathing rapid and telling. He lowered his head and their mouths joined, hers yielding under the pressure of his, then to the gentle invasion of his tongue. One part of his mind tried penning a mental list of all the reasons he should put a stop to this. She was a suspect in his eyes, and those of the FBI. As such, she might also have a connection to an attempted murder. Last but not least, he was using her to bring Mal out of his coma—his prime objective—and to get a line on whoever was responsible for the explosion. Any one of those reasons should be enough to abort the embrace. He felt her arm steal around his back and knew that nothing on earth made any difference at this moment.

Her tongue teased the tip of his, and he stifled a groan, the throbbing between his legs matching the rhythm of his pulse in his ears. It was approaching a pace he'd be hard-pressed to control—she was every bit as soft, as warm, as he'd imagined. Then as abruptly as it had started, it was over. She took a step backward, then another, her face flushed, her pupils dilated with alarm. Spinning away from him, she ran down the steps and disappeared toward the back door. Jess finally caught up with her at the car.

"Please," she said, "just get me away from here."

He unlocked the door to let her get in and loaded her luggage, glad to have something to give him time to recover.

They were three blocks away when she said, "I'd like to go to the police station. I want to talk to Detective Owen."

"Pete? Why?"

"I think I'm entitled to an explanation. The least he can do is tell me what he thinks I've done."

Jess's mental wheels began spinning in high gear. He had to stall her. Confronting Pete about the bugs would put his friend between a rock and a hard place. The relationship between the FBI, the Treasury boys, the Park Police and the D.C. Metropolitan Police was touchy enough. It was not uncommon for their investigations to overlap, precipitating territorial flaps, over which the local police often came out on the losing end. He had to keep Pete out of this if he could, or at least warn him what was coming.

"He's working the graveyard shift for the next couple of weeks," he said, "so he wouldn't be at the station this early. Why don't we go to my apartment and—"

"No!" Lisa shook her head, her jaw set. "That's not a good idea."

"How about my office? We can call the station from there, just to be sure."

"Fine. If he's not there, would he mind if you called him at home?"

This woman was going to get him killed. "One step at a time," he said, thinking fast. He had to get to Pete before she did. On impulse, he swooped into a parking lot beside a drugstore. "I'll only be a minute," he said, careful to leave the motor running. "I promised my secretary a bottle of aspirin and I keep forgetting it. Do you need anything? Bandages or something?"

"No. Thank you." Sitting back, she closed her eyes.

Good, he thought. "Be right back."

Digging for change, he sprinted into the drugstore and found the phones in the back. Pete was at home.

"It's Jess," he announced, "and I've got to make this quick. The feds ran a game on you. Lisa's place is bugged. She found one by accident and thinks you guys did it. She'll be calling wanting to know why, so this is a warning to have a tale ready to tell her."

"Back up, Jess. You saw it yourself?"

"Yes, a type I haven't seen before."

Silence spun along the line.

"Pete? You there?"

"Yeah, and trying to make sense of this. It's not the feds. I passed along your theory about the dial-a-hooker setup, but they already knew about it, and have the names of the women involved. Gillette is *not* one of the operators."

So he'd been wrong about Lisa—again. "Talk about batting zero," Jess said staring blindly at several telephone numbers scribbled on the wall. "So whose equipment could it be?"

"Ya got me, but you'd better get her out of there. We can remove the equipment and check it for prints, but you know what the chances are of finding anything we can use. What now?"

"I don't know, Pete," Jess admitted. "I had banked everything on her being in on the sex-by-phone deal. I've even had one of my guys tailing her." He left it at that. There was no way he could tell Pete he'd also bugged her phone.

"Well, keep her out of the loft until we've had a chance to go over it. The only problem is, I can't guarantee how soon that will be."

Suddenly his cop instincts warned him to watch his back. Jess whirled around and saw at once that he had blown it. Lisa, a bottle of lotion and a tube of toothpaste in her hand, stood not three feet away. From the chips of ice in her eyes, there was no doubt she'd heard his end of the conversation. Tossing his car keys at him, she deposited the lotion and toothpaste on top of a display of disposable diapers and stalked off.

Jess swore. He'd never be able to repair the damage now. "Gotta go, Pete. Lisa just snuck up behind me. I don't know how much she heard, but it was enough."

"Tell me something, partner. Do you like Gillette?"

Nodding, Jess laughed humorlessly. "Yeah, you could say that."

Pete snorted. "You big, dumb jackass. That should have told you something, don't you think?"

There was a loud click and the dial tone droned in his ear.

Chapter 7

Angie parked her cart at the bottom of the steps of the neat brick row house. Her three earlier visits had taught her a lesson—see if anyone's at home before you drag that heavy old cart up all them steps for nothing. She plodded up to the porch and knocked. The place was as quiet as a graveyard, and she peered up and down the streets. Not a soul in sight, nobody to call the cops if she tried to see in the windows. Them venetian blinds on the front were closed tight. She shuffled around to the side porch. The blinds here were lowered, too, except there was a little bitty space between two of the slats. Gluing her nose to the window, she peeked in, and grunted with disgust. No wonder nobody answered. Who would live in an empty house?

Had Lisa moved? The paper said the thirty-nine-hundred block of Kelso Place. Weren't but four houses finished on this side of the street with folks living in them. She had strained to see the names on the mailboxes. Not a one of them said Gillette—just like the razor, Wheezy had told her. This one didn't, either, but there was a big, pretty *G* on the mailbox, so it must be the right place.

Angie sat down on the front steps to figure this thing out. By the time she had, it was almost dark. That poor child. Folks thought she was dead, so they moved all her things. But now that she was alive, she would be coming back by and by. Might as well wait for her. If she didn't, she never would get shed of that blamed satchel. Shoot, with all the empty houses, she could probably find a good place to sleep, long as she got out before the construction workers showed up. She'd be a far piece from Old Dawkins and breakfast, but now that her cold was gone, she wouldn't mind the walk. That's what she'd do, find a place to bed down and just wait. Lisa was bound to show up sooner or later.

Lisa pounded on the hatchback of Jess's car in frustration, and drew back her foot to further vent her spleen, but decided there was something blasphemous about kicking the tires of a Porsche. She had forgotten she'd locked the car when she'd gotten out. Now she would have to wait for him so she could get her bags. She still had no idea where she was going, but she would be damned if she'd go one yard farther with Jess Hampton driving.

Lisa leaned against the car and rested her head on her forearms, trying to anesthetize her bruised ego. She was one giant ache—her body from the fall, her emotions from the battering they'd taken from the moment she'd found the bug. Then she'd made a fool of herself, letting Jess kiss her—and kissing him back. His conversation on the phone had inflicted the deepest of her wounds, goring her on the horns of his suspicions. She had survived, thanks to an anger of such intensity that the open sores had been cauterized, her ire as much at herself as at Jess, for almost believing what he'd said last Tuesday, for wanting so badly to believe him, for wanting him, period. The memory of the lean, hard musculature of his back under her fingers, and the equally firm evidence of his desire against her abdomen, sent a searing flame up through her torso. And all the while he'd thought she was no better than a prostitute!

She blamed herself. Jess had made no secret of his priorities. Mal and his safety were first. Catching the person who had tried to kill him was next. Nothing else mattered to him, least of all Lisa Gillette. She had known all along she had no future with him. The problem was, he had made her forget it.

He came around the side of the building and she straightened quickly, arranging her features in a blank mask, refusing to give him the satisfaction of knowing how deeply he had hurt her, how angry she was. He stopped on his side of the car and looked across at her, waiting.

Lisa exploded. "How *dare* you! How dare you write me off as a ten-dollar tramp! The unmitigated gall to feel you were entitled to sacrifice me on the altar of your ego as a former member of the D.C. Metropolitan Police! And poor, stupid little Lisa fell for the act, when all the time you were setting me up to prove your preposterous theories."

"Lisa—"

She rode right over him, rage fueling her momentum. "I guess I shouldn't complain. When it comes right down to it, being considered a prostitute is better than being called an accomplice to murder. You missed your calling, Jess. You are a superb actor. I was almost convinced you meant the things you said last week. And the kiss, that was a masterstroke. You deserve an Oscar for that alone, to say nothing of the special effects that went with it."

His face reddened. He unlocked his door, and the button on hers popped up as well. "Lisa, I'm sorry. I owe you an explanation, but please, get in the car. We'll find somewhere to talk, neutral ground, say, the park. Then I'll take you anywhere you want to go."

"Anywhere I want to go? I hate to tell you but I'm flat out of ideas. I don't dare go to Kitty and Alec's—I wouldn't subject my worst enemy to a house full of listening devices."

"We can figure out something, but please, let's get moving," he said, coming around to the passenger side and opening the door for her.

Lisa glared at him, wanting to hate him, wanting to hit, to hurt. But you could only hurt someone who cared. Jess didn't. Besides, what other options did she have? Giving him a wide berth, she got in.

Dusk had drifted over the city, the sky a violet blue streaked with clouds tinted mauve by the setting sun as Jess made his way into the capital's dearly loved Rock Creek Park. Studded with picnic grounds and trails for hiking and horseback riding, it housed the National Zoo and assorted historical land-marks, and still managed to give the impression that man had yet to leave his mark on it. During the day it was a serene oasis, at night a black hole. Streetlights were few and far between and to lose your way on its narrow winding roads was the equiva-lent of being lost in a maze at midnight.

Jess drove with confidence, meandering into the heart of the park until he found a parking lot adjacent to a small picnic area. Here at least there were lights, just enough illumination so that he would be able to see her face clearly. And she would be able to see his.

He stopped, turned off the engine and lowered the win-dows. The scents of creek, trees and grass wafted in, bathing them in their finest spring bouquets. Somewhere in the dark-ness, a lion roared. When the wind was right, the big cats could be heard for miles.

Jess released his seat belt. Freed of its confines, he slipped lower in the seat and sighed. "I've really made a mess of things, haven't I?"

Lisa considered it a rhetorical question and saw no reason to respond.

"I was calling Pete to warn him what to expect from you." He explained the uneasy relationship between the city's var-ious law enforcement agencies and the problem he thought Owen would have had if she had pinned him down about the listening devices. "It never occurred to me that the FBI might not be responsible. I'm putting Pete's career in your hands by telling you they're investigating a ring of high-class call girls whose clients include a number of men on Capitol Hill. He told me and he shouldn't have, but he did it for a reason. I'm just sorry you had to hear the whole ugly story the way you did."

Lisa chuckled without humor. "Would you believe I feel I should apologize for eavesdropping? It was an accident. After you left, I realized all the things I'd left in the medicine cabi-net. I came in to buy replacements, saw you on the phone and was coming to give you your keys. Your conversation was so...enlightening, shall we say, that I stayed to listen, which is just as well, since I know what you think of me now. You're good, Jess. You should apply for an Equity card."

"Look at me, Lisa, please." It took some doing, but she turned in her seat so she could see him. The dim glow of the streetlights emphasized the angular planes of his face and made his eyes seem ebony. "I am not an actor, Lisa, just a man who's determined to save the life of a friend and, if I can, catch the bastard who tried to kill him. From the very first, I've been sure he was a target because of the research he was doing the past couple of months before the explosion. Before then, he had been pulling together profiles of high-priced prostitutes, but the day after Thanksgiving he honed in on one particular woman."

Lisa felt a frown blossom between her brows. There was something significant about that, but she couldn't pinpoint how. Her head felt as if it were full of quicksand, most of her thoughts sinking to a murky death.

"I was a good cop, Lisa," Jess declared, "in part because I had good instincts. On the face of it, you were in the clear. All the evidence said you were. I might have walked away that first night with no doubts about your innocence if I hadn't gotten the impression that you were hiding something."

It wouldn't hurt to clear that up, Lisa thought. "So we're back to that little hesitation that bugged you so much. When Detective Owen asked if I knew Mal, something popped into my head, a kid from kindergarten or nursery school whose last name was Mallory. I'd forgotten him—or her, I don't even remember which—until that moment. That's all it was."

"You could have told me that, and I'd have believed you, but you didn't. Pete kept insisting you were clean, and I had trouble accepting it because of my hunch that you were hiding something. That hunch is stronger now than it was then, Lisa. I think you're still holding back."

She averted her eyes, unable to answer.

"So I did the only thing I could—I went with what little I knew. If Mal was digging into prostitution and you were sitting on something, then it must have been because you were somehow involved in that scene. Then Mal reacted to your voice. The *only* thing that made sense was that you were one of the subjects he'd interviewed by phone—one of the dial-a-dolly bunch. I thought if I could find out who your contact was, it would lead me to the person who'd hired the killer."

"Dial-a-dolly?" Lisa echoed, her features twisted with disdain. "Prostitution one step removed? Thanks a lot, Jess. You can't imagine how complimented I am."

"It never felt right, you're just not . . . never mind. But with Mal lighting up his monitors every time you spoke, it fit the scenario whether it felt right or not. The point is that most of this could have been avoided if you'd been up front with me."

"In other words, you broke the vase, but it's my fault because I put it so near the edge of the table."

"That's exactly what I mean. Things have taken a nasty turn, Lisa. Whoever planted the bug is fishing for something, I just can't— What's wrong? You don't look so hot."

She was surprised she had telegraphed her thoughts. "One day last week when I got back from downtown—in fact the day you asked me to visit Mal—the loft smelled faintly of musk cologne."

"Ah. That's why you mentioned it to Brad."

"He'd left some dishes for me, so I assumed he'd been wearing it. You heard what he said. It must have been whoever bugged the place. He had plenty of time. I'd been gone since right after breakfast."

"Which means they went into action the same day the *Post* printed that article. It also says they're definitely local, prepared and fast. But what the hell could they want? You're going to have to come clean, Lisa. Mal's life may depend on it."

And finding out whatever he'd come to tell her, Lisa reminded herself. It had cost Maria her life. She had stalled long enough. He had to know what Kitty had told her.

"All right, Jess. I found out—never mind how—that Mal stopped by my office to see me."

Jess's only response was to sit up straight and drape his arms over the steering wheel, his movements slow and deliberate. He turned his head and looked at her, his face immobile.

"I'd already left town, but no one at the office knew that. He said it was a personal matter, that it was important he talk to me then because he wouldn't be able to get back again until late spring. My phone was unlisted and he didn't have my home address. It would never happen again in a million years, but the person he talked to said he seemed so distraught that I might leave town before he'd had a chance to talk to me that she gave him my home address.''

"Only Maria was there and you weren't," he said quietly.

"Maria was there and I wasn't. I can't imagine what he wanted, and I don't know where the two were going. I didn't even know Maria could drive.''

"They were a few blocks from my apartment. Mal won't drive in the District and she was probably bringing him to my place. How long have you known this?''

There was no accusation, no "I knew it!" in his tone, for which Lisa gave him points.

"I found out just before I went to the hospital that first time. That's why I was there. I was terrified that he was someone I'd known. I had to see for myself.''

"Lisa, why in God's name didn't you tell me?''

She phrased her answer carefully, wanting to be certain that he understood. "Look at it from my point of view, Jess. I hit town, find my house completely empty, my name in the files of the deceased, my best friend murdered in the company of a man—a stranger—who had a contract out on his life. I've barely digested that when you jump me and accuse me of having been the cause of it all. Things were bad enough without having to endure your accusations and hostility. As far as I could see, especially considering what the police thought was the motive, Mal's visit had no bearing on what had happened to him. So I kept the information to myself.''

"God." Jess yanked open the door, got out and began to pace alongside the car, the picture of pent-up emotion, whether anger or frustration, Lisa wasn't sure. "Lisa..." He stopped outside her door and her fingers inched toward the lock. Here she was in the middle of the park after dark, a perfect place to get herself murdered.

He knelt outside her door, his face level with hers but focused on the toes of his tasseled loafers. "I'm sorry...for everything. I don't know what else to say.''

She was grateful to be sitting down. Freed of the muscle-locking tension that had gripped her, her legs felt flaccid and weak. If she'd had to get out, she'd have fallen on her face.

She considered telling him about the reaction Mal's cologne had caused, but was so emotionally exhausted that she wasn't certain she could handle it. Besides, her conclusion that she'd met Mal as a child was based solely on a sensory impression. Until she could remember more, it made no sense to bring it up.

"If it helps anything, I'm sorry, too, Jess. What do we do now?"

He stood and moved away. Lisa, no longer fearing for life and limb, opened her door and put her feet on the ground. Her knees were beginning to stiffen.

"We dig," Jess said. "There's no argument that Mal's research on prostitution got him in trouble and the fact remains that he was hot on someone's trail after Thanksgiving. If there's no reason to suppose that person was you, perhaps it's someone you know."

"I know a good many working women," Lisa commented dryly, "but not the kind of working women you mean."

"Then we have two questions—one, why did he want to talk to you, and two, where are his notes on the research he started after Thanksgiving? I think I know the answer to the second question. Mal carried an old briefcase of his father's everywhere he went. It was his working file, but it hasn't turned up and it wasn't destroyed in the fire."

Lisa remembered his questions about the number of attaché cases she owned. He must have thought Mal might have left it at her house. It explained his curiosity about the inventory Kitty had made, and that rankled, but there was no use bringing it up now. "I assume you've checked Mal's apartment."

"A couple of times, but there's one place I haven't looked— I don't know why I didn't think of it before. There's storage space for each unit in the basement of his building. He might have stashed it there. God only knows where he keeps the key."

Lisa knew what was coming and let him off the hook. "Then let's go look for it."

His eyes searched her face. "You don't mind? You've had one hell of a day already."

She swiveled, pulling her knees inside, and closed the door. "You're wasting time, Jess. It's forty-five minutes to Baltimore."

"Not the way I drive," he said with a rakish grin. Skirting the front of the Porsche, he got in and slammed his door with relish. He started the engine, then turned to her, his face set in solemn lines. "Lisa, are we okay now?"

"For the time being. Considering our history, I figure I'd better hedge my bets."

He mulled that over and nodded. "Better safe than sorry. I guess I don't blame you. One last thing, though."

"Yes?"

"Kissing you wasn't part of the performance. It ... just happened, and I apologize."

Lisa settled back in her seat, sweeping her hair behind her ears. All things considered, she mused, it was one apology she could have done without.

Clifford Mallory lived in a three-bedroom condominium on the top floor of a stately old apartment building on Bolton Hill. Lisa stood in the doorway of the high-ceilinged living room and opened her mind to her senses, hoping they might give her a clue to the character and personality of the man who lived there. The room was visually stimulating, an intriguing mixture of eclectic furnishings—antique drum tables anchoring each end of a modular sofa, a black lacquered butler's table serving as a display surface for African figurines and highly polished stones. The walls vibrated with colorful prints in magnificent frames, floor-to-ceiling shelves of well-used leather-bound volumes and a patchwork quilt Lisa guessed was at least a century old. The floors were gleaming hardwood parquet, their beauty enhanced by oriental rugs.

Jess, who'd warned her she was in for a surprise, watched for her reaction. "Not your typical bachelor pad, right?"

"It's marvelous, all of it. Did he decorate it himself?"

"Piece by piece, over the years. He made the dining room furniture—in a former life, as he put it. He's been everywhere, collecting all sorts of things. Come on."

He led her through the apartment, pointing out a samovar from Russia, a set of Japanese fans, a Chinese watercolor, a sitar from India. All the disparate elements seemed comfortable with one another, a masterful blend of the exotic with the

ordinary. But nowhere did Lisa spot anything that would indicate he had any interest in miniature reproductions, which
blasted any remaining hopes she had that Mal had come
searching for her in her capacity as an artist.

The faintest scent of his cologne lingered, as much a part of
the aura of the apartment as the decor. Jess stood for a moment in Mal's bedroom. "I keep thinking something's missing
in here, but I can't figure out what it is."

"Stop worrying about it and it'll come," Lisa suggested.
"Where does Mal work?"

"This way." Leaving the bedroom, Jess proceeded to the end
of the hall and opened a door.

Mal's office revealed yet another side of his personality. It
contained the necessities—floor-to-ceiling shelves jammed with
books; desk and chair; lamp; computer and printer; telephone. The room was Spartan—no frills, no softened edges.
The floor was bare, as were the windows, except for blinds.

"It's so different from the rest of the apartment," Lisa
commented.

"He says he works better with no distractions and prefers to
keep things to a minimum."

"And his briefcase would normally be in here?"

"I've only seen it two places—beside the trash can under the
desk and in the closet where he keeps his supplies. It's not there,
so we'd better start looking for the key to his storage locker."

"Try the kitchen. I saw a magnetic strip on the side of the
refrigerator with several keys stuck to it."

Jess left the room and a moment later stuck his head in the
door and grinned. A key dangled from his hand. "As many
times as I've seen it, it never registered. Are you coming?"

Lisa had been trying, without success, to compose an excuse to remain in Mal's office a while longer, and was saved by
the ringing of the doorbell.

"Who could that be?" Jess muttered and disappeared.

Thankful for a few minutes' grace, Lisa sat down in the big
executive chair, soaking up the atmosphere. Where at first the
office had seemed austere in the extreme, her opinion had begun to change. Permeated with the scent of old books, it had
an air of tranquility. She liked this room.

Jess finally returned, a batch of mail in his hand. "That was the lady across the hall," he explained, flipping through the envelopes. "She collects Mal's mail whenever he's traveling. I've had it forwarded to my place for the past couple of months, but she's been holding all these since right after he was hurt."

He stopped halfway through the pile. "American Express. I've paid it, but by the time I did, it was past due. This must be the original bill." He ripped it open and scanned its contents. "Interesting. Charges for airline tickets, car rentals and motels he used in late December and January. And here's the bill for his long-distance calls. Why don't you hold on to these? They might give us a clue to where he went."

"Jess," she said, voicing a thought that had just surfaced, "would Mal have confided in his literary agent?"

His expression betrayed the fact that he hadn't thought of it. "I'm sure Pete's guys must have checked, but I really don't know. He and Mal were on fairly close terms. I think his name is Wilburn, maybe Wellburn. Why don't you flip through the card file for his number while I check out the storage locker?"

"Do you think Mal would mind if I got nosy? I'd like to look through his calendar. He might have made notes on it."

"Help yourself. It's been done, but a second go-round couldn't hurt. I'll be back as soon as I can."

She told him to take his time and he left. There was no reason to hurry on her account. The limbo of her homeless state persisted in sneaking up on her at odd moments, gouging out a hollow space in her middle. She had thought long and hard over the forty-odd miles between Washington and Baltimore, but there was no one on whom she felt she could impose for an open-ended stay, no one whose privacy she would want to put at risk. She still had most of the money Alec had loaned her, but if she took a motel room, she would soon be penniless as well as homeless.

The fact that Mal's apartment was available hadn't escaped her notice. There might even be a certain irony in moving into the habitat of the man responsible for the loss of her own, but she could not bring herself to become a squatter and invade his territory. She would have to think of some other way.

Shaking off her lethargy, she reached for the card file and found the New York telephone number of a Lawrence Willborn. It was nearly seven, but Lisa had a strong feeling that the agent was probably still at his desk. The few agents she knew kept ridiculous hours. There could be no harm in trying.

She called the number and jumped when it was answered on the first ring—"Willborn and Associates"—and realized she had no idea what to say.

"Hello?" His voice thundered with impatience.

"Mr. Willborn, this is Lisa Gillette, and—"

"Lisa Gillette. I know that name. How come?"

"You may have heard it in connection with Clifford Mallory."

"Cliff— Of course, she's the woman who was—did you say *you're* Lisa Gillette?"

"That's right. Someone else was with Mr. Mallory and she was mistaken for me."

"I'll be damned. What can I do for you?"

She sagged in the chair, tension leaking from her body that she would not have to go into detail. "I'm at Mal's apartment with Jess Hampton—"

"His buddy. Yes?"

"We're trying to find out what he was working on in the weeks before he was almost killed," Lisa explained. "Mal mentioned something about researching the background of some unnamed woman, and we wondered if you could shed any light on it."

"You say you're with Hampton?" Suspicion colored his voice. "Where is he? Let me speak to him."

"He's downstairs in the basement trying to find Mal's briefcase. He'll be—"

"Mal's briefcase? Don't waste your time. He had it with him when the car blew up, or my name isn't Willborn. The thing stayed glued to his hand."

"There was no evidence of it in the debris. Jess has searched the apartment and hopes Mal might have stashed it in his storage locker downstairs. He shouldn't be long. If you'll be in your office a while longer, he'll call you back."

"I'd like to talk to him, but I have a dinner engagement, so I can't hang around. There isn't much I could tell him anyhow. Mal called the day after Thanksgiving, said he was returning the advance on the book he'd been working on, because something had come up that was more important. He wouldn't say what, only that he had some digging to do and wasn't sure how long it would take."

"He doesn't seem to have told anyone what he was up to."

"If he didn't, it's a first. He was on a high, I'll tell you that, going on about being a day late reading the paper and almost missing the biggest story of his life."

Lisa came erect slowly, as if being pulled upright by an invisible string attached to the top of her head. "The day after Thanksgiving?"

"That's right. That's the last I heard of him until the Washington police called, wanting information about the book on prostitution. Pass that along to Hampton, will you? I've got to go. Give me a call tomorrow if there's anything else you think I can tell you."

"Thank you, we will," Lisa managed and eased the phone onto its cradle.

Mal had been a day late reading the newspaper. The feature article on area miniaturists had appeared in the *Washington Post* on Thanksgiving day, the article with the sidebar about Lisa Gillette, and her photograph. Two months later Clifford Mallory had walked in the door of the offices of the *Journal* asking to see her. Hours later, he was a passenger in her car. There was no way she could pass off that sequence of events as coincidence. The *Post* article had launched Mal's research into the background of Ms. X, as Jess was wont to call her. Only now Ms. X had a name—Lisa Gillette.

She got to her feet, flipped the switch to extinguish the ceiling light and closed the office door gently. Standing in the darkness, she closed her eyes, shutting out her surroundings. She had to think, to recall as much of the article as she could. What had it contained that caught Mal's eye?

The first few paragraphs led the reader through the design process, emphasizing the demand for attention to detail and accurate measurements. Then she, as the designer, was introduced, followed by an explanation of how she'd drifted into the field, resurrecting a childhood fascination and love of doll-houses and their furnishings. There was a description of the little Victorian dollhouse she'd had as a child, unique in that it folded to become its own carrying case, a convenience she had come to appreciate as she'd moved from city to city and job to job with her mother. It had been destroyed in the accident that had killed her mother.

It was not until she had begun working for Alec as a word processor at the *Journal*, and *Miniature Mania*, the article went on, that she remembered the dollhouse at all. From that point she had begun as a collector, then a hobbyist using kits, and from there to designing her own. It had concluded with the announcement of her invitation to the exhibition in London. That was it. So what had Mal seen that others had not? Why would it impel him to put his career on hold while he looked into her background?

"Lisa?" Jess opened the door and stared into the darkness, his expression an amalgam of bewilderment and concern. Reaching in, he flipped the switch. Light flooded the room, and Lisa squinted, blinded by the sudden brightness. "Are you all right? What were you doing?"

"Thinking, that's all. The briefcase wasn't there?"

"No. I didn't think it would be, but I had to be sure. Did you find Wellburn's number?"

"Yes, I found it. His name is Willborn. I called him. I hope you don't mind."

"Why should I? What did he say."

"Mal called to tell him he was tabling his research indefi-nitely because he had something important to look into. He even sent back the advance."

"That's all?"

"More or less. I'm guessing that what Mal was working on had no relation to the book."

Jess eyed her with interest. "What makes you say that?"

Lisa ambled to the window and leaned against it. Nightfall nestled over the city, so there was little to see. The panes of glass became a mirror, reflecting a shadowy image of herself, dis-torting her face, making it rounder, younger, the face of a child.

The optical illusion was unsettling in and of itself, even more so because it triggered a certainty that she had stood like this before, looking into a window, seeing both herself and what was happening on the other side of it. She had the eerie sensation of having looked into some past life, and shook it off. She was having enough trouble with the present.

"Jess, there's something you should know."

"Yes?" His voice was quiet and full of waiting, but his reflection gave him away. He was perched on the edge of the desk, his head tilted at an angle. Tension arced around him in an invisible power field.

"Mal called Willborn the day after Thanksgiving. He said he'd been a day late reading the paper and had almost missed the lead of his life."

"That's right—he brought a paper with him, a Baltimore *Sun*. I dug up one when I was trying to figure out what he had seen."

"You were looking at the wrong paper. There was a big spread in the *Washington Post* about miniaturists on Thanksgiving Day."

He stiffened. "I'll be damned. I remember it."

She turned, tired of avoiding the inevitable. "I was heavily featured in the article—photograph, bio and all. I think that's what Mal saw, what set him off. I have no idea why, except . . ." She faltered, still hesitant to voice the frail connection she'd drawn between herself and Mal.

"Except what, Lisa? Something else you've been sitting on?" There was steel in his tone. His eyes blazed into hers.

"His cologne. I have a special talent for scents and I could swear that I met a man who wore that fragrance when I was a kid. I must have known Mal years ago, but on my honor, I don't remember him. Nothing about him is familiar to me, except that scent."

Jess didn't move and Lisa became the one who waited, braced for his anger. His eyes lost focus and he gazed into the middle distance. His response was a surprise. "It may not have been Mal."

"But you said it was a custom blend—"

"It is. Mal's father served in France during the war." He rubbed his forehead impatiently, as if massaging his memory. "He became friends with an old man whose family business was perfumes. They had been working on a new after-shave lotion—men weren't wearing cologne back then, and the old man gave Mal's father and at least a dozen other guys a bottle of the stuff."

"The cologne you brought to the hospital couldn't be that old, Jess. It was too fresh and light."

"Let me finish. It's called Liberateur—something like that, in honor of the whole regiment. The family still gets orders for it and they'll only sell it to the original twelve they gave it to, or their sons. That's how Mal got it. He said he didn't begin using it regularly until after his father died. So it may have been Mal you remember, but it could very well have been someone else."

"But it was Mal who began checking on me," Lisa pointed out. "It was Mal who tried to see me about a personal matter. I don't understand, Jess. Why aren't you angry? Why aren't you crowing? You were right all along!"

"Yes, I was." Jess looked down in thought. "But so were you, Lisa, about me. I've always been proud of the fact that ninety-five percent of the time my hunches panned out, and I wondered if I was being pigheaded about this because all the evidence said my instincts were wrong. After a certain point, my belief in myself was on the line. So I have to admit that I'm so damned relieved to be right that I don't have the energy to be angry, too. I'm bothered that you have such a hard time being open with me, but I can't blame you. And don't forget, even though Mal was digging around in your past, it had nothing to do with the reason somebody wanted him dead."

"I wish I was as sure of that as you are." Lisa went back to the window. "I have a bad feeling about this, Jess. I'm scared, and I don't know why."

She watched his image move in behind her and pull her back against him. Lisa closed her eyes, savoring the heat of his body. The urge to lean back against him waged a battle with a little voice in her head warning her she shouldn't get used to him because the time would come when he wouldn't be around.

There was also the added danger of his closeness loosening the demons of passion already rearing their tiny horns at the thought of being in his arms again. She gave the hand on her shoulder a companionable pat and moved away, eschewing the comfort he offered.

"Lisa, what's wrong?"

She paced in a tight circle, going nowhere. "I don't know. I just can't shake this feeling."

"You've had one bitch of a day. Let's get out of here right now."

"And go where, Jess? I have a problem, remember?"

"No, you don't. You're coming home with me."

"So they can bug your apartment, too? What sense would that make?"

"My apartment is my part-time residence. We're going to what I consider my real home, in the mountains. It's lovely and peaceful and miles away from trouble."

Lisa had decidedly mixed emotions about his suggestion. The mountains sounded wonderful and she was overdue for a bit of peace of mind, but with just the two of them alone there, she might be jumping from the frying pan into a white-hot fire. This man touched something in her, aroused—a good word, he decided—all the needs she'd ignored for so long. She was falling in love and had no safety net to catch her. Too many things blocked the way—questions dangling, danger lurking and the growing conviction that once the questions had been dealt with, the answers would be devastating.

But she had no control over her feelings for him, no control over anything. And nowhere else to stay.

Slinging her purse over her shoulder, she said, "All right, Jess. Let's go." Is this, she wondered, how Daniel felt walking into the lion's den?

Chapter 8

Jess had described his mountain retreat as a cabin, which led Lisa to anticipate something fairly rough-hewn and rustic. The reality, however, was far removed from her expectations, the cantilevered redwood edifice seeming to defy gravity as it projected from the face of the mountain. It was deceiving, smaller than it looked, primarily because there appeared to be only one story when in fact there were two.

The main floor was one large room, a well-appointed kitchen tucked neatly in a front corner, set off from the remaining space by a free-standing counter. The dining area was opposite, an old-fashioned maplewood table ringed with high-backed ladder chairs. Stairs to the lower level were just to the right of the front door.

The decor of the living room area was simple and effective—two long couches positioned at right angles, and a large glass cocktail table, all of which faced a massive stone fireplace in the right rear corner. A wall of sliding glass doors opened onto a deck, which seemed to soar into space. It was too dark to see the view, but it promised to be breathtaking.

The lower floor consisted of two large bedrooms on either side of a central hallway. Each bedroom had its own bath and a spacious deck, each deck inaccessible from the other and protected by the overhang of the floor above.

The biggest surprise for Lisa was the Steinway baby grand at the left rear corner of the living room. It was a beautiful instrument, its wood dark and gleaming with the sheen of years of polishing. Yet something about it evoked an uneasiness Lisa found difficult to shake off.

"You play?" she asked.

Jess, busily checking overhead cabinets in the kitchen to see what was available, answered with a distracted air. "Hmm? Not as well or as often as I'd like. I was one of those kids who had to take lessons whether I wanted to or not. How about you?"

"I never learned. It would have been difficult, considering how often we moved, and I don't remember a piano any place we lived. Jess, this is lovely, but it doesn't have the feel of a weekend retreat. The way it's furnished, you could live here year-round."

"I did at one time," he said, starting a list of supplies they would need. "I use the apartment during the week because it's convenient, especially during the winter, but once snow is out of the picture, I'm here more often. I'd do it every day, except I'm lazy. It's a long drive."

"You lived here while you were on the police force in Washington?"

"No, afterward. It's a long story and you must be out on your feet. Feel free to turn in if you'd like."

Lisa wasn't sure whether he wanted her out of his hair because she had asked one too many questions, or whether he simply wanted her out of his hair. Whatever his intent, she was a guest and obliged to be considerate. "Do you mind if I take a look at the things from Mal's?" At her suggestion, they'd brought along his calendar, and several notepads on which Mal had scribbled, as well as all the bills the neighbor had left.

"Help yourself," Jess responded. "I'm so beat that they wouldn't make any sense to me, but let me know if you find anything interesting. I left them on the desk in my bedroom."

"Okay." She started toward the staircase and paused before going down. "Jess, thanks for everything."

He looked up from his grocery list, his dark eyes regarding her solemnly. "You're welcome. Don't worry too much, Lisa. You work on the reason Mal wanted to see you and I'll work on keeping him alive so he can tell you himself." He smiled. "Good night."

"Good night, Jess."

Lisa descended the stairs, marveling at the havoc so tiny a smile could wreak on her heart. Why couldn't she have met him before her life became so complicated? Of one thing she was certain, she would not have been bored. As much as she had liked Chad Cauthen, and before him Evan Harcourt, they had always left her feeling she could have enjoyed herself just as much at home, curled up with a good book. They were nice guys, in a city where males were outnumbered three to one. Nice, available and boring. Jess could be nice and he was certainly available, but she would never be able to say he was boring.

She stood in the door of his bedroom, trying to come to grips with the difference between it and the rest of the cabin. The walls were of smooth white panels with gaps of an inch or two between them. The carpet was the same thick plush as the one in the guest bedroom, but the furnishings were nondescript. The king-size platform bed was lower than others she'd seen, barely six inches off the floor, and the nightstands were bare except for a pair of lamps that were much too tall to be practical. The bases were ceramic, and deep pleated shades masked enormous three-way light bulbs.

A desk and a chair sat at right angles to the window wall. There were no other pieces of furniture—no dresser or chest. The room had a monastic quality and glowed with light, which Lisa found mystifying, since neither of the monster lamps were lit. It was a moment before she realized that the illumination was supplied by the wall panels. She tapped one. It was Lucite. The ceiling, too, glowed softly. The whole room was one big lamp, a novel idea, and well done. Perhaps the bedside lights were old family favorites. There was certainly no need for them otherwise.

She removed the box with Mal's papers from the desk and hurried across the hall to her quarters, tastefully decorated with traditional pieces she was sure had probably come from his parents' home. After a long-overdue soak in the tub, she pulled on a knee-length T-shirt and settled down cross-legged on the bed, the stack of bills and notepads at her side.

It wasn't long before she realized that she couldn't read Mal's writing, either because she was too sleepy to see straight or because his shorthand defied translation. Setting them aside, she removed the long-distance telephone bill from its envelope. Mal had made a number of calls after Thanksgiving, but only one caught her interest, to a number in Lockwood, Virginia.

Lockwood. Where had she heard it before? There was something about it hovering just beyond the reach of her conscious mind. Like quicksilver, it slithered into inaccessible corners, too fast for her to snare. Separating the sheet from the rest, she left it on her pillow and returned the others to the box. She would pin it down before long.

She awoke several hours later, with none of the unsettling disorientation that had plagued her recently. One lamp still burned, so she knew instantly where she was this time and indulged in a muscle-lengthening stretch, pleased that she could without undue discomfort. Her palms were sore and sensitive, and might make handling her tools a little awkward, but she could live with it. It was better than the alternative and she sent a heartfelt thanks to the young man who'd risked his life to save hers.

Turning off the lamp, she settled down again. Sleep, however, had left for parts unknown. She squirmed, seeking shelter on the other side of the bed. It made no difference. Random thoughts ricocheted through her mind, refusing to light in one place.

Perhaps Jess had some milk she could warm, she thought, and got up. She had forgotten to pack her robe, but her T-shirt was long and covered the essentials. Even if Jess was still up and about, she was "decent." Easing from her room, she stepped out into the center hall, pitch-black except for a barely discernible strip of white showing under Jess's door. Whether he was awake or had fallen asleep with the lights on, she didn't want to disturb him, and tiptoed up the stairs in her bare feet.

A fluorescent tube above the sink cast a pale yellow glow, beckoning her into the kitchen. She opened the refrigerator, but its contents—an assortment of bottled juices, beer, a canned ham and a few desiccated onions—held no appeal, so she satisfied herself with a glass of water. Taking one of the stools on the far side of the counter, Lisa sipped the water and stared at the baby grand, baffled by its effect on her. Leaving her glass, she walked over to it and sat down on the bench. The lid was closed and she lifted it to expose the keys. Now that she thought about it, someone she knew years ago had a piano with a mirrored panel behind the keys, so you could see your hands as you played.

Her fingers came to rest on the keys. They were smooth, almost warm to the touch, and something stirred in her, like a nudge in the ribs, demanding attention. She closed her eyes, straining toward it, trying to discern the form it took. Inadvertently one finger of her right hand depressed a key and the note sounded softly. She drew it back, startled, hoping Jess hadn't heard it—his bedroom was directly below. The note died away, leaving her feeling that she had started something that was unfinished.

Her hand dropped to the keyboard again, wrists straight, fingers curled, and she touched the key again and knew immediately the one that should follow. From E to C-sharp, back to E, C-sharp to A, back to C-sharp. How could she know the names of the keys and which one was which?

A flare exploded in her mind. *Little Spring Song!* Three-quarter time, like a waltz. Forgetting the hour and her concerns about disturbing Jess, she began to play with one hand, tentatively, at first, then with more confidence, her left hand joining in to supply the base, fingers moving easily from key to key, phrase to musical phrase. It was a simple tune, one familiar to piano students in the earlier stages of their careers at the keyboard. She finished and started again from the beginning, remembering the simple lyrics this time, her composure deteriorating with the completion of each measure. After the second rendition, she sat for a moment, trembling with alarm. Closing the lid, she left the piano and started down to the lower floor, her mind searching for an explanation.

SILHOUETTE DELIVERS FIRST-CLASS ROMANCE— DIRECT TO YOUR DOOR

Mail the Heart sticker on the postpaid order card today and you'll receive:

— 4 new Silhouette Intimate Moments® novels—FREE
— a lovely gold-plated chain—FREE
— and a surprise mystery bonus—FREE

But that's not all. You'll also get:

FREE HOME DELIVERY

When you subscribe to Silhouette Intimate Moments®, the excitement, romance and faraway adventures of these novels can be yours for previewing in the convenience of your own home. Every month we'll deliver 4 new books right to your door. If you decide to keep them, they'll be yours for only $2.74* each —that's 21¢ below the cover price—and there is no extra charge for postage and handling! There is no obligation to buy—you can cancel at any time simply by writing "cancel" on your statement or by returning a shipment of books to us at our cost.

Free Monthly Newsletter

It's the indispensable insider's look at our most popular writers and their upcoming novels. Now you can have a behind-the-scenes look at the fascinating world of Silhouette! It's an added bonus you'll look forward to every month!

Special Extras—FREE

Because our home subscribers are our most valued readers, we'll be sending you additional free gifts from time to time in your monthly book shipments, as a token of our appreciation.

OPEN YOUR MAILBOX TO A WORLD OF LOVE AND ROMANCE EACH MONTH. JUST COMPLETE, DETACH AND MAIL YOUR FREE OFFER CARD TODAY!

*Terms and prices subject to change without notice. Sales tax applicable in NY and Iowa.
© 1990 HARLEQUIN ENTERPRISES LTD.

FREE! gold-plated chain

You'll love your elegant 20k gold electroplated chain! The necklace is finely crafted with 160 double-soldered links and is electroplate finished in genuine 20k gold. And it's yours FREE as added thanks for giving our Reader Service a try!

The light in the stairwell came on.

"That *was* you. I thought I was hearing things." Jess stood at the base of the steps, his robe loosely tied over pajama bottoms, his feet bare.

"I . . . I didn't know I could play," she said, her voice shaking. "I could swear I never took lessons, but I must have! My God, I can even see the book, John Thompson's First Grade Book with its red cover." She felt the blood drain from her head, and sat down gingerly, unable to manage the three steps to the bottom. "*Little Spring Song.* Jess, I think I played that in a recital."

Slowly a picture shimmered into focus. A stage with dark blue curtains, a baby grand piano with a stool one could spin around on. "I remember what I wore, a white lacy pinafore over red—no, a deep pink dress. It was my Alice in Wonderland dress. But I don't remember anything else! I can't remember lessons, practicing, nothing! My God, what's wrong with me?"

The panic in her eyes made Jess move quickly. He had watched her swim upstream against a tide of troubles over the past thirteen days, a good many of which he had caused. This was the second time in twenty-four hours he had seen her flounder, and from the looks of her, she was sinking fast.

"Lisa, there's got to be a perfectly rational explanation for this."

She nodded, her face buried in her hands. "There is. I'm losing my mind."

"No, you're not."

"I must be, and I can't blame it on the past two weeks. As long as I can remember, pictures have flashed in my head, things I couldn't have seen, places I couldn't have been. And this . . . I took piano lessons, Jess, but I have no idea when or where. So not only am I seeing things that couldn't have happened, I've completely forgotten things that have." She pulled herself to her feet and walked slowly to the bottom of the stairs. Moving past him to the door of her room, she emitted a dry, brittle laugh. "Maybe I shouldn't have been so quick to deny being one of Mal's ladies of the evening. For all I know, you may be playing host to the hottest property in Washington."

Her voice broke and Jess closed the distance between them, turning her around to face him. She came into his arms, her hands against his chest, and Jess held her tightly, determined to do no more than that, trying to ignore the allure of the fresh, clean scent of her hair. Lisa was drowning and he had to keep her afloat. She was obviously suffering from emotional trauma of some sort. There was a time when he'd have snorted at the suggestion that therapy might make a difference, but without it, he'd have blown someone's head off by now, possibly even his own. He was sure therapy would help Lisa, too. Perhaps if he used himself as an example, told her what he'd been through....

"Lisa, look at me," he said, his fingers lifting her face to his. "I'm no expert, but ..." He lost his train of thought, mesmerized by the luminous quality of her skin in the light spilling over his shoulder from the open door of his bedroom. In contrast, her hair appeared raven dark, flaring around her face in a glossy frame. Her eyes took in his features, and one hand stole upward, brushed past the line of his jaw, along his cheek. Forefinger extended, she smoothed his lips, focusing on them with intense concentration. The hand left his face, outlined an ear and when he felt her fingers glide from the back of his neck into his hair, every promise he'd made to avoid a replay of his earlier lapse disintegrated.

He lowered his head and her mouth was his, captured under the pressure of his lips. She surrendered with no resistance, her lips parting to permit egress, her tongue darting, dancing across the tip of his, alighting, teasing, demanding, prisoner becoming imprisoner. He kissed her eyes, her cheeks, her throat, delighting in the floral bouquet that emanated from her skin. Cradling her face between his hands, he sought her mouth and was met again with the welcome seduction of her tongue.

He pulled her even closer, glorying in the soft contours of breasts and thighs against his leanness, basking in the warmth of her body, her hunger feeding his. Her left hand slid inside his robe and found his nipple, her touch sending a bolt of lightning down through his body to his groin. The sweet torture of a full erection gripped him, betraying the intensity of his desire to Lisa, who sighed with openmouthed pleasure and moved against him, her hips locked against his. Jess groaned at the exquisite friction and the hands exploring the planes of her back moved lower to cup her buttocks, then under the interfering fabric of her T-shirt, lifting it above her waist until his fingers touched her breasts. High and deliciously full, their rosy peaks were waiting for his touch, coming alive under his teasing, pushing against his fingertips to stand at attention. Her skin, smooth and soft as chamois, begged to be stroked. He cradled her breasts, enchanted with the weight of them, aroused by the flutter of her heart beneath his palms.

Reclaiming her lips, Jess felt her relax against him, her mouth opening in eager response. She loosened his robe and her hands moved over his torso, grazing his nipples in passing, causing them to respond precisely as hers had, a first for him. Her hands traveled around to his back, scorching him as they moved, and her fingers slid under the waistband of his pajama bottoms. He removed her hand from the base of his spine and guided it to the agonizing center of his need.

Her touch was gentle and tentative at first until her shyness dissolved, and from that point, Jess, his blood igniting in a river of fire, knew he was dangerously close to losing control. She must have sensed it—hearing a click, he reluctantly pulled his mouth away from hers to pinpoint the source of the sound. Lisa had reached behind her and had opened the guest room door. Jess found himself looking directly into the interior of a pitch-dark room, an ill-timed reminder of the reason he'd been celibate for the past two years. How could he have done this to himself, to her? Stepping back from her, he dropped his hands.

"Lisa, this isn't right. Sex isn't what you need. You're reaching out for reassurance, some sign that you're not alone, and you aren't. I'm here for you and I'll support you in any way I can, but let's not do something we'll regret in the morning. Go to bed, get some sleep. Your perspective will be different tomorrow."

He risked a gentle kiss on her forehead, then backed into his bedroom and closed the door. Remembering that he'd warned himself earlier that Lisa was poison, Jess revised his opinion. Perhaps suicide wasn't such a bad idea after all.

*   *   *

Lisa sat up the rest of the night, at first in the easy chair, which she positioned in front of the door to the deck, then later outside in the chilled morning air. Her body burned with re- membered heat, her face with remembered shame. She had been as wanton as the prostitute Jess had thought she was, ravenous for his mouth, his touch, his body. She would have shared his bed—or hers—without a second thought and no re- grets, giving all she had, body, mind, soul. How could she have put him in such a position? He had reacted as any healthy male would be expected to.

He had wanted her, there was no way he could have hidden it. Remembering the throbbing length of him in those last few seconds before he'd moved away, a quiver shot through her torso and she curled in a knot in the big chair, wishing she were alone so she could scream and release her agony. That she had fallen in love with him—she knew it now and admitted it—was beside the point. He could not be intimate with a woman he didn't love. He'd even apologized, when she should have been the one begging forgiveness.

Well, he was right, it would not happen again. His role as host did not require him to see that the erotic fantasies of his guest became a reality. Whatever she could do to help bring these uncomfortable living arrangements and her dependence on Jess's help to an end she would do, even if it meant return- ing to the loft.

As for the mystery of her familiarity with the piano, she was at a loss. For the first time in her adult life, she had reason to doubt herself. All the odd flashes she'd seen in her mind over the years began to take on new meaning. As soon as she could, she would ask Alec if he knew a good psychiatrist. It looked as if she was in for years on somebody's couch.

Detecting a subtle lessening of the darkness beyond the win- dows, Lisa wrestled the big chair out onto the deck and watched the shape of the mountain become visible, its color changing from a matte black to the darkest of greens as the sun, still be- low the horizon, painted the sky in a wash of blue gray, then swirling a bit of pale orange over it all. Before long, she could make out the lush foliage below and the ragged peaks, and other homes dappling the mountainside, wisps of smoke curling from the chimneys of a few. Ground fog danced through the undergrowth, giving the scene the serenity of a Japanese landscape. She remained there, snuggled in a blanket, until the sun became a flaming orb, gilding the trees and hurling arcs of reflected light off the windows of the houses. The view was everything she had expected and she understood perfectly why this place was so special to Jess.

Jess. It was almost eight and time to stop hiding. As ashamed and embarrassed as she was, she would have to face him and apologize. She rehearsed her lines as she showered and dressed, in jeans and an oversize polo shirt. If she could keep things light, she might be able to pull it off.

She needn't have worried. The house was empty. Jess had left a note on the kitchen counter saying he'd gone to get groceries and would be back shortly. There was coffee on the stove, which he hoped would hold her until he was able to fix a decent breakfast. At the bottom of the note was a P.S. "Sorry about last night. Hands off from now on. Scout's honor."

Lisa crumpled it into a wad and hurled it across the room, swearing at herself, and at him. She needed no reminder that he didn't want her. She didn't really blame him. What man in his right mind wanted to become involved with a woman with her problems? And despite the fact that she'd had nothing to do with it, he would always associate her with what had happened to Mal. She'd fallen in love with a man who could never love her.

"Oh, Jess," she said, his name a wistful sigh. Hell on earth had taken on a whole new meaning. What she needed was time and distance, and seeing the last of Jess would speed that day along. Temper restored, she picked up his note and dropped it in a trash can, poured herself a mug of coffee and stepped out onto the front porch to sip the strong, invigorating brew. The morning promised a day to enjoy. Dew shimmered on the evergreens, each drop a tiny prism in which the sun dissolved in circular rainbows. Massive oaks and elms shared the lot with the house, and birds flitted through the canopy overhead, carrying bits of twig. It was nest-building time.

A path ran alongside the cabin. Curious as to where it led, Lisa left the mug on the porch rail and followed the path, which ended at steps made of railroad ties descending to a well-worn trail that snaked along the side of the mountain. To her right, the decks of the cabin jutted free of the ledge on which the structure was built. It was the kind of alpine setting one usually saw on postcards and calendars. Soothed by its fragrant serenity, she sat down at the bottom of the steps to take it all in. She had lost track of time when she heard Jess's frantic call.

"Lisa! Lisa, where are you?"

Hurrying back up the steps, she rounded the cabin and ran up onto the front porch, missing a collision with him by inches as he pelted out of the door. "Here I am. What's wrong?"

"Nothing. I thought—where were you?"

"Down on the steps, enjoying the view. That was all right, wasn't it?"

"Of course. Sorry. I wasn't sure what to think. Did you see my note?"

"Yes. Thanks for leaving it, or I'd have thought you had jumped ship."

"Not on your life." His dark gaze took on the laserlike intensity she found so disconcerting. "No hard feelings? About last night, I mean."

"Of course not," she said, inordinately proud that she sounded as if she meant it. "You were right, as usual. I was upset, or it wouldn't have happened. Thanks for bringing me to my senses. What's for breakfast?" The change of subject eased them over the hump.

Jess underwent a metamorphosis, emerging as a chef extraordinaire, whipping up a plate of eggs Benedict, which surpassed any she had ever had. He had news on several fronts. He had called Kitty from a shopping center to let her know that Lisa was with him and to alert her that the police would need access to the loft. "I didn't say why. I couldn't figure out what to tell her."

Lisa chuckled. "Don't worry about it. She'll concoct a reason of her own, and by the time she's told it to a couple of people, she'll have forgotten she made it up. I should have left her a message, but I wasn't thinking. I hope she wasn't worried.''

"About you? If she was, she isn't now. She seemed pleased that you were with me."

"That's Kitty, a hopeless romantic." To cover her faux pas, Lisa hurried to add, "She means well. What else is happening back there?"

He pushed his plate to one side and sat back, eyeing her warily. "Mr. Joyner asked me to pass along the good news. The people who were trying to buy your house backed out of the contract. They said they saw the article and thought it was the decent thing to do. Mr. Joyner says the real reason is that they couldn't get financing. So you can move back into your house whenever you like."

The surge of elation Lisa expected did not materialize. The thought of someone bugging her house ... "That will have to wait. It makes more sense to go back to the loft after the bugs have been removed. This has been lovely, but I can't impose on you any longer."

His expression softened, imbuing his features with a gentleness she'd seen only in Mal's presence. "You aren't imposing, and I'd just as soon you stayed here, at least over the weekend. I know it's lonely up here, but I've had the phone turned on, and passed the word I have a friend staying with me, so my neighbors will be keeping an eye out for you. I have to go into town—something's come up at work, but I'll be back as soon as I can."

Lisa nodded. Since this was Saturday, it had little impact on her schedule. The beginning of the week was another matter, but she'd worry about that when the time came. In the interim she could start on the design of the Louis XV dresser and mirror—thank goodness she had her tools and a decent supply of balsa for the mock-up.

And there were Mal's bills to go through. She might be able to work out his itinerary between Thanksgiving and the end of January. Whether it would tell her anything was open to question, but it would keep her busy.

"Do you have a map of Virginia?" she asked.

"At work. Why?"

"Mal made some calls from a place called Lockwood. I just wondered where it is." If she saw it on the map, it might ring a bell.

"I'll bring it back when I come. Now I'd better get dressed."

Jess changed clothes and headed for Washington, leaving Lisa feeling bereft. The cozy cabin seemed to double in size, the rooms yawning emptily. Determined to make the best use of her time, she loaded the dishwasher, then settled down at the table with graph paper, and the photos and measurements she'd taken in Portland of a dresser she'd been five minutes too late to buy. As usually happened when she was working, the hours flew as the delicate piece took shape on the paper. Its serpentine front required careful drafting and the detail of the elaborate molding caused a low-grade headache, but the finished product would be worth it.

The shadows on the mountain were long and deep when she had had enough. Wondering what was keeping Jess, she sliced the canned ham and made do with a sandwich and orange juice, taking it out on the deck to watch the sun begin a game of hide-and-seek among the trees atop the mountain.

It was after dark when Jess finally called. He was just leaving Security and was on his way to the hospital. Considering how late it would be when he left Greenhaven, he would stay in town overnight and return after a short meeting with his partner in the morning.

Also, he had stopped by the loft on his way in. The police had arrived just as he was leaving, but it would be a couple of days before Pete would get back to him about any latent fingerprints the perpetrator might have left.

Lisa drew out the conversation until there was no more to say, comforted by his rich baritone, wishing he were there to share the evening meal. Having little desire to cook for one, she concocted a giant salad and ate it with Mal's notes and receipts spread out around her bowl. But Jess's ghost lingered in her consciousness and she got up and, on a whim, went downstairs to his bedroom.

Turning the dimmer switch, the lighted panels worked their magic, bathing the room in a soft, warm glow. She leaned in his doorway, languishing in the scent of him, the woodsy fragrance so reminiscent of the mountain air outside. His bed was neatly made, the corners squared in sharp precision. But where did he keep his clothes? On her side of the hall, a walk-in closet opened onto the bathroom, but the arrangement here was different. His bathroom was twice the size of hers and there was no sign of a closet.

It took her five minutes to locate the slot between a pair of panels opposite the window wall. She tugged and a section slid to one side, exposing a closet, at the back of which was another door. With a guilty conscience for invading Jess's privacy, she opened it and walked into a brightly lit room.

Considering its size, it must have spanned the front of the house, a good half of it extending beyond the rear of the guest room. The walls were mirrored on three sides, and several pieces of exercise equipment were positioned around the room, with a folding cot in a far corner. The fourth wall was filled from end to end with framed photographs.

Lisa walked the length of it, examining each of the black-and-white glossies. They were shots taken in Vietnam—Jess with members of his platoon, a much younger Jess, wiry as a stalk of grass, his face smooth and unlined, his infectious grin double-width. But the ones that captured her undivided attention were a battery of photos of Jess with Clifford Mallory, who was easily recognizable by the shape of his head and round face.

She scrutinized them closely, searching for some sign of recognition. If she actually had met Mal during her childhood, this would have been how he looked then, but she couldn't be sure whether his face was familiar because he was no longer a stranger or because his was truly a face from her past. It was an exercise in frustration, and after a while she gave up on it, turning back to scan the room again.

A waist-high bookcase sat between the cot and a full-length punching bag. Expecting to see titles relating to health and exercise, she found an odd assortment of books on post-traumatic stress, phobias, Vietnam and meditation. She could understand his interest in the war and the chaos it had caused— he had lived through it. The others were a mystery. Try as she might, she could not envision Jess Hampton chanting a mantra.

On the bottom shelf were a dozen composition books. Opening the mottled black-and-white cover of one, she discovered page after page of strong, bold handwriting, each page dated, the earliest going back almost two years. Jess's journals. She would love to read them, but couldn't bring herself to poke into his private life any more than she already had, remembering how she had felt knowing someone had done much the same to her in the loft.

She left the room and went back upstairs with Mal's bills, and by the time she went to bed had sketched out his route. He'd come back to D.C. the Monday after Thanksgiving. There was a gap of several days, after which he had gone to St. Louis, backtracked to Indianapolis, then Cincinnati, and south from there to Charleston, South Carolina, and up to Lockwood. Since she had lived in St. Louis, Indianapolis and Cincinnati, she had to conclude that Mal had been tracing the moves she and her mother had made. As far as she could tell, the stops in South Carolina and especially in Virginia, where he'd stayed the longest, had had nothing to do with her.

Perhaps it was coincidence that Lockwood set off alarm bells. She was beginning, however, to look upon coincidence with outright suspicion. Every time she'd passed something off as pure happenstance over the past two weeks, it had turned out to be anything but.

Lisa slept soundly that night, but came awake abruptly, grappling to retain a fast-fading dream. The only remnant she could recall was of wandering through a dollhouse and finding a door that should not have been there and would not open. She seemed to be dreaming frequently in recent weeks, yet she could rarely remember their content. They weren't nightmares, but they left her feeling fatigued and apprehensive. Perhaps it was just as well she couldn't remember them.

Breakfast was toast and coffee, and a brief walk to help banish the jitters. She returned to the cabin with a twinge of guilt that she was as comfortable here as she'd been in her own home. Regardless, she would not move in until she could be certain it would not be violated by the persons who had invaded the loft.

But there was more to it than that. Her house would seem quieter, lonelier, her bed emptier. Thirty-odd hours spent here with Jess's presence, even while he was away, had become habit-forming. She felt a sense of sharing that she would miss. She'd be rattling around in her house like a widow, she for whom marriage to the man she loved seemed too remote a possibility to consider now. There would never be another Jess.

When she heard the crunch of tires on gravel and glanced at her watch, it was after two. She got up, stretched and opened the door, her pulse leaping at the sight of Jess getting out of the Porsche and smiling at her across the driveway. He was the picture of sartorial splendor in a charcoal-gray suit and pearl-gray tie. He wore it well, his broad shoulders shifting beneath the tailored jacket.

"Hi! How's Mal?" she called.

He crossed to the porch, his stride loose and easy. He looked tired, but his eyes were bright as they moved over her, head to toe. "Restless, and looking for you. He kept turning his head as if he was listening for your voice. I explained and he settled down right away. He's so close to coming out of it, so close."

"Oh, Jess, that's terrific. By the way, I've worked out his movements from Thanksgiving on, but now he can tell us what he was up to himself."

Jess sobered. "Don't count on it, Lisa. Don't count on anything yet. Dr. Trent says he may have no memory at all. Let's just take it one day at a time and keep our fingers crossed. Now I need to unwind. How about a walk? There's a Sunday flea market behind the shopping center. If we cut through the woods, it's about a mile and a half."

"You're on," Lisa said.

Ten minutes later, they were hiking toward the southwest through a stand of pines. The day was nippy but invigorating, the air redolent with the scent of moss and woods. Somewhere along the way, Jess took her hand, so natural a gesture that she couldn't quite pinpoint when it had happened. They continued, fingers locked, the sun, sieved by the branches, dappling their path.

"Jess, how did you find this place?"

"My granddad was born about five miles from here and I spent the summers with him until I went off to college. It's one of the best parts of my childhood, so when I needed a place to get away from it all, I scouted around and lucked out on the cabin. It was more like a shack back then, so I tore it down and put that one up."

"You built it? Alone?"

"Practically. Occasionally a couple of neighbors would come nosing around and volunteer. It took me a year, but I'm happy with it."

"Only a year? I'm surprised it didn't take longer, if you were keeping the kind of hours Detective Owen does."

A pulse jumped at his temple. "I was off the force by then. I came up here specifically to be alone and work on myself. I'll tell you about it sometime."

Lisa took the hint and let the matter drop, wondering how much emotional toll his years as a policeman had taken. So the books on meditation had had a purpose after all. She didn't dare mention them or she'd be admitting to outright snooping. She had to forget that room, concentrate on the here and now. "Enjoy him while you can" would become her motto this weekend. This was all she'd ever have.

The Sunday afternoon flea market was a cozy gathering, card tables lined up in rows the length of the parking lot behind the Piney Peak shopping center. Pedestrian traffic moved and stopped up and down the aisles. Whole families inched from table to table to examine the wares on display.

"I'm not sure about the quality of the merchandise," Jess apologized. "It may be junk, for all I know."

"But good junk, the best kind," Lisa countered, spotting a perfectly respectable Tiffany lamp in sore need of a cleaning. This was a collector's haven—thimbles, antique dolls, beer steins, cuckoo clocks, watches, glassware.

Clowns entertained the youngest browsers with balloons twisted into various shapes. A freckle-faced teenager was filling a piggy bank by applying decals to little arms and hands. At one table, a young woman with a toolbox crammed with makeup painted faces already sticky with cotton candy.

"See anything you like?" Jess asked as they ambled down the second aisle.

"Lots, but I didn't bring any money." She'd been so happy at the prospect of a stroll with him that she'd forgotten her wallet.

"I'm buying," he said firmly. "This is about as cheap as a date can get, so the least I can do is pay for a souvenir."

Lisa smiled, pleased that he considered it a date at all. "Well, if I see something, I'll let you know."

A mob of children were gathered at the table of an elderly woman drawing hearts, daisies and ducks on their cheeks. "I want a bumblebee," a strident little voice demanded. "No, not a bumblebee. I want a pretty red butterfly like that lady has. See? On her neck!"

Lisa stopped in her tracks, her mouth open, her hand flying to the nape of her neck. She had knotted her hair in a ponytail this morning, fully intending to let it down before Jess returned.

His hand cradled her arm. "Come on, Lisa, she's just a kid. She couldn't know."

Lisa shook her head quickly, her eyes wide with wonder. "No, it's okay. I could kiss her. I remember now! She made me remember!" She erupted with relieved laughter.

"Remember what?" Jess asked, pulling her to the side. Her sudden stop had caused a roadblock.

"Lockwood! Mal made calls to Lockwood, Virginia. I knew I'd heard the name before. A couple of years ago, I guess, I was in a crafts shop in Georgetown, and the woman behind the counter asked if my name was Lisa. She said . . ." The sentence trailed off. Lisa felt her face become pale and stiff.

Jess maneuvered her between the tables until they were beyond the boundaries of the vending area. "Take it easy. She said what?"

"That she had gone to school with me in Lockwood. Lockwood Elementary. I must have had my hair up, like today. She said she recognized me because of the butterfly birthmark. I told her she had confused me with someone else, that I had never lived there, and she apologized, but I could tell from her expression that she thought I was snubbing her. She was certain I was the person she remembered. I forgot about it—there was no reason not to. But Mal went to St. Louis and Cincinnati and Indianapolis, places I did live for a while. So if he went to Lockwood, too..."

"You're thinking that you might have lived there?"

"I don't know what to think. She—the woman in the store—said we'd been in fourth grade together. I started fourth grade in St. Louis."

"Then obviously the woman was wrong, Lisa."

"Was she? I remember starting fourth grade, Jess, but I don't remember finishing it. I was a year ahead of myself because I skipped a grade, so I was eight when I went into fourth grade and turned nine the summer after it. I lost that birthday—"

"Pardon me? You lost a birthday?"

"Could the doctors have been wrong?" she asked, not hearing him. "I need to talk to Mal's doctor. He would know. What's his name? I can't remember his name!"

Jess placed an arm around her waist, hoping he didn't look as concerned as he felt. She was unraveling at the seams again, perhaps with good reason, he couldn't be certain. Steadying her, he guided her toward the entrance of the flea market. He wasn't sure if she could make it to the cabin on her own two feet. Of all times for him to have suggested a walk!

He took a good hard look at her and the knot of tension in his gut eased a little. Her head might be somewhere else—she stared blindly ahead—but her legs were working, her stride strong and even. She could make it. If she couldn't, he'd carry her, simple as that.

"You mentioned doctors," he prodded gently. "What doctors, Lisa? Have you been in therapy?"

"No, I meant after the accident. I'm not sure how long I was unconscious—I was never able to work that out—but it was quite a while. When I couldn't remember the accident or anything about it, they told me not to worry about it, that it was quite common after a severe concussion. That's why I don't remember my birthday, which was the day before we crashed."

"I see."

"My ninth birthday is gone, as if it never happened, and I still tend to think of myself as a year younger than I am. But this . . ." She covered the hand around her waist with her own, moving closer to him, as if for warmth. "This is scary. It means I've lost more than a day or two, and it explains a lot of things I've never understood."

"For instance."

"Those pictures in my mind I mentioned last night. There's one where my hair is supershort, like a flat cap hugging my head, with little wisps around my ears. But my hair was never cut when I was a child. Mom wouldn't consider it. She hated my birthmark and made sure that I wore my hair long enough so that it was hidden. But the woman in the crafts store had seen it and remembered it. How could she, unless my hair had been cut? It wasn't something I'd show. I thought it was hideous, primarily because Mom said it was."

"It isn't, you know," Jess assured her. "It's a surprise at first, but the kid is right—it's like a pretty red butterfly. Go on." They were across the highway from the shopping center, heading for the path through the woods.

She stopped, her eyes lowered, her bottom lip caught between her teeth. Jess recognized a hurdle in the road when he saw one and prompted her cautiously. "And? Say it, Lisa. It's time you stopped sitting on all this."

"I saw a picture of Mount Vernon and suddenly I was walking through its rooms with a bunch of kids strung out two-by-two, holding hands, and my partner was a girl with hair longer than mine, only blond, and she wore thick glasses. I've never been to Mount Vernon. Things like that, and . . ."

"Yes? Come on, you're doing fine."

"I wake up these days," she said, her eyes pleading for understanding, "with the feeling that I've done something—I don't know—really bad, something I'll have to pay for someday. It's so strong, so overpowering. I'm terrified that it might have some basis in fact, Jess, that Mal knows what happened and that's what he wanted to talk to me about."

"Bull," he said harshly. "You're talking about your childhood. You know how kids think, blowing things out of proportion. If you did anything at all, it was probably something that made one hell of an impression on you, but in reality wasn't all that bad."

She shook her head. "I don't think so. I have the feeling this was very serious. The woman in the crafts shop—I don't know if she still works there, but if she doesn't, perhaps someone will remember her. I want to go into town with you tomorrow, Jess. I've got to find her."

"Why, Lisa? I was going to ask you to stay until we get the report from Pete. You met this woman...what? Two years ago? It's waited this long, another couple of days won't make any difference."

"Perhaps not to you. I want to go tomorrow, Jess. I feel as if I'm on a roller coaster heading toward this dark tunnel full of all sorts of terrors. I'm not used to being out of control. If I have to go through that tunnel, I want to be prepared. If you won't take me tomorrow, I'll get there without you, but I intend to go."

Jess saw the determined jut of her chin, the no-nonsense rigidity of her posture and knew there was little to be gained by arguing with her. He'd rather take her and know where she was than have her running around town, not sure which direction she might have gone. But why did he have a hunch that he might be driving her to her doom? For the first time, there was no consolation in the fact that his hunches were almost always right on the mark.

Chapter 9

Lisa ran out of Crafts 'n' Stuff and spotted the Porsche coming around the corner. Parking had been impossible and Jess had been circling the block. Squeezing between two parked cars, she waited for him to pull abreast and hopped in, waving a slip of paper. "Her name is Barbara Trainor, and she's the manager," she said, securing her seat belt. "She works afternoons and I had to convince the clerk to call her at home. Then I had to talk her—Barbara—into seeing me. She was pretty chilly at first, until I explained the problem. She lives on Holly Street, off upper Sixteenth."

Jess looked dubious. "You're sure you want to do this."

"I have to, Jess. If she's wrong, there's no harm done. I almost hope she is."

A blast of a horn behind them served as a reminder they were blocking traffic, a capital offense on Georgetown's busy streets. He pulled away and headed uptown. "God, I wish I could go in with you, but I can't afford to miss this staff meeting."

"I'll be fine. After I'm finished, I'll get a cab to Security Specialists and wait in your office for you."

"You might be there awhile," he warned her. "This is an important planning meeting and may last all day, but I'll leave as soon as I can. Then we'll run out to see Mal." He raced past a Metrobus, beating it to the light, his face set in a scowl.

Lisa squeezed his arm. "Come on, Jess. Everything will be fine. What's there to worry about?"

"Only a dozen different things. I'm a firm believer in Murphy's Law and this is exactly the type of situation for it to kick into high gear."

Laughing at this variation on superstitious behavior, Lisa settled back in her seat, bemused at her discovery that under his cool exterior, Jess Hampton was a worrywart.

Barbara Trainor lived in a two-story detached brick house shaded by fine old trees, the diminutive yard graced with azaleas about to burst into blossoms. Lisa waved Jess away and rang the doorbell. The deep front porch was much like her own, giving her a moment or two of homesickness.

The door was opened by the same attractive woman she remembered, statuesque, her skin the color of pan-browned butter. She wore a green-and-white caftan with flowing sleeves, her hair in a topknot, which showed her slender neck to best advantage. "That was quick," she said without preamble, and stepped back from the door.

"That's what happens when you're in a Porsche driven by a man who thinks you're being hardheaded by not listening to him, so he takes it out on the accelerator."

Barbara burst into laughter. "Your husband?"

"No, which may be just as well," Lisa said, relaxing a little. She hadn't been sure what kind of reception she'd get. "We met two weeks ago and, for the most part, we've been fighting ever since. Thanks for seeing me, Mrs. Trainor."

"Stop that. My name is Barbara, remember? Oh, that's the problem, isn't it? You don't."

"Precisely, and it looks like you may be the only person who can help me. Before I waste any more of your time, do you still think I'm the girl you knew in Lockwood?"

Her gaze crackled with curiosity. "You really don't remember? No fooling?"

"Cross my heart."

"Honey, come on back to the kitchen," she said, waving Lisa through a charming peach-and-pale-green living room. "We're gonna need room to spread out and plant our elbows. I've got a pot of coffee on, and a few Danish I hid from the kids." The dining room was pure Duncan Phyfe, making Lisa's mouth water.

"How many do you have?" she asked, following Barbara into an airy yellow-and-white kitchen aromatic with the smell of a full-bodied coffee. "Kids, I mean?"

"Three, and one in the oven. They're seven, six and four. This last one is an 'oops,' but what the hell. Maybe this one will be a girl. Sit," she said, nodding toward a breakfast nook in the recess of a sun-washed bay window. A thick leather-bound photo album and a stack of papers took up a corner of the table. Lisa slid onto one of the benches and waited while Barbara poured coffee and set a plate filled with an assortment of pastries in front of her.

"Now," she said, sitting opposite Lisa. "You aren't going to throw a fit when I show you what I have, are you?"

"I make no promises. I'll tell you one thing, though—I'm really nervous about this."

Barbara's mocha-brown eyes softened. "I owe you an apology. I was really put off that day in the shop. I thought…well, you can guess—here's this black lady talking about knowing me from some backwater town in Virginia. But I was sure it was you, Lisa. You haven't changed. I'd have known those fantastic hazel eyes even if I hadn't seen the birthmark. Here, let me put my money where my mouth is."

Pulling the photo album to the center of the table, she opened it, flipped to the middle and turned it around so Lisa could see it. It was a class picture, taken on the steps of a school, the words Lockwood Elementary inscribed on the lintel above the doors. Thirty-odd children, scrubbed, brushed and dressed in their best clothes, grinned up at Lisa, their faces bright as morning sunshine.

Barbara placed a finger above the child near the end of the second row. Lisa stared into the wide, smiling eyes of a little girl in a plaid dress with a Peter Pan collar. Her hair, anchored by perky white bows above her ears, was long, dark and wavy, disappearing behind her back. This was not a case of someone with whom she shared a resemblance, not a doppelgänger. This was Lisa No-Middle-Name Gillette. She felt her stomach flutter nervously and swallowed, her mouth dry as dust.

As if to prove her point, Barbara removed the picture from its transparent sleeve and turned it over. Typed on a sheet of paper glued to the back was the legend—Mrs. Briscoe's Fourth Grade Class, September 30, 1969. Beneath it were the names of her pupils, by row. The third from the last name in row two— Lisa Gillette.

Lisa brushed a hand over her eyes, her trembling fingers dancing against her lids. "Barbara, this doesn't make sense. I started fourth grade in St. Louis. I distinctly remember Mom taking me to register."

Without comment, Barbara extracted a sheet of paper from the stack on the corner of the table. "Each class published a little monthly newsletter, allegedly to improve our writing skills—ha-ha. This was the first one for that year." She held it at a distance, as if she might be farsighted. "Under Newcomers. 'Welcome to Lisa Gillette,'" she read, "'a new student from St. Louis, Missouri, the Show Me State. Lisa has been with us for a week, and has already shown us what a bright student she is.' That's the first item entered into evidence—my husband's a lawyer, so we tend to talk that way around here. There's lots more. My mother never threw any of our school things away. Here, take a look at these."

"These" were nine more issues of Mrs. Briscoe's fourth grade newsletter, all of which had a short column with the byline, Lisa Gillette, and were profiles of her classmates.

"Bucky Ingland," Lisa said, her voice hoarse with astonishment as she read her contribution to the January issue. "I remember him. Bugs Bunny teeth."

"Right. His mother finally slapped braces on him and you wouldn't believe what a hunk he turned into. We had to stop calling him Bucky."

"Barbara, this is crazy! I remember him so clearly—now. But the rest . . ."

"Keep looking," her hostess ordered. "And eat. I've got to get rid of these things."

Lisa obediently removed a Danish from the pile and nibbled at it absently as she paged through the photo album. The next set of snapshots that brought her up short were Polaroids, groups of children on a lush green lawn, the backdrop a stately white mansion she recognized immediately. "We went to Mount Vernon?" she asked.

"Our spring class trip."

"Wait." Lisa held up a hand, a fog lifting in her mind. "Somebody got sick and threw up all over the bus."

Barbara's eyes widened and she erupted in peals of laughter. "Rudy Thomason! I'd forgotten that! So it's coming back to you?"

"In bits and pieces," Lisa admitted, elated and increasingly unsettled at one and the same time. To a certain extent, it was like witnessing the salad years of a stranger, yet there was an increasing familiarity about everything she saw. Continuing her perusal, she nodded as still more recognizable scenes appeared between the sheets of plastic. But the contents of the next to the last page drained all heat from her body. She gasped, her hand over her heart.

"Mrs. Waxter." Her eyes were glued to a tiny sparrow of a woman in the first of two photos. She stood at the end of a row of students, the girls in frilly dresses, the three boys in dark pants, white shirts and ties. The children were arranged on a stage, in a semicircle before a grand piano, its lid raised.

In the second picture, an almond-brown pigtailed girl sat at the piano, her round face twisted in fierce concentration, her fingers curved above the keyboard.

Lisa looked up in amazement. "That's you! We took piano lessons after school from Mrs. Waxter! This was the end-of-the-year recital. Barbara, until a couple of nights ago, I didn't even remember that I knew how to play!"

Solemnly Barbara turned the page to indicate the recital program. The second listing down showed that Barbara Whitaker had played *Impromptu* by John Thompson. Fifth was Lisa Gillette playing *Little Spring Song*. Lisa squeezed her eyes closed.

"Are you all right?" Barbara asked worriedly.

"Fine, just...I don't know...flabbergasted, and relieved, and scared spitless." She removed a napkin from the holder Barbara extended and braced herself for whatever might come next. Scanning the program again, she said, "I don't understand. If I played in the recital, where was I when the picture was taken?"

"You're there. Look again."

Flipping back, Lisa checked the grouping before the piano. She was indeed there, at the end opposite Mrs. Waxter, taller than the others in her patent leather sandals and Alice in Wonderland dress. She was surprised she hadn't recognized herself. Here was the image that had haunted her in lightning flashes of memory, the small face framed by a sleek, dark haircut that made her eyes look even larger. Lisa folded her hands in her lap. The trembling had begun again.

"Something wrong?" Barbara queried.

"This picture. My hair. I could have sworn..." Haltingly she tried to explain her mother's attitude about the birthmark.

"Well, there wasn't much she could do except cut it." Barbara grinned. "It was full of rubber cement."

A flashgun exploded in Lisa's head. "Of course! Roger Carruthers! We were learning about—" she snapped her fingers, gathering the strands of the memory "—about Vikings! We'd made helmets out of construction paper, with horns and everything, only mine kept falling off because my hair was so thick. Roger came up with the bright idea of using glue to hold it on, and I let him do it. *I let him do it.*"

"Honey, if I'd been in your shoes, I'd have let him do it, too. Roger was so cute, he made your teeth ache. But your head was a mess afterward. It looked like your brains were oozing out. Boy, was your mother mad! She chewed Mrs. Briscoe out so badly, the woman cried."

Lisa slumped against the padded cushion behind her. "My God, Barbara, I remember. I felt terrible for Mrs. Briscoe—she wasn't even in the classroom when it happened." She paled, recalling her mother's fury at her for her part in the silly scheme. Eloise Gillette had been completely out of control, literally raving.

She yanked herself into the present. "I even remember the beautician who cut my hair. Her name was Dolly, and she really sheared me. I wondered how you could have seen my birthmark."

"Once seen, never forgotten. What happened to you, Lisa?" she asked, getting up to refill their cups. "You just disappeared. One day you were at the YW day camp with us—school was out by then—and the next day you were gone."

"I really don't remember, but I assume we left for Mom's next assignment. On the way, she skidded off the road and hit a tree. She was killed and I wound up in an orphanage. The courts didn't know what else to do with me. My father was dead, and I had no one else."

"Oh, Lisa, I'm sorry. We always wondered. I'm sure you never mentioned you were moving, or we wouldn't have been surprised when you didn't show up again. You became the mystery of our childhood—that's another reason I never forgot you. All your neighbors missed you."

"You lived nearby? I'm sorry, it's just something else I don't remember."

"I lived at 306 Halstead—we were the first black family in the neighborhood—and you were four doors down at Mrs. Howard's at 316. She's still there. The next time I go home, I'll be sure to tell her I've seen you. She was so worried."

"Why? She must have known we were leaving."

Barbara regarded her with a speculative air. "I don't think she did, Lisa. It's been twenty years, but I remember Mama saying how hurt Mrs. Howard was that y'all hadn't even said goodbye."

"We didn't? That doesn't sound right. Maybe she misunderstood, or forgot Mom had told her."

"Maybe," her hostess said after a tactful silence. It was obvious she thought otherwise. "Is there anything else you'd like to know?"

Lisa, taking that as an indication that she'd worn out her welcome, checked her watch. "I'm sorry, I've blown your whole morning."

"I'm not rushing you. This has been a real kick for me."

"You've been so helpful," Lisa said, meaning it. "If you really don't mind, I'd like to jot down some of this while it's still fresh, like the approximate date we arrived, a few names."

"Would you like copies of all this stuff? Bill has an office in the basement with every toy imaginable, including a copy machine. I can do that while you finish your coffee—and another Danish, *please*," she added fervently. "Back in a jiff." Sweeping the piles from the table, she left the room.

Lisa finished her cup, listing her former landlady's name and address, neither of which seemed familiar. The things she and Barbara had discussed seemed to hang in a vacuum, isolated events with nothing preceding them, gaps in between them and no finish for them at all. She remembered the recital and after that, awaking in the hospital in Delaware, two blocks from the orphanage that became her home. What had happened in Lockwood to cause her to eradicate so much of it?

The reminder of her mother's tantrum reared its head once again. It was the only time Lisa had seen her display such rage . . . or was it? It seemed there'd been another occasion but when, where and why were shrouded in a miasma of thick black smoke, which roiled and swirled through her mind, as if whipped about by an ill wind. Or was that a part of the crash scene, which had always been hidden from her?

How was it she remembered the school, but nothing about where she and her mother had lived? Would a return trip help to jog her memory? Why had Mal gone there? How was it that every time she stumbled on an answer, she wound up with a dozen more questions?

Footsteps sounded on steps nearby and Barbara appeared bearing a sheaf of papers, which she plopped on the table. "The copies of the photographs aren't that hot, but Bill's machine isn't exactly top of the line. They're distinguishable, but that's the best I could do."

"You are a sweetheart," Lisa said with feeling. "One last thing, and I'll get out of your hair. Where the heck is Lockwood?"

Barbara giggled. "A spit in the wind south of Portsmouth. It's really a bedroom community with pretensions of grandeur—planned zoning, open spaces, population control. Are you thinking of going?"

"I might."

"I'd better draw you a map," she said, accepting a blank sheet from Lisa's pad. "You'd never find it otherwise. If you're nervous about going alone, I drive down every other month to check on Mama. I was just there last weekend, so I won't be going again until June when school is out."

"If I go, I expect it'll be sooner than that."

"Well, okay." She concentrated on her efforts for a few minutes, then passed it over. "Look, honey," she said solemnly, "if and when you decide to go, give me a call. I can set it up so you can stay with Mama. She'd be delighted to have you."

"Barbara!" This was totally unexpected, and warmed Lisa no end.

"I'm not kidding. There are only two motels in the vicinity. One's a little mom-and-pop operation, clean, but far from fancy. The other rents by the hour, if you know what I mean. I'd also be willing to call Mrs. Howard for you. Better to warn her than have her flop over dead at your feet out of shock, because she'll recognize you immediately."

Lisa collected the papers, slid them into her bag and stood. "I can't tell you how much I appreciate everything you've done."

"I just hope it's helped. Where are you going now?"

"Over toward Wisconsin. I'm supposed to meet the demon with the heavy foot when he gets out of a meeting."

"Give me a minute to change shoes and I'll take you. You could get a bus or a cab, but you'd have to walk all the way to sixteenth to do that and I have no idea how often the buses run."

"Barbara," Lisa protested, "you've done enough."

"I have to go out anyway. It's time to pick up my youngest from day-care, which he refuses to miss, whether I'm off or not. Besides, it looks like rain."

As good as her word, Barbara ferried Lisa to Wisconsin Avenue, and let her out on the corner nearest Security Specialists.

"Hey," she said as Lisa closed the car door, "do me a favor? Keep in touch? I mean it. Here's my card with all my numbers, including the car phone. It's been so nice meeting up with you, and I'd hate to lose track of you again."

Lisa's smile was broad and genuine. "It's a deal. I'll call you as soon as I've moved back into my house."

"Why did you move out?"

"That's a whole 'nother story, as the kids say. Let's save it for next time. Thanks again."

She watched as the trim blue car merged into traffic and sped away, then glanced around for a restaurant. She had no hesitation about camping out in Jess's office at Security Specialists, but wanted a few moments alone to align her thoughts in case he had a yakky secretary who would distract her. A dark-windowed diner in the next block looked perfect, and she hurried toward it, just beating the first few drops of rain.

Ordering a cup of tea to keep the proprietor happy, she took the table farthest from the window and removed the copies from her purse, going over them again, sheet by sheet. Their impact was no less unsettling the second time around, and she sensed the opaque door of her memory opening a little wider, permitting a clearer view of her days at Lockwood Elementary.

It was not until she reread the first class newsletter that she became aware of something she had missed before. Barbara had read only the beginning of the blurb on her. The remainder sent a jolt through her, causing the cup to shake in her hand. She placed it gingerly on the table, dabbed at the liquid she'd spilled and picked up the sheet.

"...has been with us for a week," it read, "and has already shown us what a bright student she is. Lisa was born in San Francisco, California. She has traveled all over the country with her mother, who works with computers. We are pleased that she has joined us here at Lockwood Elementary. Welcome, Lisa!"

San Francisco! Why in the world would she have told them that? She didn't remember anyone even asking, though that was no guarantee of anything. Regardless, she'd have had no reason to lie.

It pulled at her, and no matter how she twisted and tugged at it, it didn't make sense. She remembered her mother's litany about wanting to have her baby at home rather than in Scranton. Her mother wouldn't have told them San Francisco, so where had the information come from?

She couldn't leave it alone. Going to the cashier, she asked the location of the nearest public phone and was directed to a hall leading to the rest rooms. She dug out a quarter, and taking a chance, dialed the number of Barbara's car phone.

"Trainor," came the crisp reply.

"Barbara, this is Lisa. Sorry to bother you so soon, but I have a question."

"It's no bother. Hush, baby. Mama's on the phone. What is it, Lisa?"

"The Newcomers' column. I just read that first one all the way through. It says I was born in San Francisco, but I couldn't have told anyone that, because it's not true."

"Mrs. Briscoe must have goofed. The way it worked, any time a new pupil showed up, his teacher made a note of anything she could use for the Welcome column, so it would be a nice surprise for the kid. Face it, honey, for some it was the only time they'd see their names in print. It's funny, though. Mrs. Briscoe wasn't the type to have made that kind of error. Another idol bites the dust. Anything else?"

"No, that's it. Thanks again. Happy motoring." Lisa hung up, far from satisfied. The problem was easily solved—her school records were back in the warehouse, repacked once she'd no longer needed them. Digging for more quarters, she called Security Specialists and was told that the staff meeting was still in session. She left a message for Jess that she was on her way to the warehouse, but would be waiting for him when he was free. Then, feeling guilty for having ducked out on her friends without a word, she dialed the office and traded insults with Alec, and followed up with a call to Kitty, who was in one of her chatty moods.

"Lisa, where *are* you? Sara's here and we could all go to lunch together."

"Sorry," Lisa burst her bubble as gently as she could, "but I can't. I'm on my way to the warehouse to pick up a couple of things and from there to Jess's office. We'll be running out to the hospital, then back to his place in the mountains."

"Well, I can't blame you for preferring Jess to either of us. He is such a find. I'm so happy for you, sweetie. He's just the kind of man you need."

"He might argue that point vehemently, so don't get the wrong idea. The only reason we're together is to help Mal."

"Of course, darling," she cooed. "Did he tell you the police were here? They tramped around upstairs for a couple of minutes and left. What in the world were they doing?"

Lisa hated to lie, but to tell Kitty would be akin to publishing it in the *New York Times*. "It was all a misunderstanding. It's been cleared up now. Tell Sara hello for me, and I'll call you again soon."

"How long will you be staying with Mr. Tall, Dark and Handsome? And did he tell you you can come home now?"

"I'm not sure and yes, he told me. I'll probably go there when I leave Jess's. By the way, Mal's almost conscious."

"So my little secret will be out soon," Kitty responded, sounding aggrieved.

"I'll do what I can about that. Behave yourself. Bye." She replaced the receiver quickly, her tolerance for Kitty's self-centered attitude shorter than usual.

There was something else she could get while she was at the warehouse, the cosmetics case containing a few papers and souvenirs of her mother's. It had been years since she'd opened it—there'd been no need, and the only personal item she remembered clearly was the bulletin from her father's funeral service. The rest were résumés and work-related documents. Perhaps it was time to go through them again.

She flagged a cab and arrived at her storage container a half hour later. Noon traffic had been at its worst and the trip had been made at the equivalent of a crawl. Her footsteps seemed to echo through the cavernous building. Many of the storage containers that had formed aisle B, the row on which hers was situated, were now gone, and aside from the watchman dozing in the front office at the entrance, the place was gloomily void of human life.

She unlocked the huge sliding door of her container, groped for the light switch and located the box she needed with a minimum of searching. The cosmetics case, heavier than she remembered, was on the bottom, of course, which meant unpacking and repacking. She added her school records to her already bulging bag, and pushed the carton back in place.

She first heard the footsteps as she reached for the light switch, but saw no reason to be concerned about the crunch of hard-soled shoes on the gritty concrete floor. Her only thought was that it was not the watchman. He'd had his feet up on the desk, very sizable feet shod in crepe-soled oxfords. Opening the door, she stepped out, secured the lock and started for the entrance.

Lisa had quite a distance to go, perhaps seventy yards, and there were only two containers on aisle B between hers and the entrance. She was about halfway there when it occurred to her that the sound of her footsteps had actually become more audible. She wore running shoes, which were fairly quiet before but seemed louder now—each step produced a more staccato edge. She checked her heels, thinking she might have picked up a stone or a tack, but found nothing unusual. Continuing toward the entrance, she listened, puzzled. There was no reason for the click of her heel against the cement. Perhaps it was the person she'd heard before.

She turned around. No one was in sight, but she could only see the length of the aisle she was on. Hurrying a few steps farther, the footsteps fell between hers. It was definite—she was not alone. She stopped. So did the other footsteps. Her heart beginning to pound, Lisa ducked between a pair of containers and waited. At first there was only silence, but before long, she heard it—the sharp strike of a woman's high heel, slow and considerably quieter, as if she walked with stealth, trying to mute the sound of her shoes.

I've got to get out of here, Lisa thought. Darting over to aisle A, she knew she'd made a mistake. This was the side of the building with no windows at all. It was much gloomier here and if there was someone behind her, she wanted to be able to see who it was. It might be a warehouse employee, or someone searching for their storage unit, but instinct told her that was wishful thinking. She looked back and saw movement, someone in a dark coat moving quickly out of sight. The entrance was opposite aisle D. What had possessed her to go in the opposite direction anyway?

Running quietly past three containers, she returned to aisle B again, the stalker hurrying to locate her. Then both sets of footsteps were drowned out by the welcome rattle of the roll-up door, the approaching rumble of a big engine and the asthmatic wheeze of brakes. An air horn blasted the silence. A moving van had arrived.

Zigzagging between containers, Lisa worked her way over to aisle C, hearing voices engaged in raucous dialogue, one, that of the watchman. A cab door slammed, gears groaned as they meshed and the van drove slowly in Lisa's direction, the big semi growling past her. The driver honked, and she waved but never broke stride, sprinting toward the watchman's glass cubicle.

"Hey! No running," he scolded as she approached.

"Someone came in a few minutes before the van arrived," she panted. "Did you see who it was?"

The muscles of his face tightened. "What are you talking about? Nobody gets in here without me seeing them."

"I had to wake you up when I arrived, so anybody could slip in here while you were napping, and someone did. I'd advise you to do some checking."

He rushed away, mumbling loud enough for her to hear. "Crazy broad. Nobody came in here. Nobody passes Stoney without he sees them."

Lisa couldn't have cared less what he thought of her. Hitting the street at a run, she jogged toward the nearest corner, where a bus was approaching, joined the few waiting and hopped on. She had no idea where it was going, but whatever its direction, she would stay on it.

It went south, then west, and once she was in familiar territory, where the streets were busy with late lunch-hour traffic, she got off, flagged a cab and arrived at Security Specialists twenty minutes later. Jess stepped out into the hall as she entered the front door.

"I got your message," he said, scanning her from head to toe. "Hey, are you all right?"

"Sure," she said brightly. The trip across town had been rife with second thoughts about her experience. There was no way to be certain of the identity and purpose of the woman in the warehouse, and Lisa, in the bright light of the outdoors, had begun to feel silly. "I got spooked in the warehouse, I guess because it's the first time I'd been there alone. Then I took the wrong bus coming here and got lost. Have you been waiting long?"

"I haven't been waiting at all. The meeting's still on. I took a break."

"Mr. Hampton." A young woman came out of his office, model thin and crisply immaculate in a severely cut suit softened by a frilly white blouse. "Mr. Owen has called three times," she said, sternly thrusting several pink messages at him. "He said it was imperative he speak to you as soon as you were free." Her blue-gray eyes flicked toward Lisa and scanned her with lightning speed before they returned to Jess. She did not look pleased, whether because of Lisa's presence or because her superior was neglecting his duties wasn't clear.

Jess must have picked up the vibrations. "Cecile, this is Lisa Gillette. Lisa, my administrative assistant and taskmaster, Cecile Kilroy. Lisa will be using my office until this blasted meeting is over."

"Ms. Gillette," Cecile murmured, her tone decidedly noncommittal. "I'll clear your desk for her, Mr. Hampton." Performing a smart about-face on her three-inch heels, she went back into the office and closed the door with a good deal more force than was required. So much for my concern about a yakky secretary, Lisa mused.

Jess's thick brows rose in surprise. "What was that all about? She knows there's nothing on my desk. Come on." Opening the door, he led Lisa through the outer office, past an unsmiling Cecile, into his own.

I'll have to do something about her, Jess thought. Cecile was a professional and good at her job, but she was possessive, and any woman who crossed his threshold, for whatever purpose, was considered a threat—to what, Jess wasn't sure. "How'd it go with Mrs. Trainor?"

Lisa collapsed into his chair. "She was right. I lived in Lockwood from mid-September until late June of the next year. She showed me the proof—I have copies of everything. That's where I took piano lessons, Jess. And that's the year my hair was cut."

This confirmed his theory. Something traumatic had happened to her in Lockwood and she'd done a masterful job of blocking it out. "You still don't remember any of it?"

"A lot of it came back to me, but not all, by a long shot. We can talk later. You'd better get back to your meeting."

He nodded absently and thrust his fingers through his hair. "Let me get the call to Pete out of the way first." He picked up the phone and tapped out the number, grateful that he'd managed to remove the bug he'd planted in Lisa's telephone before Pete's men had arrived. "With luck," he said to her while he waited for Pete, "we'll be finished in there in about a half an hour."

"There's no hurry. I got a few of my mother's things from the warehouse to go through, and I yanked my school records again. I—"

He held up a restraining hand as Pete came on the line. "Homicide, Owen."

"Jess, Pete. You're a hard man to catch. What's up?"

"Where's Gillette?" he asked brusquely.

"She's right here. Why?"

Lisa looked up at him, openly questioning.

"Bring her in. Item one—the bugs were clean, but Quarles hit the jackpot for us with the space heater."

"A print?"

"A partial, but enough. For your information, it had been rigged to fry anyone who plugged it in, but that's beside the point. We know who he is now, a very nasty character named Ralph Youngblood, a free-lancer who usually operates out of the New York area. The important thing for you to know is that his apartment was searched. Fortunately for us, he's the sort who likes to keep souvenirs of the hits he's made. They found a stash in the ceiling above his closet. It included, among other things, a *Post* article about Gillette that goes back to November of last year, and an index card with her address, phone number, a description of her car and her tags."

"You're kidding." Jess sank into the chair at the corner of his desk, feeling a tightness across his chest. He kept his face averted, past being able to control his expression.

"There was a lot of other garbage up there in that closet, but nothing on our buddy. We've been barking up the wrong tree from the git-go. *She* was the target, not Mal. You and your damned hunches."

"To hell with that! The question is *why*? And who hired him?"

"We hope she'll be able to tell us, but she may not know herself. Bring her in, Jess."

Using the desk as a crutch, Jess pushed himself to his feet and pressed his fingers above the bridge of his nose. "I don't think so, buddy."

"What's that supposed to mean?"

"Are you going to be there for a minute? Let me call you back."

"Not on your life. I'll wait."

"Your choice." Punching the hold button, he looked down at her. "Think back to Friday, Lisa. Your fall. Tell me precisely what happened, starting from a few moments before."

His manner must have convinced her not to waste time with questions. "It was time for the train. I stood up—I'd been sitting on a bench—and moved to the edge of the platform. There were a lot of people waiting and we were all bunched up together. The lights blinked, and a kid thought he'd caused it and everyone laughed. The person behind me must have been carrying something in their arms, because I felt it in the small of my back, and suddenly I was falling forward onto the tracks."

He sat on his next question for a few seconds, but he had to be clear on this point, even if it meant alarming her. "Is there any possibility you were pushed?"

She blinked, her eyes widening. "I don't know. Jess, what's going on? What did Detective Owen say?"

"In a minute. Has anything else suspicious, or out of the ordinary happened recently?"

She looked away, her face troubled. "Well . . . the bag lady, I guess."

"What about her?" Jess had been informed of her encounter with the homeless woman. It had been a two-sentence comment in his co-worker's concise reports. That seemed so long ago.

"She—her name was Angie something—rammed a man with her grocery cart. She said he had followed me in and out of Westlake's, that he'd had a gun and was about to rob me. I didn't take her seriously. Should I have?"

"Perhaps. The news from Pete isn't good." He started to press the button to continue his conversation with the detective, but was forestalled by Lisa's surprisingly strong grip on his wrist.

"There's something else," she said. "In the warehouse. I'm not sure, but someone may have been stalking me."

Jess clamped his jaw tight in exasperation. "What happened?"

He listened to her description of the events without comment, then turned his attention to the phone. "Pete, I'm back. She stays with me, and we'll be heading out to the cabin as soon as I hang up. Your boy is in town."

"Who? Youngblood?"

"Roger, buddy. He may be working for or with a woman." He outlined the reasons for his opinions tersely, watching fear work its effect on the color of Lisa's eyes. "And you don't have the manpower for round-the-clock surveillance."

"We could put her under protective custody in a safe house somewhere."

"Where she'd be a veritable prisoner? The cabin's as safe as any place you'd use, and she'll be able to move around."

"It's her decision, not yours," Pete argued. "Ask her."

Covering the mouthpiece, Jess struggled manfully to keep his voice neutral. "Pete just reminded me that what you do is up to you. You're free to use the cabin for as long as you like, but if you'd feel safer in protective custody, please, Lisa, say so. I'll understand."

Her eyes were hooded, her face as tightly closed as a vault. He waited, determined not to influence her. As a result, he was astonished to hear himself saying, softly, "Stay with me, Lisa."

The change in her expression reminded him of the way the sun popped from behind the mountains in the morning, flooding the valley with light. "I'll stay."

God, he thought, if anyone so much as touches her, I'll kill the son of a bitch. "She votes for the cabin," he said into the phone.

"You realize that places her outside our jurisdiction. Don't be a hero, Jess. Alert the law in your area. Youngblood's rap sheet would make your blood freeze like dry ice. See if she has a clue as to why she's the bull's-eye. Whoever's paying Youngblood's bill is someone local, and must know he—or she—will be tried for murder, too."

"You're talking to a former cop, remember? And wasting precious time, too. Any chance of getting a description of this guy?"

"Caucasian, 52, five-eleven, 170. Brown hair, light brown eyes. A nothing-looking guy, which makes our job that much harder. I'll issue an area-wide alert, but that's the best I can do."

Jess nodded. "I know. We're on our way back out of town right now. I'll keep in touch."

"Do that."

Jess disconnected, already plotting ahead. The Porsche was too visible. The pickup would be perfect but it was parked behind his apartment. He hit the intercom button. "Cecile, ask Lem if I can trade cars with him for a while."

She gasped. "Trade your Porsche? But you've *never* let—"

"Just do it, please, as quickly as possible, but make sure he drove his car and not his wife's. I need something heavy and fast."

Lisa stood. "Jess, tell me what's going on. What did Detective Owen say?"

Jess looked across the desk at her, ripped by indecision. Whatever she'd been through as a child had been too upsetting for her to deal with and she was just now coming to grips with it. Given her history, the truth about her present situation might push her over the edge. Damn, what should he do?

Coming from behind the desk, she confronted him, her eyes locking with his. "Jess, listen to me. I've learned a lot about myself over the past two weeks, and one of the most important lessons is that I can take it. I may sag now and then, but the droop doesn't last long. I've also learned that I've been running from something for twenty years and didn't know it. I assume I ran because that's what it took for Lisa, the child, to survive. Well, it's caught up with me, and it's okay, because Lisa's an adult now. No more running, Jess, from whatever's back there in the past and whatever's facing me today, or waiting around the corner in my future. I want to know everything. *Everything*. End of speech. What's going on?''

Jess, impressed by the even timbre of her voice, had just learned a lesson of his own. He loved Lisa Gillette. Nothing he could do about it, but he loved her. And for all the credit he'd given her for having kept a stiff upper lip, he'd been selling her short. The past two weeks had been a crucible for her, and she stood before him having emerged from it with the tensile strength of steel. She seemed strong enough to take Pete's news, and he hoped he was right, because she had to know, for her own protection.

The intercom burred, sounding like a hive of angry bees. Jess leaned down and pressed the speakerphone button. ''Yes, Cecile.''

''I have Mr. Silas's keys for you. His car's in its usual slot.''

''Terrific. Thanks, Cecile.'' He disengaged the speaker and straightened up. Lisa had not moved and skewered him with her steady hazel gaze. She was waiting.

As if of their own volition, his hands reached toward her and he very deliberately lowered them. She needed no comforting grip on the shoulder, no supporting arm. ''Lisa, you were the target, not Mal.''

Her pupils dilated with shock. ''Me? I?''

''The hit-man—his name is Youngblood, likes to keep mementos of his hits. He had the Thanksgiving article with your picture, a description of your car and your tag number on a three-by-five card.''

''Nothing about Mal?'' It had the urgency of a plea.

''Nothing. He meant to kill you.''

''But Maria and I...'' She sat down again, gingerly, as if she might shatter. ''I was about to say that Maria and I looked nothing alike, but how do I know? I hadn't seen her since she took her vows. All I remember are those big eyes smiling goodbye through the grate. When we were kids, people visiting St. Mary's thought we were sisters."

She bowed her head for a moment. Jess wasn't sure whether she was crying or praying, but before he could move to find out, she swiveled around toward him. There were no tears on her cheeks. Her face was still, but her eyes were hard and cold. Jess's spirits plunged. In Greek classical theater, when the news was bad, the messenger who'd delivered it caught it in the neck, or the back, or however they dispatched the poor fool who had earned their displeasure. He had no fear for his life, but she certainly looked as if she didn't like him a hell of a lot.

"We should leave," she said tonelessly. "I didn't mean to hold things up."

"You haven't. Lisa . . ."

One side of her mouth tipped up. "It's all right, Jess. *I'm* all right—terrified, and confused, all the things I should be. I'm also very, very angry. I am sick of people playing God with my life. I do not like feeling helpless. I've had enough."

He nodded. He knew that kind of anger intimately and should have recognized it. Four years before, he'd been where she was now, only he'd been busy denying that anything was wrong. She was handling it far better than he had. God, he loved her, but there was nothing he could do to soothe her pain. If she wanted his help, she would ask. More than likely she would work it through on her own. Either way, she'd make it. The tempered steel had cooled from the heat of the furnace. The edges had been sharpened. She was now ready for battle. That was all to the good, since she might well be fighting for her life.

Chapter 10

Lisa, stretched out on the back seat of the unobtrusive old German-made car Jess had borrowed from his partner, used the long trip back to the mountains to rethink, regroup and adjust to the new reality that would rule her life for the immediate future. Everything was changed, yet nothing had changed. Maria was dead because of her, and Mal's life and his physical and mental condition now irreparably altered, because of her. Only the bottom line was different—everything had happened because someone wanted *her* dead.

It apparently made no difference that they had murdered the wrong woman the first time. Barbara's description of her latest pregnancy seemed to fit this scenario to a *T*. Maria's death was an "oops!" So was Mal's wrecked life. So was the future she would never have with the man with whom she had fallen in love—assuming she survived to have a future at all. Jess would never be able to forget that Mal was an invalid because *someone had wanted her dead*. And the killer was still trying. Why? What had she done to warrant a death sentence?

Jess stopped at the sheriff's office, with Lisa only dimly aware that he'd left the big station wagon, and with no inkling as to how long he'd been gone when he finally returned. He drove directly to the cabin, helped her inside and prepared a meal, which she tried without success to eat.

"Talk it out, Lisa," he said, clearing the table. "Blow up, cry, but don't hold it in. It'll only make things worse."

"What's the point, Jess? I feel as if I'm a character in some sci-fi movie, and everyone's read the script but me. Every time I think I have a handle on what's happening, someone changes the script and throws in a new wrinkle. I don't know what's true anymore."

"What do you mean?" He brought two glasses of wine to the table and placed one in front of her.

"If you'd asked me to tell you about myself a couple of days ago, I'd have said, okay, born here, lived there and there and there, except I'd be leaving out one, maybe two, chapters because I don't remember them. I would have said the few friends I have I value highly and, as far as I know, I've made no enemies, and that would be wrong, too. I've made one hell of an enemy, and don't know who it is or what I've done, and you can take the last part literally. My session with Barbara proved that."

He picked up the glass of wine and put it in her hand. "You said you had copies of what she showed you?"

"In my bag." Too drained to get up, she nodded toward the leather tote she'd been using since her return. It sagged against the railing at the top of the stairs where she had dropped it and her mother's cosmetics case on her way in the front door.

Jess brought her purse to her. She slid the papers out onto the table and pushed the larger sheets across to him. "See for yourself."

"Where'd the other piece of luggage come from?"

"The warehouse. It's crammed with stuff that belonged to Mom."

Jess flipped through the pile in silence, examining the copies of the photographs, reading the recital program and newsletters, while Lisa removed her school records to find the carbon of the registration form for Lockwood Elementary.

"I see why Barbara recognized you," Jess said. "You haven't so much changed as mellowed."

"Another reason she remembered me is because as far as she and the people in the neighborhood were concerned, Mom and I just disappeared. The lady we were boarding with didn't know we were leaving. It sounds as if we just packed up and left in the middle of the night."

"Perhaps your mother was out of money and couldn't pay the bill."

"I doubt that. I've got her wage stubs in that cosmetics case. I went through them when I was packing to move into the house, and I was bowled over at the salary she was paid."

"What exactly did she do?"

"Analyzed the computer needs of a business, suggested the kind of system they'd need, saw them through the procurement process and set up the appropriate programs. There weren't many women doing that sort of thing back then."

"So money shouldn't have been a problem," he said thoughtfully. "Odd that she chose to use boarding houses instead of short-term rental apartments. What's this about you being born in San Francisco?"

She pushed the registration form across to him, her finger above the line requesting her place of birth. San Francisco. "All the others say Pittsburgh. So which was it, California or Pennsylvania? Or was I born in a plane en route across country?" she asked, unable to suppress her bitterness.

Jess got up and ambled to the sofa. After a heavy silence, he said, "Lisa, this has all the classic symptoms of a woman on the run—the constant moving, staying in boarding houses where she'd be harder to trace, the conflicting information about where you were born. It sounds to me as if she was trying to distance the two of you from something or someone. A scandal, perhaps? What do you know about your father?"

Lisa stirred restively. "He was killed when I was three. He was a building contractor on the site at a housing development. A severe windstorm came through, and a tree fell on the roof of the house he was in. He and another construction worker were killed." Retrieving the cosmetics case, she removed a sheet of paper from a pocket in the lid and took it to him. "This is from his funeral service."

Originally it had been a mimeographed eight-and-a-half-by-eleven sheet of paper folded in half to make a four-page bulletin. At some point, it had been torn in two, leaving only pages three and four intact, the order of service on one side, the names of pallbearers and flower bearers on the back.

Jess sat on the edge of the cushions, his elbows on his knees. "Lisa, with the front part gone, your father's name and his obituary have been lost, even the name of the church and its location. This may hurt, but we should consider the possibility that he may have committed suicide."

Lisa's mind churned with panic. All the givens of her past were being challenged. There were children at St. Mary's who had been deserted by their parents, and Maria had been left in a bassinet in the back of a parish church. Lisa had taken comfort in the fact that she had once been a part of a family and that she had lost her parents to God—they'd had no choice about leaving her. To have suspicion cast on the death of her father was the equivalent of a catastrophic breach in the foundation on which her life was built. Suicide had never occurred to her.

"But Mom didn't just pack up and move to another area where we wouldn't be associated with something like that," Lisa pointed out. "We never settled any one place for very long." Her relief at finding a flaw in Jess's logic was short-lived. She had just added fuel to his argument that Eloise Gillette had been running from something.

She picked up the sheet and scanned it again, turned it over to read the names of strangers who had helped lay her father to rest. A line at the bottom brought a smile of elation.

The family requests that in lieu of flowers, friends offer a donation toward the furnishing of the new Sunday school wing. Checks should be made out to the New Jericho Building Fund—Gillette Room.

"Here's the name of the church! Maybe it still exists, Jess. The minister may remember him or know someone who would."

Jess drained his wine and stared moodily into the empty glass. "A good idea. It won't hurt to try. You might also ask the minister if your parents were married there. You may have been christened there, too."

That thought held great appeal. Considering that there was now more doubt than ever about where she'd been born, Lisa found herself longing for some proof that she'd been carried to a church in a christening gown to be blessed. It would be a clear indication that she'd been wanted and loved.

Jess dug out a telephone directory and they settled on the sofa with the phone between them. Lisa found the area code, called Information and held her breath while she waited for the number. New Jericho Presbyterian Church was listed, not in Charlotte, but in a nearby suburb.

"Don't let that throw you," Jess said. "Figure they moved. It's been twenty-six years, remember? Go ahead and call while I change clothes. This suit is stifling."

The telephone was answered by a Reverend Putnam who responded to her request with a puzzled silence. "I'm not sure I understand. You want to know if your parents were married at New Jericho, and whether you were christened here? I take it they aren't available to ask."

"My parents died when I was a child. They were from Charlotte, and my father's funeral was held at New Jericho—I'm hoping it was their home church. I'm also curious about how he died."

"It might help if you explained why, Ms. Gillette."

Lisa told him as little as she could, employing some judicious editing along the way. "I know so little about my parents, and anything that might help me find out where I was born would be especially helpful."

"Well, I've only been here eight years, but our records go back to the year one. I'll see what I can do. Let me have your number. I may not get back to you immediately, but I'll certainly look and call you as soon as I can."

Lisa thanked him and hung up, butterflies migrating from one side of her stomach to the other. Jess bounded up the steps looking much more at home in a faded black sweat suit and running shoes. He was far from relaxed, however, prowling around the house with the air of a caged panther. Lisa watched him from the dining room table, admiring his loose-hipped stride. It was a while before she began to suspect that there was something on his mind.

"A penny," she said.

He circled the room and stopped at the kitchen sink with his back to her. "Lisa, are you ready for whatever this man tells you?"

"You think he'll come up empty?"

"I think he'll have something and it won't be good."

"Why?" Leaving the sofa, she hopped onto a stool at the counter.

"I keep thinking back to what a hard time Mal was having trying to decide whether to tell you what he'd learned. He kept saying it might cause you—I think it's safe to assume it was you—more grief than you deserved, so it must have been bad news. Are you sure you want to know?"

"I'm sure. I owe it to Maria and Mal, but most of all to myself. I think you're right—my mother was on the run. I've been running, too, from whatever happened in Lockwood. Maybe that's why there's a price on my head. Perhaps someone wants revenge. Maybe, just maybe, I deserve what's happened to me."

"No one," he said, his voice grating, "deserves to be hunted the way you've been."

"Someone out there disagrees with you. Regardless, I'm through running. You're so strong, Jess, you don't know what it's like to—"

He pushed himself away from the sink, impaling her with a hard-edged gaze. Leaning over the counter until his face was inches from hers, he said, "Don't tell me I don't know what it's like. It's time you shed your illusions about me, Lisa. I came home from Vietnam, Jess Hampton, *mucho* macho. I was a man, all right, a man with a hair-trigger temper. At first, it would only get the best of me every so often, but before long, I was eating rage for breakfast, lunch and dinner, blowing up for no reason at all. I had screaming nightmares that launched me out of bed like an Atlas rocket. I'd sit up, walking the floor, anything to keep me out of the bed."

"Oh, Jess," Lisa whispered.

"One day I was going into a deli and a little kid—six, maybe seven—was standing outside. He had a red plastic squirt gun and as I opened the door, he pointed it at me. The next thing I know I'm on my belly on the sidewalk with my weapon drawn and my finger on the trigger. Pete was my partner and the only reason I didn't shoot that kid was because Pete kicked my gun out of my hand. I quit the force that day."

Lisa reeled from the impact of his words. Why had it never occurred to her to ask the reason he'd left the job he seemed to have loved so much?

"I had been running ever since I got home from 'Nam," he continued, "running from the memory of those two days as a captive, being tortured. Running from the terror and rage I'd felt at being totally helpless in their hands. I ran from knowing how close I was to madness while Mal and I were hiding, out of my mind with fear and pain and fever—me, Jess Hampton, Macho Man."

So this was the source of the pain, the traces of which were only now beginning to recede from his features. Lisa wanted so badly to go around the barrier that separated them and wrap her arms around him, but the fear of rejection kept her firmly on her side of the counter.

"You did something about it," she said.

He stepped back, his ferocity waning. "I came out here and lived like a hermit for months, so I had to face myself, acknowledge how I'd been affected by what I'd been through. Once I'd passed that hurdle, I was open to accept help. I went into town every day to a counseling center for Vietnam vets. I listened, and learned that I wasn't alone and never had been, that my reaction was human, that *I* am human, not Superman."

Lisa disagreed, but kept silent.

"Rebuilding this cabin was therapy, too," he continued, moving from behind the counter to lean against the end of it. "As neighbors came to help, I had to start tearing down all the invisible walls I'd constructed to separate myself from people. When Lem offered me a slot at Security Specialists, I was ready to take it. It's been a long haul, Lisa. I haven't slain all the dragons yet, but I'm working on it, and the only reason I'm still at it is because I ran from them for so long.''

He cradled her face in his hands, his thumbs caressing the line of her jaw. "So I do understand. I've been where you are, and I admire you for the way you've handled yourself. Whatever happens, I'm backing you. You came to mean a lot to Mal, or he wouldn't have had any hesitation about talking to you. He would want me to help you. I just want you to know who I really am."

And why you're in my corner, Lisa thought. Because of Mal. In which case it was all the more important that she ignore the chaos his nearness evoked. She moved a step backward, planning to ease slowly from his grasp. "Thanks for telling me," she said, "but it doesn't change my opinion of you. If anything it . . ."

Her intent had been to assure him that his account of what he had been through merely proved her point—his was a unique strength she wished she had. Somewhere between the intent and the words remaining to be spoken, however, the rhythmic stroke of his thumbs across her cheek erected a roadblock into which she crashed headlong.

"If anything . . ." he prompted her.

The thought had disintegrated into a meaningless pile of debris, a hapless victim of the collision. Giving in to the impulse that had dogged her from their first meeting, she reached up, her fingers trembling as she soothed the furrows between his brows, a simple gesture that took on an intimacy she hadn't anticipated. Jess must have sensed it as well. He stiffened for a second. Then, with a deep breath, he relaxed, as if shrugging off some irksome restraint. Mesmerized by his night-dark gaze, her face still captured in the warm prison of his palms, she watched helplessly as he stepped even closer.

He lowered his head and, unable to resist the lure of what was to come, Lisa moved into him eagerly, her lips parting, meeting, melding with his, her slender frame becoming pliant in his arms, a willow yielding to the rising storm of his embrace. She pressed against him, delighting in the hard planes of his chest and stomach, and felt a silent roar of joy at the sudden rigid evidence of his wanting, its impatient throb between her thighs as it strained against the layers of fabric that separated them.

He raised his head long enough to pick her up and carry her down the steps to the guest room, where he lowered her carefully onto the bed, then knelt beside her, his upper body covering hers as he bent to kiss her mouth and eyes, her temples and earlobes, feasting, tasting, his fingers tugging gently at the zipper of her beige jumpsuit until it was open to her waist. He helped her out of the sleeves, pushed the thin straps of her teddy aside and brushed a kiss across each bare shoulder, his tongue darting across her skin to dip into the hollows at the base of her neck, making her pulse flutter and leap.

Sitting up, he removed her shoes, lowered the zipper as far as it would go and, reaching under her, supported her hips with one arm as he pulled the jumpsuit down to her ankles and discarded it, bending to kiss each bruised knee and to smooth the length of her calves, the arch of each foot. Missing the feel of him, Lisa extended her arms, and he responded by pressing one outstretched hand against his lips, his breath warming the still-sensitive palm. Slowly, deliberately, he eased the lace-edged teddy down to her waist, under her buttocks and off.

"My God," he whispered.

She was now completely nude and his eyes traveled the length of her, enrapt. Leaning down, he buried his face between her breasts before beginning a leisurely journey toward the cinnamon-tinted peaks. Lisa felt her breath catch, her back arching in anticipation of his reaching his goal, her nipples pouting, straining for attention. He closed on his target, his tongue darting, tickling, circling, first one yearning bud, then the other. Lisa's body sang with pleasure, the pulse in her ears setting the tempo, the song a paean to passion. She caressed his face, raked her fingers through his hair, clutched his head to intensify the rush of pleasure.

Suddenly his sweat suit was an intolerable barrier. Pushing him away, she sat up. He made no move to help her as she drew the sweater over his head and tossed it aside, delaying her assault on the bottoms long enough to tweak his nipples and run her palms across the hard, muscular planes of his chest. He watched her, his eyes smoldering, a small smile playing along his lips, as if he recognized her desire to undress him in the same manner as he had undressed her.

For the most part, his upper body was free of hair, but Lisa thought she detected the beginnings of a suspicious darkness just below his waistline. Untying the cord, she pushed the pants down around his hips and grimaced with frustration at yet another barrier, the dark blue fabric of his low-cut briefs. But her suspicions were confirmed. An arrow of coarse dark hair, its tip just under his navel, disappeared under the elastic band of his shorts, pointing the way seductively to the prize she sought. Without being asked, he stood. Lisa scooted to the edge of the bed and lowered the sweatpants and briefs to his feet, trying with difficulty to avert her gaze until he was completely unclothed. Then she looked.

"Jess, you're beautiful."

His skin was a burnished tan in the glow of the sunset, the broad set of his shoulders tapering to a lean, flat abdomen and narrow hips, his legs long and sinewy. Between them, projecting from a nest of midnight-dark hair, was the symbol of his manhood, the proof of his desire for her, magnificently erect, waiting. She touched him, enchanted by the velvet texture of his skin, shivering with pleasure at the turgid power alive and throbbing beneath her fingers. She stroked the smooth sheath and his breath whistled between his teeth, their eyes meeting, and Lisa rose, his gaze pulling her to her feet. They stood, skin against skin and she marveled that one could derive so much pleasure from such simple contact. His pleasure, however, was a cause of some concern. She wanted so desperately to ensure that she wouldn't disappoint him, and for the first time since he had kissed her tonight, had second thoughts.

"Jess," she said, searching his face, "I haven't had much experience at this."

He smiled down at her. "I'm glad to hear it." Then, as if sensing he had not taken her seriously enough, he sobered. "Lisa, are you telling me you're a virgin?"

"No. It's just that . . . well, I must have been doing something wrong . . . before."

"Why, darling? What happened?"

"Nothing."

"Nothing? I'm not sure what..." He broke off, his face clearing. He stared at her intently. "Ah, for you. Not ever?"

"I'm pretty sure it didn't. It seems to me I would have known, don't you think?" she asked, as if seeking confirmation.

The smile returned, and he shook his head in wonder. "Oh, Lisa, how precious you are, how..." He gave up on words, and let his lips on hers speak for him. The heat between them began to build again. Her arms around his neck, Lisa felt herself lifted off her feet and lowered onto the bed, Jess bracing himself above her.

He peppered her face with tiny kisses, etched the feel of his lips across her breasts, then slowly, leisurely, down along the center line of her body. Lisa shivered, her eyes widening as she looked down at him. He dipped into the perfect indentation of her navel, then buried his nose in the silky triangle of down between her thighs. He nestled between them, his fingertips gently probing the dark tendrils and fleshy mound dampened with her liquid satin.

A whimper slipped past her clenched teeth, her pressure point responding to his touch, and she stiffened, the whole of her body in the grip of a battery of new sensations. Anxiety slithered along her spine until his lips closed around the pulsating fullness and his tongue sought and found the source of the well of her sweet honey. The whimper became a moan of ecstasy, the whole of her being melting under her skin as Jess drank from the well.

His mouth became the center of her universe, sent her floating into worlds unknown, flinging her closer and closer toward the sun. Her skin burned, her body writhing to embrace the artful play of his lips and tongue, evoking sensations beyond any she could have imagined. Her breasts were cupped in his palms and his fingers brushed across their tips, igniting tiny flames, which made her gasp with surprise. She stroked his arms, kneaded the hard muscles of his shoulders, but invariably her hands returned to grasp his head, the damp riot of springy dark curls pressing against her fingers.

Lisa was overwhelmed by the sheer intimacy of the experience, tossing off all restraints and inhibitions as Jess administered to her with unflagging patience, seeming to put his own needs on hold. She was a goddess at whose fountain he worshiped, paying tribute to her body with such generosity that it burrowed straight to her soul. He loved her, he had to. No man could give such a gift so lightly.

Jess had settled into a languorous rhythm, laving, massaging her with a maddening gentleness, nudging her slowly toward the edge. The layered folds of her mound had begun swelling at his very first touch. Full and plump now, they separated, laying bare the secret nest they had protected, leaving the seat of her desire even more vulnerable to his caresses. With unobstructed access to the tiny pink pearl, he rolled it against his tongue, causing it, too, to blossom, rising to meet him.

"J—Jess!" Lisa cried, a white heat settling at the base of her spine. She gasped for breath as molten lava began to seep into the cradle between her hips. It swirled through her, burning, searing, as it moved, intensifying at the juncture where Jess's mouth seemed melded to her flesh. Finally the heat became too much. A volcano growled, rumbled and erupted, spewing its glowing liquid into the deepest recesses of her abdomen where it spread in a hot, glowing reservoir and became a miniature sun.

Lisa welcomed it, opened herself to it eagerly. Fingers entwined in Jess's hair, she thrashed in his grasp as he fought to prevent the violence of her movements from breaking the bond between them. Higher and higher she soared until the sun was all there was and, crying aloud, she fell into it, bathing in the exquisite torture of the flames, feeding them and being fed in return. Time was transformed, drawing out the moments of her release, stretching seconds into minutes, hours, years. Shuddering, Lisa struggled for breath, until slowly the flame died, leaving her warm and aglow in the arms of exhaustion. Then, shaken and astonished by a sudden urgent need to know the feel of Jess inside her, she reached for him.

"Yes," he said, and positioned himself above her, his instrument of desire seeking entrance, bathing her with its own silken dew. He looked down into her face and was at first more surprised than anything else to find her features so indistinct. His gaze flew to the double doors, which opened onto the deck, and the vista outside chilled his blood. In lower elevations, the sun would still be visible, hanging low in the western sky, but here, where the mountains were highest, a false dusk descended as soon as the sun slipped below the nearest peak. The mountain opposite was now a looming ebony presence, its mass bathing the valley in deep purple shadows. It would soon be completely dark.

There were no lamps lit in the room—there'd been no need for them when he'd brought Lisa to her bed. The one on the nightstand was within his reach, but turning it on would expose his neighbors across the glen to an X-rated performance he doubted they'd appreciate. No, he couldn't touch that light. And he wasn't sure how much longer he could stay in this room. He could barely see into the corners.

The sudden realization of his predicament had shattered his concentration, diluting the intensity of his hunger. Lisa, however, was waiting, open and ready for him, and he wanted her almost as much as he wanted the light. He had to do this, had to last. Closing his eyes against the smothering darkness, he buried his face in the shimmering blanket of her hair, hearing her breath dance in her throat as he balanced above her, intoxicated by the liquid heat waiting to ease his egress into paradise. And realized he needed to delay a little longer.

He knew that he would peak easily and quickly—it had been too long and he was overdue. He had to be sure that she reached that point as soon as he did, if not before. He wanted her to know the joy of coming to climax with her body joined to his, pulling him in toward her center. In order not to rush her or, worse, leave her unsatisfied, she had to be as near to the edge as he feared he already was. With that in mind, he turned his attention to the rise and fall of her breasts, losing himself in the unblemished velour of her skin, the gratifying and immediate response of her nipples to his fingers, to the feel of them under his tongue.

But Jess, for all his good intentions, had failed to reckon how severely Lisa would test his self-control. Her hands, far from idle, molded his shoulders, tripped down his spine and traced the curve of his buttocks. His skin pebbled at her touch, setting off alarms everywhere she touched. She probed, smoothed secret recesses, triggering to his astonishment, miniature explosions in places he'd never experienced before. He couldn't delay any longer. Once again, he moved into position to join with her, holding himself on a leash so tight the blood rushed in his ears.

"Jess," Lisa moaned, her hips arching toward him, "please, your face..." Her voice was a whisper, the plea thick with emotion. "I want to see your face as you're entering me. I want to see your eyes!"

He forgot. Teetering at the edge of a pool filled with the nectar of the gods, Jess simply forgot. Spurred by her complete abandon to him, her willingness to show how avidly she wanted him, he wanted nothing more than to please her. Raising his head, he opened his eyes to look down at her and the doors of the prison of darkness slammed shut. Panic grabbed him by the throat and squeezed. His vision began a torment of its own. Lisa's face, a pale oval blur, swam before his eyes, then seemed to shrink and disappear. The walls undulated, moving in on him. He had to escape. Rolling off the bed, he was out in the hall in two strides, not stopping until he reached the door of his room. Throwing it open, he stood, pulling the sweet, bright air into his lungs, braced in the doorway like a Samson holding its vertical supports upright.

"Jess, what is it? What's wrong?"

He heard the soft thud of her feet as they hit the floor, and he turned around, slowing his telltale breathing with Herculean effort. She came to the door of her room and stopped, staring across at him. "Are you ill?" she asked, her eyes round with concern. She was an alabaster goddess in the soft glow spilling into the hall, her body smooth and glistening with their combined perspiration. She was lovely, perfect, and at the moment, more vulnerable than he'd ever seen her. And it was his fault.

For half a second he considered pulling her across into his bed. There would be something so right about it—it's where he'd dreamed of burying himself in her. But suppose she asked him to turn off the lights?

"Oh, God," Jess groaned. "Lisa, I'm sorry. I swore I wouldn't..." He paused, in search of words which wouldn't wound, while at the same time wouldn't give him away. "I didn't mean for any of this to happen. I feel like a class-A bastard for . . . well, taking advantage of you. Things just got out of hand. I just hope you can forgive me."

Her face was perfectly still, color draining from her cheeks. "Forgive you?" she asked, dully.

"You deserve a man, a real man who can make a commitment to you with no reservations. You're too special a person to settle for a quick roll in the hay. The problem is, I shouldn't have stayed up here with you. I should have left."

"No, I shouldn't have come. Give me a few minutes to pack." She turned back into the darkened room.

He started across the hall, thought better of it and backed away. "You can't leave now, Lisa. There's that call you're waiting for. Besides, we agreed, this is the safest place for you."

She appeared in the doorway again, clutching a gown to her front as if to shield her nakedness. Her eyes seemed dulled, the usual gleam no longer visible. Her chin came up and she squared her shoulders. "I'm at a disadvantage, at least for tonight, but I'll leave tomorrow."

"Lisa . . ."

"Stop kicking yourself, Jess," she said, her voice hard, a nononsense edge to it. "I'm an adult and I have to take the responsibility for my actions. Things couldn't have gotten out of hand if I hadn't let them, so there's no harm done. In fact, I rather enjoyed it." A bitter smile lifted the corners of her mouth. "I must say, you're awfully good at what you do. Your technique is flawless and your performance masterful."

It was Jess's turn to feel the blood drain from his cheeks. "Seems to me we've been through this before," he said hoarsely, "but that was not a performance. I—"

She held up a hand. "Jess, I really don't want to hear it. I'm going to take a shower and lie down. If the phone rings, I'd appreciate it if you'd call me. Good night." She stepped back into the darkness and closed the door.

Lisa went directly to the bathroom, turned on the water full force and stepped into the shower stall. Crouching in a corner, she let the tears come, wrenching, scalding tears of bitterness and shame, her sobs reverberating in the small enclosure. It all had meant nothing to him. A quick roll in the hay. How naive she'd been. She'd brought it on herself. Cramming a towel in her mouth to stifle the sounds, she cried and cried, and became an intimate acquaintance with the kind of pain a broken heart can cause.

Jess took to the outdoors to dissipate his self-hatred and humiliation, hitting the path around the mountain at full speed until his lungs were aflame and the muscles of his legs rebelled in anger. It helped not at all, especially with Lisa's scent still lingering in his mind. There was no running from that. Bent double with a cramp in his side, he struggled up the walk to the porch and slumped against the door.

Why hadn't he simply come clean with her? He'd told her most of it—why couldn't he have told it all? Why hadn't he said the one thing that mattered most—he loved her, and if she'd give him time, be patient, one day—better still, one night—he'd come to her, make love to her, bare his body, his soul, give her all he had. Why hadn't he said that? Why?

He knew she would have understood his problem. She'd said it herself—she was an adult. She was also a warm, compassionate person. His problem wouldn't have mattered to her. But it did to him. It was a chink in his armor, his Achilles' heel. It could reduce him to a blob of gelatin, as it almost had this night. He couldn't allow her to see him like that—not that it mattered now. After what he'd done to her, the abrupt manner in which he'd left her bed and the lame apology he'd offered, she probably didn't want to see him again under any circumstances. He'd lost her. The pain of that realization even eclipsed the agony he'd suffered with that bullet in his hip years before. And he deserved it. He'd earned it.

Going back inside, he went downstairs to work out his turmoil on the punching bag. It couldn't hit back and he always won his bouts with it—a hollow victory, but still a victory, and he was in sore need of one tonight.

Lisa, in the easy chair in her room, sat up with a jolt, trying to determine what had awakened her. Perhaps it was the sensitivity below her waist, an awareness of muscles she hadn't known she'd had. She had Jess to thank for that. Also, thanks to him, she would sleep sitting up. Neither fresh linen nor a generous dusting of the sheets and pillows with her perfumed talcum powder had had any effect. The bed still smelled of him and it was more than she could bear.

A distant sound gnawed a hole through her woolgathering. The phone! That's what had roused her. Leaping to her feet, she pelted up the stairs, wondering why Jess hadn't answered it—there was a phone in his room. The living room was empty, the table exactly as she'd left it. Perhaps he'd driven back into Washington. She hoped he had. The thought of facing him made her queasy.

The telephone was still on the coffee table. She snatched it off the hook. "Hello?"

"Miss Gillette?" The voice, unfamiliar, was that of an elderly woman.

"Speaking."

"My name is Emma Northridge. I've been a member of New Jericho since Hector was a pup, and Reverend Putnam thought I might be able to answer a few of your questions."

"Oh, I do appreciate your calling," Lisa said, moving from the sofa to the floor.

"What is it you want to know now?"

"About the Gillette family."

"Oh, yes. You think you might be related?"

"It's a possibility."

"I see. Well, William and Eloise were married in the old church—not this new one—years ago. They had a daughter—Lisa, her name was, the same as yours, isn't that a coincidence? A pretty little thing, and her brother looked just like William."

Lisa almost dropped the phone. "There was a son?"

"Oh, yes, younger by no more than a year, a year and a half. Both the children were still in diapers, practically, when William was killed, a terrible accident. They were just building the Golden Oaks shopping center when the roof collapsed on him."

"A shopping center?" Lisa repeated.

"Yes. Such a waste of a good man. I'll never forget his funeral, the biggest New Jericho had seen. There were folks there I'd never seen before."

Lisa wondered if the woman's memory was faulty. Her story was close to that of her mother's, except for the addition of the son. "What happened to Mrs. Gillette and her children?"

"Oh, they moved soon after, but always kept in touch. The last I heard, Bill, Jr., was in Denver—something to do with the Air Force Academy—and Eloise is living with Lisa in Roanoke. Lisa married a foot doctor and she has four children. I have their address if you'd like to get in touch with them."

"Thank you, but this must not be the family I'm related to," Lisa said, her voice shaking. "I do appreciate your calling, Mrs...." She couldn't remember the woman's name. "Thank Reverend Putnam for me. Good night."

Numb, Lisa sat, the phone in her lap. Eloise Gillette lived with her daughter, Lisa, in Roanoke. There could be no mistake. But two Eloise Gillettes with daughters named Lisa?

Dragging herself to her feet, she walked over to the table where her mother's cosmetics case sat, its lid open. Pulling it to her, she fingered the initials that had gleamed in gold when she'd traveled with her mother. E.E.G. The case had been one of a set of matching luggage, a graduation present, she'd said, the only piece the fire after the crash hadn't destroyed.

Lisa checked the pocket in the lid first, removing a baby picture of herself with thick, dark hair, chubby hands curled into fists. Written on the back in an unfamiliar hand—*Our precious daughter, an hour old. June 24, 1961. 7 lbs, 9 oz. The image of us, isn't she?* Lisa smiled. In her opinion, she'd looked like an Eskimo baby.

Setting the picture aside, she removed the file folders and envelopes and saw that there was a new addition to the cosmetics case, a yearbook bound in dark blue leather, the letters embossed in gold across the cover. Where had it come from? And to whom did it belong? Not her mother, who had gotten her degree from Duke. This was from a Chilton College, wherever that was.

Lisa opened the book, suddenly fearful. She'd had enough surprises for one day. On the inside cover was a handwriting she'd come to know recently and well. The message left her gaping.

> Ellie—so, you didn't get to march with your class. Who cares? You gave yourself a miracle for a graduation present. She's so beautiful! As soon as Len sees her, all will be forgotten and everything will be fine again. J.C.!

"J.C.?" Lisa said. Of course, she thought. James Clifford Mallory. So he had known her mother. And me, she added. Mal must have left it for her, and Kitty had packed it with other old mementos. But had her mother gone to Chilton and not Duke?

Lisa flipped to the *G*s with more than a little trepidation and was almost relieved that there was no Eloise Endicott. There was, however, a blank place where a picture should have been, with Camera Shy printed across it, and the name of the missing graduate. Ellen Elisabeth Girard. Major—Mathematics. Minor—Business. Vice President, Student Government; Vice President, Senior Class; Vice Chairman, Computer Society; Vice President, Math Club.

Lisa's hands flew to her mouth, remembering. She'd come running in from school, happy, excited, to announce that she'd been elected vice president of Mrs. Briscoe's class, even though she didn't know what a vice president was supposed to do. She'd been so proud of herself and so sure her mother would be, too.

Eloise Endicott Gillette's voice rang in her ears. "What'd you expect? Coming in second runs in the family. It was the best I could do, so there's no reason to think you can do any better."

A whirlwind roared in Lisa's head and she jumped up, covering her ears, but the voice went on, perpetually, inexorably denigrating. Another time—"I don't know why I bother with you. You spoil things. You've been a thorn in my side from the day you were born." Yet another time, raving madly—"It's all your fault. You did this! You caused it! It's the second time you cost me the man I loved. You always ruin everything!"

Lisa collapsed in the middle of the living room, lowered her forehead to her knees and fought for quietude, trying to remember more. Nothing came. It was maddening, as if some unseen presence hurled random pieces of a jigsaw puzzle at her, the picture of the whole comprising the days of her life. How was she to complete the puzzle with so many pieces missing? How many of them had her mother kept from her? And why?

Anger raged through her like a flashflood. Her mother had lied to her, lied to everyone! Lisa went back to the table and stared down at the open page. Ellen Elisabeth Girard. It fitted. The initials, E.E.G. The offices she held, vice president of everything. Her major. She was good at math, something she'd reminded Lisa every time her daughter had brought home less than a perfect arithmetic paper. It all tied in.

Not only had she lied about where she'd gone to college, she'd lied about her name. Eloise Endicott Gillette on all her résumés, her driver's license. She'd lied about her husband, borrowed the name of a grieving widow, probably because, among the woman's misfortunes, she had the same initials as Ellen Elisabeth Girard, who had a set of matched luggage she would not give up. And no wonder she'd torn the front off the bulletin. The second page would have featured an obituary and a list of survivors.

"My God," Lisa murmured, shaking with fury. "Is Lisa really *my* name or did you borrow that, too? Who am I?" If Eloise Gillette's life had been a lie, so had her own. There'd been no loving father, no family life at all, only an attractive, auburn-haired woman, aloof, unfeeling. Mom never really loved me, Lisa thought, suddenly bereft. She never even liked me. I tried so hard, but I could never please her, never.

Closing the book, Lisa dropped it back into the cosmetics case. She would have no need to look at it again, ever. Her mother had saddled her with a faked history, and her memory had absconded with what little she had left. Lisa sat down and began a list of the cities in which her mother had worked. She'd been too young to remember Milwaukee and Ann Arbor, but there were bits of Cincinnati she could call her own, and Indianapolis and St. Louis, although she couldn't recall leaving the latter.

What memory she had of Lockwood—school, the recital, the trip to Mount Vernon—amounted to a total of several disconnected days. Lockwood was the key. Since it was the only period for which she could not account, it may well have been hiding the reason someone was trying to kill her. She had to go to Lockwood as soon as she could arrange it. But what would she do once she got there? She was no expert at this kind of thing. Jess would know how to handle it, but she wasn't even sure she could ever look him in the face again.

She had to. One, she was marooned here with him. Two, she needed his help. Any personal relationship with him was out of the question now, that was obvious, so what now? Her only satisfaction was that he had wanted her, if only for that fraction of an hour. She would never forget the cashmere softness of the skin and the pulsating hardness under it, how it had felt as it had touched her in all her hidden places. But that was history. She desperately needed to put some distance between them, if not physically, then emotionally. She had to deal with him on a completely different level if she was to survive being here with him.

The answer to her dilemma eluded her until she'd closed the cosmetics case and picked up her purse. Her checkbook. It was the only way. He wouldn't like it, but if he thought about it, he'd realize it would simplify matters, put their relationship in a safe, cozy pigeonhole.

Gathering her belongings, she turned out the lights and went downstairs. A glimmer of light showed under the door of Jess's room, so he hadn't left after all.

Then she heard it, a hoarse cry, an anguished groan. Depositing her load on her bed, Lisa moved back out into the hall, hesitant, debating whether to knock. Was he ill? Thinking back to his harsh breathing and the pallor of his face as he'd stood in the doorway earlier, she wondered if she had misjudged him. The possibility that he had left her bed because of some untimely physical ailment brought a sense of relief that made her blush with shame.

He moaned again. Lisa tapped softly and opened the door. Jess lay prone, his nude body at an angle across the low bed, the tangled sheet wrapped around one leg. He whimpered, his head thrashing as he buried one side of his face, then the other, in the pillow. The walls glowed dimly, like a warm, soft night-light but with enough illumination so that she could see that his sheets were damp and perspiration gleamed on his skin. Did he have a temperature?

Lisa approached the bed and leaned down to place the back of her hand against his cheek as gently as possible. His skin was warm, but certainly not hot. He muttered something and she shook off her shameful disappointment. He wasn't sick, he was having a nightmare. For half a heartbeat, she considered leaving him to it but, shaken by her streak of meanness, decided that if she could interrupt the flow of his bad dream, he might settle down without waking at all. Lowering herself to her knees, she laid a gentle hand across his forehead and smoothed the damp tendrils from his brow. His breathing slowed and he seemed to relax.

Lisa stood, looking down at his broad shoulders, her breath catching at the faint dark circles across his tautly muscled back—she'd missed them before. Cigarette burns. So this was what his captors had done to him. Her eyes strayed to his narrow waist, the swell of his buttocks, the long, clean sinew of his legs. His left buttock was marred by a deep scar, the souvenir Mal had left. It took nothing away from him. In fact, the reality of his nude body awakened her hunger for him again. It was time to leave.

At the door, she placed her hand on the dimmer, then withdrew it. If she turned off the lights, it would give her away. She would prefer he never know she'd entered the room. She stepped out and eased the door closed.

Jess rolled over and sat up, his body trembling. He had awakened at her touch and hadn't dared move. It had taken every ounce of willpower he'd had to fake being asleep, but if he'd opened his eyes, if he'd seen her, nothing could have stopped him from pulling her down to him. He'd have finished what he'd started before, entering her, giving her pleasure, declaring his love with every stroke. Fortunately she'd gotten up just as he'd reached the outer limits of his restraint. Then he'd realized the very real danger facing him.

It would have been perfectly natural for her to turn off the lights as she left—most people did it automatically. He had been rigid with panic. If that light had gone off, he would have disgraced himself, leaping for the switch in one record-setting long jump, crying perhaps, certainly shaking—as he was now— a basket case. He was weak with gratitude that she had left the lights as she'd found them, and his trembling hands and sweat-soaked body confirmed that he'd made the right decision when he'd deserted her earlier.

How could he go to her until he was the man she deserved? He couldn't. Simple as that. Not now. As long as they were under the same roof, there were other things he'd force himself to concentrate on, like the killer out there hoping to get Lisa in his sights. He had to protect her. He loved her. The way things stood between them, there was a distinct possibility that she would never know. And if he didn't catch that SOB in time, it was a certainty.

Chapter 11

Lisa was dressed and waiting when Jess came up to leave at six forty-five, looking every inch the businessman—navy suit, crisp white shirt, gray-and-blue striped tie. He started when he saw her sitting at the dining room table, his demeanor subdued. He seemed very much on his guard. After an awkward moment, he set his handsome gray attaché beside the door and said, "Good morning. I didn't think you'd be up. Did you get any sleep?"

"Enough, thank you." She sounded stiff and formal, even to her own ears, but if she was to pull this off, she had to set the proper tone. "I couldn't be sure what time you'd have to leave, so I set my watch for five-thirty. I need to talk to you."

His eyes became even more wary, but he nodded, crossing to the counter where the coffeepot emitted the heady aroma of its freshly perked contents. "I need to talk to you, too. I guess now's as good a time as any." After filling a mug, he turned to face her from where he stood, his intention to keep his distance obvious. "To prove I'm not a chauvinist, how about I go first?"

"Fine," Lisa agreed. She doubted anything he said would alter her intentions.

He stared down into his cup. "Lisa, one of the prime rules of investigation is that you don't...you *can't* become emotionally involved. It's a distraction I can't allow and neither can you. Last night was an unforgivable lapse on my part, and I will do whatever is necessary to see that it doesn't happen again. Your cooperation would make that easier."

"My cooperation? You've got it," Lisa said. "To be honest, your lapse, as you call it, put things in proper perspective for me."

"How?"

"By reminding me where I fit into the scheme of things. My being here is an awkward situation, but the reality is that I need the sanctuary you're providing. I also need the benefit of your professional expertise. It looks as if your reading of my mother's actions was right on target, so you could probably make sense of—"

"What do you mean, right on target?" he interrupted, showing signs of animation for the first time. "Did the minister call back? Have you learned something new?"

"Yes, but let's get this out of the way first," Lisa said, annoyed that she'd almost strayed off the straight and narrow she'd set for herself. "It's a poor choice of words, Jess, but I have a proposition for you."

"What kind of proposition?"

"We're both professionals, and when it comes to business we play by the rules." Reaching into the pocket of her blouse, she removed the check she'd written and placed it on the table. "I'd like to hire you." Jess turned the color of marble, but Lisa pressed on. "I'd like to retain you as a consultant or a private investigator, you choose the title. Since you're supplying me with a safe house, we can figure that into the bill, over and above your per diem and expenses."

"Oh, we can, can we?" His face was tight, his tone lethal.

"It's precisely the kind of relationship we should have had all along—it would have saved us a lot of aggravation. Anything personal between us is impossible. We started out antagonists, and have used each other for our own ends ever since."

"And last night?"

"A perfect example. We used each other to satisfy needs of the moment. It had no further meaning and complicated things, sending us both on a guilt trip, but the fact that you put a stop to it is to your credit, and I'm grateful. But why not do what we should have done from the beginning by making this a contractual arrangement? I'm sure we'll both be more comfortable. A contract—written or oral, it doesn't matter—puts a distance between us, draws the line."

Jess turned, tossed his coffee in the sink and rinsed out the mug, his posture rigid and unbending. "It does indeed."

Lisa felt a little of her tension recede. There was no mistaking his attitude about her idea, but he seemed to be agreeing with her. "Would you object to making a trip to Lockwood as soon as possible a part of the bargain? I'm sure it's the answer to the whole mess, especially since Mal went there, too. Oh, and I can only afford to give you a retainer right now, but if you'll bill me—"

Without warning, he slammed his mug down on the counter. It shattered, spraying chips of stoneware and drops of water all over his shirt and tie. Crossing to the table, he picked up the check and ripped it in half. "All right, I deserved this," he said, his voice a low growl. "I hurt you last night, and you've just returned the favor in spades. I am not for hire, Lisa."

Lisa stood her ground, refusing to relent. "If I've insulted you, I'm sorry. That was not my intent. But if you won't accept my terms, I can't stay here. It'll just make things worse between us. If you'll let me get my things, I'll ride into town with you."

"The hell you will." His eyes spat fury. He strode to the door and yanked it open. "You have every right to be upset with me, but not so much that you'd put your life in danger. If being here with me is so repugnant, you can rest easy. I'm going to be tied up in meetings for the next four days. I can't afford to miss them because we're in the running for a contract with the government, and I owe it to Lem to see that we get it."

"Four days?" Lisa stared at him, appalled.

"The meetings are scheduled to run from eight to six, so it's stupid for me to make the trip back out here every night. I realize that means you're stuck here, but it's the best place for you. The sheriff has his guys keeping an eye on the place."

"I can't—"

"Youngblood's mug shot has been faxed to every police station between D.C. and New York, and Pete's boys are combing hotels and motels, leaving his picture with desk clerks. It's just a matter of time. When the meetings are over, if you still want to look into the Lockwood end of things, fine. But it'll have to wait, so you might as well relax. I'll call when I can." With that he went out and closed the door firmly.

Lisa was only a couple of steps behind and followed him out to the car. "Jess, listen. If you don't want to work for me, fine. Just take me as far as Barbara Trainor's and I'll figure out what to do from there, but I can't stay here and do nothing. At the least I can start trying to find out my real name."

"What the hell does that mean?" he asked, tossing his case onto the back seat.

"Mom lied about my father, lied about her own name, so it stands to reason she lied about my name, too. I want to know who I really am."

Jess climbed under the wheel, shut the door and lowered the window. "It doesn't matter what your name is, what your mother was up to, any of that. You've made yourself who you are. I've got to go, Lisa."

"Then take me to the hospital. I'll sit with Mal."

He started the engine. "Don't make this any harder than it is already. I'm sorry if I've spoiled it for you here, but it doesn't change the fact that it's the only place I feel you'll be safe. And nothing is more important to me than that. I'll check in with you when I can." He put the car in gear and Lisa, giving up, stepped back out of the way, watching until his taillights disappeared into the trees.

"Goodbye, my love," she whispered. Well, that was that. Going back in, she sat down to map what needed to be done. It was time to follow her mother's advice and rely on herself. She would need help to implement part of her plan, but after that she'd be on her own. Perhaps that was best. She'd managed before she'd met Jess Hampton and she would again. One day she might even wake up and find that the pain of having loved him was bearable. Picking up the phone, she dialed the Joyners'.

Alec answered, groggy and grumpy, his "Hello," a snarl.

"Hi. This is Lisa."

"No kidding. Haven't we done this scene before? What time is it?"

"Morning. The sun's up. You should be, too. Alec, I have a favor to ask."

"Shoot. Hush, Kitty, it's Lisa."

She explained her plans and what she'd need from him.

"Are you sure about this? What does Hampton think?"

She hated having to lie, but it was simplest. Tarred with my mother's brush, she thought. "He understands. He'll be tied up in meetings for several days, so he agrees that there's no reason for me to sit around twiddling my thumbs until he's free. Will you be able to come get me?"

"Yeah. Where is this place?"

She gave him the directions, assured him she did not need Kitty to go with her—God forbid—and told him she'd be waiting. A call to Barbara was next. At least she would not have to lie to her.

Half an hour later, she was ready, her few clothes in one bag, the copies Barbara had given her crammed into the cosmetics case with her mother's papers and the yearbook. After one last look around to be sure she hadn't forgotten anything, she crossed the hall, opened the door of Jess's bedroom and stood gazing in for a long moment.

She'd have given anything to share his bed, but as her mother used to say, she was old enough not to let her wants hurt her. Some things weren't meant to be and the combination of Lisa and Jess was one of those things. Closing the door, she went upstairs to compose a note for Jess.

Alec arrived at eleven-forty, still grumpy and disgruntled. A tour of the cabin improved his mood considerably so that he was almost civil by the time she locked the front door and followed him to the car.

"Kitty's picking me up at a restaurant in Crystal City, if she doesn't get lost in Arlington or somewhere, so you and I can bypass D.C. altogether. Are you sure you don't want someone to go with you? The magazines can get by without me for a day or two."

"I'll be fine. It's not like I'm driving across country."

He grumbled, stuck his pipe in his mouth and slowed to make the turn onto the winding country road. A beige sedan sat on the shoulder just beyond the driveway, its hood raised like a gaping mouth. The driver, his cap pulled down over his eyes, was slumped low in his seat, as if asleep.

"A hell of a place to break down," Alec remarked. "It's a long walk to the nearest gas station."

"That's probably an unmarked police car. Jess said the cabin is being watched."

"Well, I have to tell you, seeing him catnapping on the job does not fill me with confidence. I'd better honk so he'll know you're leaving." He gave a blast of his horn, which brought the man upright in his seat. Alec slowed as he drew abreast and Lisa lowered her window. The man stared at her with pale eyes that were surprisingly alert. Lisa realized he'd been faking.

"I'm leaving," she said, "so there's no need for you to hang around any longer. Tell the sheriff thank you for me."

"Be glad to. Where shall I tell him you're going?"

"Lockwood, Virginia. Thanks for looking out for me."

He smiled and tipped his hat. "My pleasure, ma'am. Have a safe trip."

Alec waved and drove away, heading for Route 70. From there, he flirted with speeding tickets all the way to northern Virginia, past the Pentagon, arriving in Crystal City with a smug grin. Lisa made short work of the farewells, enduring a spate of caveats about driving too fast, picking up hitchhikers, speaking to strangers. Planting a loud kiss on his cheek, she pushed him out from under the wheel, took his place and sped off. She wasn't sure how long it would take to get to Lockwood, perhaps three hours, and she wanted to get there before dark. If she fell behind schedule, however, it didn't matter. She would not be heading north again until she had some answers.

Jess rubbed his eyes and shot a surreptitious glance at the clock. He'd been baby-sitting with the visitors all day, showing off the facility, playing host at lunch. It was almost five, and he wondered how much longer they'd want to hang around. They seemed impressed, and it looked as if he and Lem would win the contract to set up a training program for government security guards. They were in the lounge now, going over enrollment figures, the catalogs and personnel folders of instructors. There was no reason he couldn't leave them for a couple of minutes, maybe phone the hospital to see how Mal was doing, since he probably wouldn't get there tonight. He was tempted to check on Lisa, but doubted she'd welcome the intrusion. Damn, he'd messed up with her! Even if he was honest with her now, it was too late. He'd lost her, he was sure.

The spike on his desk was stacked with messages. He flipped through them, categorizing them in order of importance. The one from Alec Joyner was a puzzler. What could he want? Perhaps a message for Lisa. He pulled the phone across the desk and slumped into one of his visitors' chairs.

"Mr. Joyner, this is Jess Hampton. What can I do for you?"

"Oh. Thanks for returning my call. I just need the phone number of Lisa's motel. I should have gotten it myself, but she took off like a bat out of hell, probably to avoid running into Kitty."

Jess came erect. "Wait a minute. What motel?"

"In Lockwood. She decided not to stay at—"

"Just a minute. Are you telling me Lisa's gone to Lockwood?"

Alec growled. "Are you telling me you didn't know she was going? She gave me to understand that you couldn't go, something about your schedule. Damn that hazel-eyed witch! She knew I'd believe anything she told me. I even loaned her my car."

Hazel-eyed witch. An apt description. Shrugging out of his coat, Jess grabbed a notepad, scribbling a message for Lem as he talked. "I would never have let her go alone, Mr. Joyner. Whatever happened to her there was so traumatic that she's blocked it all these years. God knows what she'll learn and how it might affect her. She's strong, but—"

"Hampton," Alec interrupted him, "is there a possibility this mess she came back to might be connected with that place, or am I reaching?"

Loosening his tie, Jess paced in front of his desk. "I don't know, but I don't want her down there alone. Hell, I don't even know where it is!"

"South of Portsmouth is all she said. Probably a suburb. I can drive down there, but I'll have to rent a car. Kitty's needs a tune-up and I wouldn't trust it to go that distance without some sort of calamity."

"Never mind, I'm going," Jess said, decision made. "I'll fly down to Portsmouth, charter a plane, if I have to. What time did she leave?"

"A little before two. She should be there by now."

"Okay. The woman Lisa met with yesterday can tell me everything I need to know. Lockwood's her hometown. Depending on the time, I'll call you when I get there."

"Please do, Hampton. We thought we'd lost her once, and once is enough."

"I get your meaning. Talk to you later."

He yelled for Cecile, who was on her way out of the door, and pressed her into service to find a flight to Portsmouth. He snatched Lem out of the conference room and explained his need to leave.

"Go, man," his partner said without hesitation. "I can handle things here. I mean it. You may be too stupid to admit you're in love with the woman, but if this doesn't make you face up to it, nothing will. If there's anything I can do, give me a call."

Jess belted him on the shoulder. "I owe you. I'll be in touch."

He sprinted back to his office and opened a phone book. Five minutes with Barbara Trainor on the line and he had everything he needed to know. "Cecile!" he yelled, forgetting the intercom. "What've you got for me?"

She had a flight leaving in an hour and a half, and a rental car reserved for him in Portsmouth. Jess grabbed the slip of paper with the information as he sprinted past on his way out the door. With luck, he'd be in Lockwood before Lisa went to bed. He was sure she wouldn't start her search until tomorrow and he would be with her when she did.

* * *

The Traveler's Haven was precisely as Barbara had described it, a mom-and-pop operation. Lisa was welcomed by an apple-cheeked woman, a Mrs. Zimmerman—"Just call me Mrs. Z.—everybody does." She was as round as she was tall, her ample proportions swathed in a giant chef's apron with God Bless the Cook emblazoned on it.

The main building of the Haven contained a small lobby crisscrossed with rough-hewn beams, a homey dining room and the Zimmermans' living quarters. A patio off the dining room offered red-and-white checkered tables, lounge chairs and umbrellas. A dozen tiny cabins formed a horseshoe behind the registration building, each with a diminutive front porch.

Mr. Z., who could have passed for his wife's twin, met Lisa at cabin 6, and helped her with her bags. After reciting what must have been an often-repeated spiel—to wit, the dining room contained ice and vending machines and was open around the clock, but meal service began at seven a., ended at ten p. and the special for the day was pot roast—he wished her a relaxing stay, refused a tip and waddled out.

Lisa examined her quarters. The cabin was roomier than she had expected, with a queen-size bed, an old-fashioned maple dresser and mirror, a chintz-covered easy chair and the ubiquitous television tucked away in the niche of an armoire with a pullout shelf, which could be used as a writing surface. The bathroom was immaculately clean, with a generous supply of fat white towels, and the medicine cabinet contained miniatures of everything someone in transit might need—soap, shampoo, mouthwash, toothpaste, lotion.

It would soon be dusk, after which sight-seeing would be impractical, so Lisa unpacked and went to the dining room, where Mrs. Z. allowed as how Lisa was far too thin and loaded her plate as if she were feeding a long-distance hauler.

Returning to the cabin, Lisa prepared herself for a royal chewing out from Jess and was disappointed and relieved when, after dialing the cabin, Security Specialists and his apartment, there was no answer. Perhaps he and his partner were wining and dining their visitors. She was disabused of this theory once she'd talked to Alec and Kitty. Jess was very likely on his way, and to say that he was none too pleased that she had sneaked out on him, Alec warned her, was an understatement.

"Damn it, Alec, I didn't want him to know. He...he's done enough for me. What about his meetings? He can't afford to miss those."

"He didn't mention any meetings, but if he's coming, he obviously thinks you're more important than they are."

Kitty took the phone. "Lisa, how long are you staying?"

"Until I have some answers. Don't worry, I'll keep in touch this time." After the fiasco she'd come home to from New England, she'd learned her lesson well.

"Good, but don't forget Sara's invitation. It'll be worth coming back for, even if you turn around and head south again the next day. There'll be all sorts of influential people there."

"We'll see, Kitty. I'd better go. Does Alec know what time Jess left?"

"Sometime after five. He may by flying down. Lisa, you aren't in any danger down there, are you?"

Lisa laughed, describing the Traveler's Haven and its proprietors. "I might as well be at your house. The only danger I'm facing is gaining two pounds a day. Hang up, Kitty. I'll talk to you tomorrow evening."

So Jess was coming. She wasn't sure how she felt about it. He would be furious with her—so what else was new?—but he would not change her plans. She was tired of living with the blanks, tired of running. It was time to find out what she'd been running from and nothing he could say would make any difference. The least she could do was to reserve a room for him. If nothing else, it would alert him to the fact that she expected him and destroy the element of surprise. She sprinted to the office.

"He's only a friend, this gentleman?" Mr. Z. asked delicately. "So it wouldn't matter if I put him in, say, number 12?"

"Not at all. In fact, he might prefer that."

"Cabin 7 next door to you is available. Why don't I put him in there?"

Another matchmaker, Lisa thought, and gave in. "That will be fine," she said primly, filled out the reservation card and beat a hasty retreat to her cabin.

She took a long, leisurely bath, pleased to see that her knees were healing nicely, gave her hair a brisk brushing and organized all the documents she'd brought with her. By ten, unable to fight her fatigue, she stretched out across the bed. If she left the lights on, Jess would see them and knock to let her know he'd arrived.

She would even sit still and let him blow off steam. Then she would assert her independence and tell him to go. There was no reason for him to stay and jeopardize the government contract. There was no reason for him to burden himself with her problems at all. She was in no jeopardy here, and besides, she was no longer his concern. His help was not needed. If she said it with enough conviction, he'd get the point and leave.

"Oh, Jess, why couldn't you love me?" she whispered. With one last satisfying yawn, she fell asleep.

Jess waited patiently through Mr. Zimmerman's speech, thanked him and said good-night, fuming, ostensibly because his flight had been canceled and he'd had to scare up a charter puddle jumper to get here. In reality, he was so angry with Lisa, and hurt, that he had to focus on other sources of annoyance.

He checked his watch as he tossed his attaché on the bed. Almost midnight, far too late to call the Joyners. Lisa's lights were on, but that didn't mean she was awake. Besides, if he saw her tonight, he was bound to say something he would regret, so he might as well let her sleep. He'd asked for a wake-up call at seven-thirty, at which point he'd rouse her and arrange to meet her for breakfast. By that time, he'd have a cooler head and would be able to face her without throttling her.

Unpacking a shirt, he showered, pleasantly surprised at the coziness of the room and the generosity of his hosts, considering the dearth of occupants. There were only three cars in front of the cabins—his rental, the car Lisa must have driven and the beige sedan outside of number 5. Odd that they were all bunched up together. Considering all the vacancies, he'd have thought the Zimmermans would have left a few empties between them. Still, he was glad to be right next door to her.

He pulled on pajama bottoms, turned off the ceiling light and left the lamp by the chair burning. He glanced out the window—Lisa's windows still glowed softly—and went to bed. In less than five minutes, he was asleep.

Lisa stirred in her sleep and rolled over onto her stomach, the pervasive aroma of musk cologne filling her nostrils. Frowning, she fought her way to full consciousness, her senses registering that the scent was not a dream. She was not alone.

"About time you woke up."

Fingers with the strength of iron encircled her wrist. Lisa flipped over on her back and looked into the face of the man who'd been parked at the end of Jess's driveway, the man she'd shouted her destination to. She'd led Ralph Youngblood right to her door.

She opened her mouth to scream and he clamped the other hand over it as she stared up at him, taking in his sandy hair, features that wore no expression, rendering his face unremarkable and indistinguishable from a host of other nondescript middle-aged men. Displaying a supreme lack of interest in what he was doing, he crammed the top of a pair of panty hose in her mouth, circled her head with the legs, tying them above the nape of her neck.

Lisa's heart lunged, her pulse booming like a tom-tom in her ears. Where was Jess? He couldn't have arrived or he'd have knocked or called her to let her know he was here. How sad that she would die without telling him that no matter how he felt about her, she loved him, that with him she'd learned a little about the glory of being a woman.

Holding both wrists in one large hand, the man flipped her over onto her back, neatly sidestepping the kick she aimed at his groin. "Don't give me any trouble, please," he said, his voice gentle, ash dry. He yanked her into a sitting position and removed his tie, using it to secure her hands in front of her. That done, he whipped off his belt, wound it around her ankles and buckled it.

Lisa rolled toward the far side of the bed, but he stopped her, grabbing her hair and backhanding her across the face. Dazed by the blow, she lay still, blinking to clear her head. He used the time to pull the chair over to the bed and sit down heavily, patting his pockets. Extracting a roll of mints, he popped one into his mouth.

"Antacid," he said in his flat, dry voice and pressed his fingers into the base of his breastbone. "Ulcer's acting up. Now." He settled in the chair, making himself comfortable. "I'll talk, you'll listen. Normally I prefer to do a job from a distance—it's safer—but since you've been a source of considerable aggravation, and I have a deadline, I'm forced to do it this way. I must say, you've had luck on your side. I saw the space heater by your bed and did a little trick with the wiring. What happens? The nights warm up and there's no use for it. I nudge you in front of a subway train and an idiot mailman jumps down to save you. But your luck has run out, Miss Gillette. You die here, tonight."

Lisa listened, her face throbbing, her mind reeling at the surface gentility of the man. If she'd passed him on the street, which she well may have the day she had met Angie, she probably wouldn't have noticed him, much less have pegged him for a cold-blooded killer. But cold-blooded he was. There was no life to him, no sign of anger, regret, enjoyment, nothing. She could not let his demeanor paralyze her. She had to do something, struggle, fight, anything. Raise enough racket so someone would hear. Youngblood would probably succeed in killing her, but she wouldn't make it easy for him.

"Understand, at first there was nothing personal about this," he was saying. "It's what I do, and I'm well paid. As for who paid me, well, I'm not really sure. It has to be someone from the old days back in Newark and that narrows it down a good deal. Most of our little gang are dead. Only a couple have done well enough to afford the kind of fees I charge. But I'll find out, that's for sure. And if it's who I think it is, I intend to make good use of our relationship, which is another reason for cleaning up this bit of untidiness. That's you, of course."

Lisa took little satisfaction in the thought that whoever had hired him was in for a lifetime of being blackmailed. What good was sweet revenge if you weren't alive to enjoy it? But to die without knowing what you'd done to deserve being killed...

"By the way, I'm sorry about your friend. The problem was, the photograph I was given didn't do you justice. I see now that you are much more vibrant than she was. The resemblance was very superficial."

He dared to talk about Maria to her? Lisa was filled with rage that she'd been right—Maria was no more than an "oops!" to Youngblood. It lit her fury, ignited her resolve. Forcing an attitude of defeat, she turned her face away, her lids lowered. If she could make him think she'd given up, that there was no more fight left in her... She suspected she didn't have much longer. She had to be ready for him.

He discontinued his stomach massage and began pocket-patting again, pulling out a small leather kit, which he placed on his knee. He opened it carefully, removed a small bottle of liquid and pried loose a hypodermic syringe from its custom-fitted niche. Lisa froze, her eyes glued to it.

"Now the way this works, I use a bit of chloroform in the bottle here to put you under but just barely. The point is to avoid any sign of a struggle. I shouldn't have hit you—your cheek's a little red, but we can work around that. After you're out, I make a nice, tiny hole and inject you with...nothing. Air. And you die. I leave your body in such a position that it looks as if you hit the corner of the nightstand as you fell out of bed. And I leave. No muss, no fuss. By the time you're discovered—and since you drove down alone, that may be quite a while—I will be home. No one saw me arrive—no one will see me leave. All very tidy. Then I confirm the identity of my employer and gain a benefactor—for life. So."

He leaned forward and Lisa, her legs already bent, whipped around on her back and kicked him squarely in the stomach. He doubled over and she lashed out again, connecting with both feet at the crown of his head, which sent him and the chair over backward with a great clatter against the hardwood floors. She squirmed off the bed and hopped toward the door, hoping to make it before he recovered, but she had underestimated his stamina. Grunting with effort, he was already levering himself to his feet. She would not be able to get out before he caught her. Her last chance would be to attract enough attention to bring the Zimmermans or a nearby guest running.

Lisa did the only other thing she could think of. It would be awkward with her hands tied, but she had to try. Grabbing her mother's cosmetics case from the pullout shelf under the television, she hurled it at the window with all her strength, shattering it with a sound that seemed to blast through the still night air. Someone had to have heard it.

"You *bitch*!"

Youngblood spun her around, his hand slashing her across the face. His mask of aloofness was gone, his face twisted with angry determination. Her knees buckled from the blow and she collapsed, rolling immediately onto her back and blinking to clear blurred vision. She had to see his next move. Evidently his plans to leave her as bruise-free as possible went out the window with a hundred shards of glass. "You will suffer for that," he snarled. Yanking her to her feet by her hair, he doubled his free hand into a fist and drew it back.

Before he could strike, something hit the door with an explosive thud. The frame splintered, the door blasted open and Jess vaulted into the room, colliding with Youngblood, whose fingers, entangled in Lisa's hair, pulled her with him to the floor. He released her and she scooted backward out of the way, tears flowing with a relief that lasted no longer than a second or two. Youngblood was in far better physical condition than his plumpish exterior would lead one to believe, and there was no doubt that Jess would be well matched.

They grappled, each straining for dominance as they rolled across the small room. Lisa watched, helpless to do anything. Her hands and feet were numb and beginning to swell, but she felt the pain in some other dimension, her focus on the fight to the death being staged in the middle of the room.

Jess aimed several vicious blows at Youngblood's head, who countered with a well-placed fist to Jess's midsection before writhing out from under him. To Lisa's horror, the sandy-haired man rolled quickly over onto Jess's back and, as if by magic, a gun appeared in his hand. Terrified for Jess, Lisa screamed against the gag in her mouth and he reared, dumping his opponent onto his side. Seeing the gun in Youngblood's hand, he grabbed the man's wrist, and a war for possession began, Jess trying to wrestle the weapon from him.

"What the Sam Hill...?" Mr. Zimmerman stood in the doorway in a voluminous striped robe, a baseball bat in his hand. He gawked at Lisa on the floor at the foot of the bed, straining against her bonds, then at the life-and-death struggle in progress. "No, sir, not in my motel," he said grimly and stepped into the room. He raised the baseball bat and the thought occurred to Lisa that he might have no idea which one to hit. Evidently he had the same thought, because he hesitated, the bat above his head. Lisa, watching him anxiously, was gripped by an overwhelming sense of déjà vu. She forgot the belt around her ankles, the tie imprisoning her wrists. Something exploded in her head with such devastating force that the simultaneous discharge of Youngblood's revolver made no impression on her. The dam had been breached. Images flooded her mind, tossed and tumbled in a torrent of emotions, old and remembered, taking on new meaning with the wisdom of experience. Circuits overloaded; she slumped over onto her side, closed her eyes and tuned out.

His ears ringing from the shot, Jess released his hold on Youngblood's wrist, pried the gun from the man's hand and slid it across the floor out of reach. Not that Youngblood would be reaching for anything ever again.

"You all right, Mr. Hampton? The missus was calling the police when I left."

Jess looked over his shoulder at Mr. Zimmerman and nodded. "Better get an ambulance, too," he said. "Where's Lisa?"

"At the foot of the bed. Looks like she fainted." He squeezed past the two men and picked up the phone.

Jess turned back to Youngblood to check for a pulse, which was weak and thready, his respiration nonexistent. Jess opened his shirt and grunted. Administering CPR would make matters worse, given the location of the wound dead center of his breastbone and the rapid spread of blood from shoulder to waist, but he had to do something. As tempting as it might be to let the bastard die, he couldn't. In the distance, the wail of sirens cut through the night.

Tilting Youngblood's head back, he cleared the airway. Immediately the man's eyes opened and his damaged chest elevated. He was breathing again.

"An ambulance is on the way," he said, reaching up to snatch a pillow from the bed and placing it under Young-blood's head. "Who hired you? Come on, man, you want to take the rap all by yourself?"

Youngblood focused on him, made an obscene gesture with one hand, smiled and died.

Jess swore, and sat back on his heels. Hearing tires screech to a halt in the parking lot and footsteps pounding toward the cabin, he stood.

A tow-headed youngster in a policeman's uniform, his face white as bond paper, dashed into the room, his weapon drawn. "You!" he snapped at Jess. "Over there, against the wall."

"Take it easy, Clint," Mr. Zimmerman, coming out of the bathroom with a dampened towel, said quickly. "He shot the man in self-defense. Looks like he saved the lady's life, too."

A second officer, older, panted in. "What the hell . . . ? You all right, Mr. Z.?"

"Fine." He handed Jess the towel. "You might want to clean yourself up before Miss Gillette comes to and sees all that blood on you."

"Thanks." He swabbed his bare chest and wiped his hands, crossing to the foot of the bed where Lisa lay curled in a knot, her eyes closed. He picked her up and placed her on the bed, alarmed at how pale she looked. He untied the gag, pulled it from her mouth as gently as he could, then freed her hands and feet.

The ambulance had arrived, but the attendants moved at a leisurely pace. It was obvious there was nothing they could do for Youngblood. They tended to Lisa instead, pronouncing her unharmed but probably in shock. Jess sat on the bed and cra-dled her in his arms, while he supplied an explanation for the older of the two policemen, introduced as Harris.

Lisa didn't stir until the arrival of the medical examiner. Opening her eyes, she looked up into Jess's face. "You're all right," she said hoarsely.

"I'm finc. Youngblood's dead. Don't look," he ordered, trying to shield her from the carnage. "How do you feel?"

"Stiff. My throat—" She broke off and sat up. "Oh, God. Jess, she killed him."

"She?" Jess smoothed her hair out of her face. "Lisa, are you sure you're all right?"

"She killed him. He came to get me and she killed him and they hid his body behind a secret door."

"What's that?" Harris asked, leaving the medical examiner's side. "We got us another murder?"

"I remember now." She moaned. "They didn't know I was watching. She . . . she bludgeoned him to death."

"Lisa!" Jess held her tightly. "Slowly. What are you saying?"

"Oh, God, Jess. Mom. She killed my father!"

Chapter 12

The police cruiser proceeded through the quiet streets of Lockwood at a leisurely thirty miles per hour. Lisa, imprisoned behind the wire grid in the back seat with Jess, pressed her foot against the floorboard as if giving the gas to a phantom accelerator. "Can't you go any faster?" she asked, chafing at the snail's pace.

"Look, lady," Harris said over his shoulder, "I've extended all the courtesy to you and Hampton I intend to. When it comes to Hampton, I've got a good excuse—he's a former officer and Owen's story about what's been happening got him off the hook. But I'm having one hell of a time believing I let you talk me into waking up these people at damn near three o'clock in the morning. If Mrs. Howard and Mrs. Whitaker hadn't vouched for you, we'd be heading for the nearest giggle palace right now. The Forsythes are being awful nice, letting you barge in on them this time of night. If this turns out to be a bunch of bull, I can kiss my job goodbye."

"But if she's right," Jess said, "you'll get credit for solving two cases of murder, one that took place in your own back yard and the other in D.C. The D.C. cops will be awfully grateful to you."

"Yeah, you said that before. I don't give a hangnail about your D.C. boys' problems, I've got enough of my own, and I'm tellin' you, we ain't got no unsolved murder cases on our books. She can't be remembering right."

"Some of it's a little fuzzy, but I remember enough," Lisa responded grimly. "Eddie—I can't recall his last name—lived in the house directly behind Mrs. Howard's."

"That would be Woodyard Street," Harris supplied. "How is it you know Lena Howard again?"

"My mother and I boarded with her. All the neighbors were nice to us, but Eddie treated us as if we'd lived there all our lives. He..." She closed her eyes for a moment, sorting things out. "Of course! He had an old upright in his basement! That's why Mom agreed to let me take piano lessons—he let me use it to practice on. And Mom fell in love with him. She used to talk about how we'd be able to settle down like regular people once Eddie was free. I was too young to realize that she meant he already had a wife. I guess they were separated and getting a divorce."

"So your mother intended to marry Eddie," Jess said.

"Yes. Then his wife came back, on my birthday. Mom and I were downstairs in Eddie's rec room having cake and ice cream, when this woman I'd never seen before marched down the steps, said she was moving back in and told my mother and me to get out. She and Mom got into an argument, and Eddie—he wasn't saying much of anything—told me to take the present he'd given me home and he'd come over later to find out how I liked it. He let me out the basement door, but I crouched in the stairwell outside, trying to hear. I couldn't figure out what was going on, who the woman was and why she and Mom didn't like each other. Then..." Lisa frowned, trying to interpret with hindsight.

"Then?" Jess asked.

"It was dark," she said slowly. "I was trying to peek in the window of the basement door when I realized that someone had come down the steps behind me. He was a stranger, but I had seen him a couple of times, in the park or outside the playground, I'm not sure which. He said he wanted to talk to me, that he'd been trying to find me for a long time."

Harris grunted. "Sounds like the typical line freaks use to talk kids into coming with them. Did he specifically say he was your father?"

"He never got the chance. Eddie heard his voice and opened the basement door." Lisa felt a tightness grip her chest as pieces of the jigsaw puzzle dropped into their proper places. "The man—my father—took me by the arm and we went back into the rec room. He told Mom he'd come to get me and that if she made any trouble, he'd call the police."

"Well, I guess that means he wasn't your garden variety child abductor," Harris commented. "We're almost there, so how about speeding things up. What happened then?"

Lisa began to tremble. "Mom was livid. She yanked me away from him and practically threw me out the door. I was to go on to Mrs. Howard's or I'd be in for it. I went up the stairs to the yard, but as soon as she closed the door, I hopped down into the window well so I could see.

"I couldn't hear much, they weren't talking that loudly at first, but Eddie must have asked him who he was, because he took out his wallet and showed his identification. Mom was yelling that he shouldn't believe anything the man had to say, that it was all lies and..." She swallowed around the knot in her throat. "Eddie said it wasn't right for her to keep me from my father. My dad started to put his wallet away—he had his back to Mom—and all of a sudden, she just went crazy. She jumped on him from behind, clawing at his eyes and screaming she would never give me up, that keeping me was her... her revenge. He had to suffer for what he'd done to her."

"Good Lord," Jess murmured. "A custody battle?"

"I... I guess so. Mom was raving, literally hanging onto his back, drawing blood with her fingernails. He shook her off, but she kept coming at him, kicking and clawing, and his face was bleeding. He pushed her away and she fell. Mom screamed at Eddie that he was a kidnapper, to do something, and Eddie... I don't know, I guess he felt he had to come to her defense. There was a fireplace in the rec room and Eddie grabbed a poker and hit my father just as he was turning around. He just... crumpled, like a doll."

"Well, that's not exactly cold-blooded murder," Harris said, turning onto a quiet tree-lined street. "Manslaughter, sure, but under the circumstances, Eddie could probably have gotten off with a suspended sentence."

Lisa shook her head. "He wasn't dead. He got up on all fours and Mom snatched the poker out of Eddie's hand and hit him, over and over, like someone trying to kill a rat or a snake, until..." She began to sob quietly against Jess's shoulder.

"Damn," Harris muttered.

"It was so awful. His head..." She sat back, her eyes closed. "Eddie finally grabbed the poker from her and started toward the phone, but his wife opened the door and pushed him out, saying she would take care of everything, there was no reason for him to be involved, because he had too much to lose. She said all she had to do was tell the police that she and Mom had caught the man trying to molest me and no court in the land would blame her for what Mom had done. He tried to argue with her, and she asked him if he thought Mom was worth the ten years he'd spend in jail for obstructing justice."

"What kind of logic is that?" Jess demanded.

"She told him that if Mom had no legitimate right to keep me, how would it look if he admitted he had struck the first blow to prevent my return to a legal parent. At least that's what I think she meant. Anyway, he just stared at her for a long time and then went up the stairs."

"Spineless jackass," Harris growled.

"As soon as he left, Eddie's wife pulled a big wall hanging off the wall and there was a door behind it, which she opened, and they dragged my father through it. Mom came out and got the poker and took it back. After a few minutes, they both came out, closed the door and put the wall hanging back. My dad's wallet was on the floor—he had dropped it when Mom jumped on his back—and they built a fire in the fireplace and burned it. That's about all I remember. I must have gone on back to Mrs. Howard's."

"Assault and battery," Harris recited, "accessory after the fact to murder, obstruction of justice. This Eddie and his missus made a bad situation worse. This must be the place—there's Mrs. Howard and Mrs. Whitaker."

Lisa dried her eyes and peered out at the two women standing at the curb. Barbara's mother was a picture of her daughter thirty years hence, the same features and honey-brown skin, the slender neck and regal carriage. Even in curlers, she was an arresting woman.

But the sight of Mrs. Howard, delicate as a hummingbird, her hair now snowy white, opened the floodgates of Lisa's memory. How could she have forgotten the image of this tiny woman waiting at the front door for her to come in from school, cookies or brownies fresh from the oven filling the house with mouth-watering aromas? They had spent afternoons together at the kitchen table, Lisa regaling her landlady with her adventures of that day, adventures in which her mother had shown little interest.

Jess helped her from the car, and Mrs. Howard squinted up into her face, turning her so she could see her more clearly in the glow from a nearby street lamp.

"Lisa," she said, extending her hands. "Bless my soul, it's my little Lisa all grown up, and prettier than a morning glory."

Lisa leaned down and kissed her cheek. "I'm so ashamed that I'd forgotten you. I used to pretend you were my grandmother, did I ever tell you that?"

Mrs. Howard beamed up at her. "No, but you didn't have to. I knew. Oh, Lisa, I'm so glad you're back."

"But do you know why I am?"

"Noreen told me you'd lost your memory, so I assume you're trying to piece things together. But you and your mother lived with me, Lisa. My house is the next street over."

"I remember. It's...complicated. Maybe we can talk later." Lisa hugged her gently, then turned to Mrs. Whitaker. "I have to be honest—I don't really remember you, even now, but without Barbara's help, I probably would never have made it here."

Mrs. Whitaker patted her arm. "I'm glad. She's right. You look the same, and you're the image of your mother. She told me about your problem. If there's anything I can do, let me know."

Lisa thanked her, introduced Jess to them, then looked up at the shake-shingled two-story house, filled with doubts. Lights shone behind the first-floor windows. "I thought it was white clapboard."

"It was," Mrs. Howard assured you. "The Forsythes remodeled it. They're waiting for you."

The Forsythes were a middle-aged couple, the man tall and balding, his wife an attractive woman with salt-and-pepper hair. They eyed her warily, but greeted her with graciousness.

"I'm sure there's some mistake," Mrs. Forsythe said as she led the entourage to the basement. "We've lived here going on eighteen years. Except for the acoustical ceiling, we've done very little down here and I'm certain there's no hidden door."

Lisa stood at the foot of the stairs, her mouth as dry as if she still wore the gag. It was much as she remembered it—the cream-colored tile floor, the fireplace, the location of the door to the outside. The major difference was the walls, covered now with paneling, perhaps birch veneer. The furnishings were country-comfortable, the chairs and sofa with flounced gingham skirts.

"The piano was here at the foot of the steps," Lisa said. Walking over to the small, high window, she pointed. "That's the window well where I hid and watched."

"Er... watched what?" Mr. Forsythe asked nervously.

Harris cleared his throat. "There's a strong possibility a capital offense was committed here, Mr. Forsythe. Do you remember the names of the previous owners?"

"Oh, I can tell you that," Mrs. Howard said. "The Schefelds—Edward and Peg Schefeld. Edward was a teenager when he moved here with his mother, Crystal. He didn't marry until after she died, and I swear Peggy must have snagged him in a weak moment when he was trying to figure out how to use the washer. He taught at the community college."

"Sheffield?" Lisa turned to Jess. "That name is so familiar, as if I've heard it recently."

"It's not the usual spelling," Mrs. Howard said. "S-C-H-E-F-E-L-D. He pronounced it like Sheffield."

"What happened to them?" Harris asked.

The tiny woman frowned. "Let me see. They moved when he took a position at some university in Michigan, I think it was."

Lisa, listening with half an ear, had moved slowly around the room until she stood dead center of the rear wall. "There," she said, nodding toward the spot. "That's where the door was."

"Oh! Wait a minute." Mrs. Whitaker pressed her fingers against her temples. "Oh, dear. Lena, wasn't Eddie's mother one of the ones who had a bomb shelter built under their backyards? Remember? Sheila Coatsworthy did, too, and wound up using it as a wine cellar."

Mrs. Howard blinked at her. "You're right! It was the talk of the neighborhood. That was when things were so bad between us and Russia and folks panicked, since we're so close to Portsmouth and the Navy shipyard and all."

Mr. Forsythe stared at them, round-eyed. "You mean, there's a bomb shelter back there somewhere? Why the Sam Hill didn't the Schefelds mention it when they sold the house?"

With another round of throat-clearing, Harris clasped his hands behind his back. "Most likely because of that felony I mentioned. This young lady claims she witnessed a murder in this room. I admit I didn't believe her at first, but what with this bomb shelter business, well, we'll have to check it out. If you like, we can apply for a search warrant."

The Forsythes, pale and shaken, engaged in a bit of silent communication and nodded. "No need for that," Mr. Forsythe said. "I'll get a hammer. If there's anything in there, I want it out, now." Opening the exterior door, he disappeared outside.

"I think I'll go on home." Barbara's mother, her face ashen, followed him to the door. "I love reading murder mysteries, but that's fiction. I don't have the stomach for the real thing. Lisa, I meant what I said. If you need anything, just call." With a nervous waggle of her fingers, she was gone.

"I'll see her out," Mrs. Forsythe said weakly and hurried to catch her.

Lena Howard sat down near the bottom of the stairs. Clearly she was staying to see things through. Lisa joined her, and the little woman gave her a pinched smile and patted her hand.

With Jess's help, Mr. Forsythe pried a section of paneling and molding away to expose a lower-than-average door built flush into the wall, the knob of which had been removed to present a flat surface for the paneling. Harris retrieved a utility lamp and a crowbar from the cruiser and went to work on the door, which popped open in a matter of seconds. The room was immediately suffused with a musty odor that emanated from the rectangle of opaque darkness beyond. Lisa shivered and wrapped her arms around her knees.

Jess, his face damp with perspiration, stepped back from the door and gestured at Harris. "It's all yours."

"Yeah." The officer tugged at the waist of his trousers, picked up the utility lamp and stepped through the opening. Mr. Forsythe, his lips pursed, went in behind him.

From her place on the steps, Lisa could see the beam of Harris's lantern as he played it around the walls and ceiling of a short hallway, then around the inner sanctum itself.

"Are you all right?" Jess asked her. His skin looked as if it had been pulled taut over the bones of his face, emphasizing the angular character of his features.

"I think so."

"There's the switch," Mr. Forsythe's voice echoed hollowly, and the interior of the bomb shelter was awash in a pale yellow light.

Jess peered in, took a deep breath and proceeded through the hallway. His muffled conversation with Harris and Mr. Forsythe lasted a good while. For Lisa, the wait seemed interminable, yet ended far too soon. Jess was the first to leave the chamber. Breathing deeply, he stood outside the door, leaning against the wall on one long arm. Sweat gleamed on his face. His shirt was soaked.

Lisa's stomach fluttered with tension. If a former policeman was as affected by the secret of the bomb shelter, it must be every bit as horrible as she remembered.

After a minute or so, Jess straightened up. "It . . . he's there, very well preserved. The air has been cool and dry, which helped." He crossed to the stairs, his gait unsteady. "Harris feels there's no need for you to identify the man—his wounds fit the description of the events. It's no wonder you blocked it all out. If you had remembered any of it, you might have remembered it all, and I guess that was too much for you to handle."

Mrs. Howard took her hand. "Lisa, I'm not sure I understand what happened here. Eddie killed that poor man?"

"No. My mother did. She and Eddie's wife—Peg—put him in there. He . . ." She swallowed. "He was my father."

"Oh, child, how awful for you! So that's why you and your mother disappeared. I told that writer that if I had known about the accident, that you were all alone, I'd have adopted you myself."

Lisa blinked. "What writer? Clifford Mallory? He talked to you?"

"Well, yes." She added a worried frown to the dozens of wrinkles that etched her parchmentlike skin. "He didn't tell you?"

"He was badly hurt a couple of months ago," Jess said, his intense gaze turned up full force. "He's been in a coma ever since. We knew he'd been to Lockwood, but it would be helpful if you'd fill us in on his reason for coming to see you."

Lisa held her breath, incredulous that Mrs. Howard had the answers she'd been seeking for so long.

"My word! I hope he'll be all right. I don't understand what . . ." She shook her head. "Never mind. He said—now, let me see. He said a little girl named Lisa Gillette had lost her mother back in 1969 and had been raised in a Catholic home for orphaned girls. He thought that she . . . this is silly, I mean you . . . had lived in this area for a spell before the accident, but he hadn't been sure. The poor man had spent the last month or two checking all the schools in Portsmouth to see if there was any record of your attendance."

"Why Portsmouth?" Lisa asked.

"He'd found out that's where Eloise worked when she was here, so he just assumed she lived there, too. When he had no luck, he began checking schools in all the suburbs and found your records at Lockwood Elementary, which of course listed my address. It turns out what he was trying to do was to make out whether the child who had lived here in Lockwood and the one in the orphanage were the same person."

"The article mentioned that's where I'd grown up," Lisa said to Jess.

"All I could do was show him snapshots I'd taken of you. He had your picture from the orphanage school. I saw right off that it was you. Lisa, if I'd only known . . ."

She slipped an arm around the old woman's shoulders. "It wasn't a bad life. Did Mal say why he was going to all that trouble to begin with?"

"Something about seeing to it that your mother rested in peace, which, of course, she can't possibly, not with this soiling her soul. How did the accident happen?"

"She skidded off the road. It had been raining." Something buzzed in Lisa's subconscious, a familiar, frantic beating of wings against the door of her memory. But what else was there to recall?

Harris and Mr. Forsythe came out of the bomb shelter, the latter fairly green in the face. He darted out of the basement door and quietly relieved himself of the contents of his stomach.

Harris stood wide-legged, hands on his hips. "Miss Gillette, I owe you an apology and you've got it. Every blamed thing you said is borne out in there. I'm just sorry you had to witness such an awful thing. Now that it's out in the open, maybe you'll get a little peace of mind."

"That will remain a precious commodity until we nail the person who hired Youngblood," Jess said, helping Lisa and Mrs. Howard to their feet. "It has to be one or both of the Schefelds."

"Yes, sir, and we'll find 'em. Might take us a while, but we'll do it. The important thing is to spread the word that the body's been found, thanks to Miss Gillette, and that'll take the heat off this little lady. No sense in bothering with her now that she's spilled the beans."

Jess led the procession up the stairs. "Maybe. I intend to keep her under wraps until the Schefelds are behind bars."

"Couldn't hurt. I'm about to call the boys from the crime lab and I'll get a cruiser here to take you back to the Haven. You can sit outside in mine until they get here. Get yourself some rest, both of you, and tomorrow—I mean, later this morning—come by the station so you can sign your statements. In the meantime, we'll get to work and try to track down the

Schefelds. No tellin' how the courts will handle this, but there's no statute of limitations on murder, and they're both accessories after the fact.''

"You're welcome to stay with me," Mrs. Howard said. "I have plenty of room."

Jess gave her a smile that would have melted an ice cube. "Thank you, but I think we'll go on back to the motel. I suspect Lisa would like to be alone."

That was as far from the truth as it was possible to get, but Lisa gave her former landlady a hug and assured her she would see her again before she left Lockwood. Mrs. Howard shook Jess's hand, said good-night and cut through the Forsythe backyard.

Waiting in Harris's cruiser, Lisa curled up in the back seat in Jess's arms. "I was so sure everything would be over once I'd figured out what had happened here, but it isn't. The worst part is knowing that I met my father, watched him die and I'll never know his real name."

"Don't give up yet. His prints may have been on file for any number of reasons, and I'm pretty sure they won't have any trouble getting a good set from the body."

"I wonder what he was like."

"Let's hope Mal will be able to tell you."

"Jess." She sat up. "Mal couldn't have known what Mom did here—it's a cinch Eddie and Peg will never tell. And he couldn't know that I had no memory of living here. So what could he have wanted to tell me?"

He pulled her back into his arms. "Lisa, who's to say you don't have other relatives—aunts, uncles, grandparents, who've been hoping you'd turn up one day? Mal might feel reluctant about telling you your mother had abducted you, but if you have family who've been searching for you all these years, he would consider the bad news about what she had done a fair trade-off, if it reunited you with the rest of your relatives."

"But wouldn't he have gone to them first?"

"That would be chancy. Suppose he came to you with this story, and you decided your first loyalty was to your mother? Your family would have very little good to say about her, which might be hard for you to take. They're strangers—you've gotten along without them all this time, you might prefer to leave things alone. Coming to you first would give you the option, without raising the hopes of your family. It's pure supposition, Lisa, but it fits the way Mal thinks and what he'd do, given the circumstances."

The possibility that there might be people out there somewhere who wanted her stunned Lisa into silence, which lasted until the second cruiser arrived and ferried them back to the Traveler's Haven. There they found that the Zimmermans had taken matters into their own hands. As a crime scene, cabin 6 was off-limits and they had moved Lisa to cabin 8 on the far side of Jess. He went in with her and, taking no chances, checked it thoroughly before saying good-night.

He was about to leave when Lisa stopped him. "Jess, would you mind staying a little while? I really don't want to be alone right now."

"Are you afraid?" He stepped back into the room and closed the door. "I can sleep in that chair tonight, if it'll make you feel better."

"It's not that. I . . . just need to talk and sort things out."

"Finally!" He took a seat and she wandered aimlessly around the room, trying to put her thoughts in order. Halting in front of the dresser, she gazed at herself in the mirror.

"Funny, I don't look any different. I don't feel any different, either, but it seems to me I should."

"Why, Lisa?"

"For one, I'm the daughter of a murderer."

Jess frowned. "You aren't concerned about inheriting her tendencies, are you? Blood will out, and all that bull?"

"No. I loved my mother, but she wasn't sane, Jess. The picture I have of her with that poker is of a woman gone mad."

"It sounds to me as if she went over the edge when she abducted you. She fed on hatred, so her final act was simply an extension of it."

"I know that," Lisa said. "The thing that hurts the most, and always has, is that she never loved me. The only reason she took me with her was to hurt my father. She made him pay for whatever she thought he'd done by not letting him know where I was all those years. But she made me pay, too, Jess. She fed me and clothed me, but she never showed me any affection. She never even hugged me."

"Never, Lisa?" His voice was full of doubt.

"Not once. The most profound impression she left with me was that I . . . I'm not sure how to say it. She made me feel that I was unworthy of love."

Jess stared at her openmouthed, clearly appalled.

"Those early years at St. Mary's, I never expected to be adopted. I *knew* I wouldn't be. Face it, if my own mother couldn't love me, how could I expect it of anyone else?"

"Lisa, you aren't serious!"

"Yes, I am. I've been close to marriage twice, but I convinced myself those men weren't right for me—"

"Maybe they weren't."

"—that they were boring. The truth is, I was afraid to commit myself because I knew that sooner or later their blinders would come off and they'd see me for what I was—or am—a nice enough person on the surface, an enjoyable date, but deep down . . ."

"I've never heard such rot in my life," Jess said, getting up. "Take the Joyners. I saw what they went through when they thought you were dead. You can't tell me they don't love you."

"They do, and no one was more surprised than I was to find that out. But I'm still my mother's daughter, and the inheritance she left me runs deep. I keep thinking that one day Alec and Kitty will wake up and realize their mistake."

Jess crossed to her and shook her gently. "This is ridiculous. You can't believe what you're saying. I've never met anyone more deserving of love than you are."

Lisa gazed up at him, her hands against his chest. "Am I? This is a night for honesty, and I figure I have nothing to lose by telling you that . . ." She swallowed, knowing she had to finish this. "I've fallen in love with you. You don't love me and that's all right," she added quickly. "I have to share the blame for what happened to Mal, and I know how much he means to you. I'd be an idiot to expect you to feel anything for me, and I'm amazed at how generous you've been. You saved my life tonight. But if things were different, Jess, if we had met before all this, could you have loved me?"

Lisa told herself she meant it as a rhetorical question and almost believed it. His reaction, however, convinced her she'd pushed him too far. His hands gripped her shoulders with a crushing pressure, and his eyes seemed to emanate a scorching heat. He released her, his fingers sliding up into her hair.

"The question is not," he said, his thumbs stroking the nape of her neck, "could I love you, but do I, and how much."

Lisa was certain she had misunderstood, until his mouth covered hers, his lips parting, his tongue seeking, no, demanding entrance, gliding along the soft inner surfaces of her top lip, teasing the sensitive tissue of the lower, making contact with her tongue with the hunger of one who has fasted for an eternity. It was a gentle devouring, which loosened all the passion Lisa had promised herself to keep under lock and key. Paroled, they began a celebration of their freedom as her arms met around his neck. Her hunger for him burst its bounds, spreading from her eager mouth down along the secret passages that tunneled through her body and came to rest, to root and grow in the most secret passage of them all. Past controlling, her hips locked against his and began to move, seeking and finding the throbbing hardness that signaled his wanting. With an open-mouthed sigh of satisfaction, she dropped her hands and clutched the taut muscles of his buttocks, pulling him even closer, her head lolling back as the full effect of the feel of him overwhelmed her. Her legs buckled. His arms tightening around her, he fell with her across the big bed.

They became slaves to impatience as they unzipped, unbuckled and peeled away layers of fabric, each undressing the other. When their clothes littered the floor around the bed, the flurry of violent activity ceased, as if they had made a joint decision not to rush. Jess, on his knees, lifted her, shifting her position on the bed so that her head was on the pillow. Gingerly he lowered himself onto her body, looking deep into her eyes. Lisa, exalting in the glorious burden of his weight, let her palms glide along the length of his torso, feeling his muscles tighten in response. Sizzling from the heat emanating from his body, she pulled his open lips down to hers. Languidly they spoke of their love with silent tongues that sought and soothed, probed and played over inner recesses, meeting, greeting, welcoming invasion.

Jess ended the embrace, sliding low enough to take the creamy fullness of one breast into his mouth, his tongue flicking over its peak with a butterfly's touch, and Lisa's slender frame convulsed, currents of electricity arcing from the hot, wet circle of his lips to the honey-dewed triangle between her thighs. "Jess," she groaned, "oh, my love."

He lifted his head. "Again," he demanded, his voice thick with emotion. "Say it again."

"Jess, Jess, my love."

"If you only knew how often I dreamed of hearing that, and of doing this." In explanation, he grazed in the valley between her breasts and brushed each rosy bud with a farewell kiss. His mouth moved to the base of her throat. "God, I've been such a fool," he murmured. "I fought this for so long, saying it was too soon, saying I wasn't ready." Balancing the weight of his upper body on his forearms, he smoothed her hair from her temples. "But I *am* ready, Lisa. Are you?"

"Yes!" Lisa, dangerously close to meltdown, wedged one hand between them, moving lower and lower until her fingers curled around her target, skin soft as chamois pulled taut over a length of iron-hard flesh. "Oh, yes!" Her hips thrust upward to meet him, magnet seeking metal. The proud rosy head, moistened with a blend of his milk and her honey, settled at the yearning mouth and forged inward, the pressure gradually increasing until Lisa, every fiber focused on the site with self-centered concentration, felt herself opening to him, opening wide, taking him in greedily. The pleasure of his company was so intense that tears formed behind her lids.

Jess, however, had done no more than effect entry with the remainder of the journey yet to be made. He lingered there, immobile, flames of desire flickering in his eyes. "You're crying. Should I stop?"

"Jess, please!" Driven by a hunger to be filled, engorged, her hips rose again toward his, leaving no doubt as to the meaning of her plea. But Jess rose with her, foiling her attempt to swallow him with one hurried lunge.

"Shh, my love," he quieted. "Let me do this my way. I don't want to hurt you!"

"I don't care! Oh, Jess, don't tease me!"

"Shh," he said again and slowly, deliberately, pushed forward, muscles quivering to retain control of his egress. He moved into her a fraction of an inch at a time. Lisa gasped, overcome by the delicious stretching required to accommodate him, an introduction to a new definition of the word fullness. She felt the inner passage yielding, the velvet walls lengthening and closing in around him, receiving him in a warm, snug embrace. When at last the wiry brush of his coarse dark hair meshed with her own downy nest, she felt complete, all the tension subsiding—the waiting draining from her pores. She closed her eyes, ecstatic. This had been *her* dream, the melding, the bonding, which knows no equal.

Jess's lips caressed her lids. "Are you all right?"

"Yes." Her response was a long, shuddering rendering of the word, speaking volumes. "Only..." Opening her eyes, she squinted at the path of light the bedside lamp painted across her face. Freeing one arm, she reached for the chain. Jess froze as she pulled it.

"No! Don't!" The anguished cry sliced through the darkness that blanketed them. Lisa felt his body spasm and leave her, his feet hitting the floor with a thud.

"Jess! What's wrong?" Light exploded in her face and Lisa blinked, gaping with alarm. Jess, on his knees in front of the nightstand, pulled the lamp toward him and rested his forehead against the heavy brass base, his eyes squeezed tightly, his shoulders heaving as he struggled for breath.

"Jess, are you all right? What is it?"

"Oh, God! Lisa, I'm sorry. I don't know what else to say."

Pulling the sheet around her shoulders, she sat up, determined to ignore the silent screams of her body. For the moment, her feelings didn't matter. The man she loved was in an agony of another kind.

"Jess, talk to me! Sauce for the goose, remember? Tell me what's wrong."

He released his death grip on the lamp and sat back on his heels, cursing himself with a self-hatred that left her shaken.

Questions tumbled through her mind like laundry in a dryer, before understanding struck like a bolt of lightning, clarifying the significance of several baffling incidents.

"Jess, are you afraid of the dark? Is that it?"

He turned to look at her, his tortured features betraying his humiliation. "Yes. I am."

Of all the emotions warring within her, for some reason exasperation won out. "Then make love to me with the lights on, for Pete's sake!"

His eyes widened with astonishment. He stared at her for an eternity of seconds, then sat down hard and dissolved with laughter that lasted far longer than Lisa thought was warranted, since she couldn't, for the life of her, figure out what was so funny. Perhaps sensing her rising annoyance, he sobered and came to sit on the end of the bed.

"I would gladly make love to you with the lights on, my darling. The point is, it shouldn't matter if they're on or off. I'm not simply afraid of the dark, Lisa, I'm terrified of it, the kind of terror that strips me far more bare than I am now. I can tolerate a dimly lit room—just barely. It's taken me two years to get that far."

"Then this is something recent?"

"Post-Vietnam. The tunnel did it."

"What tunnel, Jess?" Lisa settled back against the pillow, the sheet covering her legs.

"That's where Mal and I hid from the VC. It hadn't been used for a long time. They had taken the generator with them and ripped out the wiring, so there was a complete absence of light. It was like your very worst nightmare, like being buried alive, crushed under the weight of the walls of a cave, suffocating slowly. The scars it left turned out to be a hell of a lot deeper than the ones on my back."

"But how did you get on the police force? Or didn't you tell them about it?"

"It wasn't a problem at first. I was edgy in the dark, but that was all. It crept up on me gradually, like some insidious disease. It's better than it was, but a pitch-black room? Just looking into the interior of that bomb shelter tonight, know-

ing Harris expected me to go in with him, I was close to passing out. If he hadn't found the light . . .''

"Oh, Jess, you could have told me," she said, scooting down
to the end of the bed.

He got to his feet immediately and went into the bathroom.
"You weren't the problem, Lisa. I was," he said, coming out
tucking a towel around his hips, as if his nudity embarrassed
him. "There was a time when I slept with two-hundred-watt
bulbs in every lamp in the room. Now I can get by with the
equivalent of a night-light. My bedrooms are on dimmers and
I'm gradually fading toward black. But not yet, Lisa. I can't
tolerate full darkness yet, and it makes me feel like such a child.
I swore I'd never touch you until I'd licked this and felt like a
man again.''

"What?" Outraged, Lisa hopped off the bed to confront
him, one long finger poking him in the breastbone. "How dare
you emasculate yourself because you came up against something that got the best of you!" A bemused expression on his
face, Jess backed up a step, but she followed, bearing down on
him. "How dare you denigrate your manhood! How dare you
call into question the virility of the person who made my body
sing last night, who brought me to climax for the first time in
my adult life? That wasn't a man, in its fullest meaning?"
Furious at him, she snatched off the towel and hurled it toward the bathroom door.

"Lisa, take it easy."

She had backed him up against the side of the bed. He could
go no farther. "You saved my life tonight. Are you saying that
was not the action of a man determined to protect the woman
he loved? Are you saying that this—" she cupped her hands
between his legs, her eyes flashing angrily even as her fingers
smoothed and massaged "—this marvelous instrument is that
of a child? If that were true, would this be happening?"

His body had responded immediately to her touch. He had
never completely lost his erection and it stirred, throbbed, rose,
stretched, in answer to her caresses. Her hand danced from tip
to root and farther, coming into contact with the dark, ripe
fruit that nestled in her palm. She moved her fingertips across

the corrugations of the baby-smooth skin, testing their weight, fascinated by the combination of their fragility and potency.

"Lisa, don't." Jess sounded breathless, the protest a hoarse groan.

Giving him no warning, she released him, pressed both hands against his shoulders and pushed, sending him sprawling on his back across the bed. She climbed up and straddled him, astonished at how wanton she felt, how little she cared, her thighs outside his, the soft velvet she'd smoothed moments before nestling comfortably between the swollen folds of her pouting mound.

"I don't need the darkness, Jess. I have no shame with you. I love watching you, I love seeing your body and how it reacts. Like your nipples."

She bent to tease them, her tongue darting around them, across them, feeling them begin an erection of their own. His hands measured her breasts as they grazed his abdomen. He outlined her narrow waist, caressed her back, molded the curves of her hips and buttocks. She squirmed against the rigidity tucked between her lower lips, panting with the delicious friction of the external caresses. A brush of soft, firm tissue against her own fleshy projection and she froze, perilously close to climax. As fiercely as she wanted it, had not for one second stopped wanting it, she was determined to avoid the solitary flight into ecstasy this time. He was fully, powerfully, erect now, a magnificent exclamation point, and the ache in her loins took on an urgency that brooked no delay.

"Please, Jess," she gasped, releasing control to him, "you have to help me."

Fingertips tracing delicate circles around her nipples, he enfolded her breasts in his hands, fondling the lush, firm flesh. "What is it you want, Lisa? Tell me."

"You, inside me. *Now!*"

"You really don't mind the lights?"

"Jess! To hell with the lights!"

With a throaty chuckle, he grasped her hips, lifting her, settling her on the peak of his tumescence. Slowly, slowly, he lowered her, the muscles of his arm rippling with the strain. His eyes, dark as moist earth, glowed as she eased herself down onto him, down, down, until she felt the tip wedged tightly, kissing the mouth of her womb. The fullness had returned with far more intensity, and a flush began at the point of contact, warming a part of herself she hadn't known existed. Never, never had she imagined it could be like this.

Staring down at him, she began to move, as did he, responding to her need and his, rising, falling, advancing, receding, until the movement was all, nothing else existing, no one else existing. There were only Lisa and Jess, locked in a lovers' knot with no beginning, no end. They moved as one, Lisa's senses feasting with the feel, smell, taste, sight, of the man she loved loving her. His turgescence supported her, his thrusts meeting hers, the smoldering embers in his eyes catching fire as he watched her ride him with sensuous abandon, watched the inner glow begin to suffuse her face, watched her mouth open as the moment approached, embraced her, enslaved her. She was not alone. Jess's muffled cries were in perfect harmony with hers as the explosion consumed them, seared flesh and bone in exquisite agony, welded them together until they were seamless, truly one body.

Later Lisa lay cradled against his side, listening to her heart return to normal. Jess, his fingers enmeshed in her hair, nudged her. "Has your question been answered to your satisfaction? In case you forgot what it was, you asked if I could love you."

She sighed and stretched. "Your answer exceeded my wildest dreams, and considering how many times I've dreamed of tonight, that's going some." Propping herself up, she gazed down at him. "I must say, as I told you last night, you're awfully good at this."

Jess was silent for a moment, then exploded with laughter, pulling her down on top of him. They roared together, one feeding the other, until tears joined the perspiration on their faces, their sides aching. They tumbled over each other like playful kittens, almost falling off the bed. It ended when Jess's laughter died, and the flame, reborn, flickered white-hot in his eyes. The dance began again. And again, a long, leisurely partnership where urgency had no place, except for the last few moments when the meaning of urgency and need and passion and hunger blurred around the edges until they merged into a single giant flame that burned with blinding incandescence. As a source of light, it was all the illumination either of them would ever need.

Chapter 13

The idyll at Traveler's Haven ended two days later due to an early-morning call Jess made to Greenhaven. He broke the news to Lisa over breakfast, their first in the Haven's dining room since their arrival.

"Mal's out of his coma," he announced, his voice tinged with relief and regret. "He's been sleeping normally since last night."

Lisa had decidedly mixed feelings, too, since it meant that their romantic sojourn in Lockwood was over. "That's great news, Jess. I'm just sorry you weren't there when he woke up."

"I'm not." He captured one hand and brushed his lips across the back of it. "I stayed because this is where I wanted to be."

"But we should go now, shouldn't we?" Lisa leaned against him in the booth, fighting the impending demise of the glow that had warmed her since the night before last. "We'd be selfish to stay any longer."

"If it were anyone but Mal," Jess said, burying his mouth in her hair, "I'd say to hell with it—we're overdue for a little selfishness. I wouldn't trade the past two days for anything, Lisa. I just wish we could have two dozen more."

Lisa nodded agreement. "But it is Mal. He's your best friend, and you're very important to him. Besides, if it weren't for him, we would never have met. So we'd better go. How is he? What about his memory?"

"They don't know much yet. The first time they asked him, he nodded that he remembered what happened, but the next time he said he didn't. He may be translating information incorrectly or responding incorrectly. They won't be sure until they run tests on him. Then comes all sorts of therapy. The rough stuff is just beginning for him."

"And we should be there. I'll go pack."

Jess placed a finger under her chin and turned her face toward his. "I am one very lucky man. I'd kiss you, but if I did, we'd never get away from here."

Lisa fought and lost the battle against the pool of molten lava forming at the base of her spine. "Checkout time isn't until noon. It's eight-fifteen."

"Let's go," Jess responded, smiling down into her eyes.

They made it to the reservation desk to settle their bill with seven minutes to spare.

The Zimmermans' farewell present was a picnic basket packed with the most popular items on the menu. "A little something to remember us by," Mrs. Z. said. "Promise you'll come back and see us. Next time, we'll put you in the honeymoon cottage."

Jess smiled. "It's a deal. We'll be in touch."

They headed north again two hours later, obligatory visits to Barbara's mother and Mrs. Howard made, along with an awkward farewell at the Forsythes', who were giving serious consideration to moving. Alec and Kitty had been brought up-to-date with a call that cost almost as much as had the cabin for the night.

Lisa followed Jess to the airport, where he turned in the rental car. Their only concession to prolonging their time together was a leisurely return to the District, using the lovely, less-traveled back roads rather than the interstate. Jess, however, was uncharacteristically silent for the first half of their journey, and Lisa, increasingly uneasy about the cause, lasted fifty miles before getting up the nerve to ask, "Jess, what's wrong?"

He reached over to grasp her hand. "We've got problems."

"What kind?" Her stomach fluttered nervously.

"It'll probably be a long time before Mal will be in any condition to live alone again, if ever. A nursing home's out of the question—I wouldn't do that to him. The truth is, I'd always planned to move him in with me, but now..."

"What, Jess? I don't understand the problem."

"Well, the location for one. My apartment won't do. It's too small. Sure, there are two bedrooms, but we—you and I— would have no privacy at all. The same goes for the cabin. Besides, it's too far from civilization, and Mal's strictly a city boy. But I'm getting ahead of myself. How do you feel about the three of us living together?"

Lisa's heart thudded with disappointment. Of all the scenarios she'd envisioned over the past couple of days, the possibility that Jess would expect her to move in with him had never occurred to her. "I'm not sure what I think," she answered truthfully.

"Your house won't work because it's two stories, right? If Mal's in a wheelchair, he's stuck. There's always one of those elevator chairs, but... Lisa, I know how anxious you are to move back in, and I guess it makes sense, for the time being anyway, but would you mind terribly giving it up eventually?"

"My house?" she gasped.

"Just listen. I have a two-acre lot in Howard County, nowhere nearly as isolated as the mountains. Columbia's five minutes away, and the commute into the District would be about forty-five minutes. We could design and build a house and tailor it to our needs, with a private wing for Mal and an indoor-outdoor pool—swimming's bound to be part of his therapy. I like the idea of a separate wing for any kids we have, too."

"Kids?" Lisa gaped at him.

He looked back, uncertainty pulling his brows together. "No? I just assumed...maybe I shouldn't have. I mean, we haven't talked about it, but from the expression on your face, I guess we should."

"Jess—"

"I don't mean right away," he said hurriedly. "I'd like to spend a little time being a husband before I become a father."

"A husband?" Lisa squeaked, on the verge of exploding. "You mean, marriage?"

Jess whipped the steering wheel to the right, bumping off the road onto the shoulder. Putting the gearshift in Neutral, he faced her, an indignant expression on his face. "Did you think I meant we'd just be living together, no strings? I'm sorry, Lisa, but I'm too old-fashioned for that. I want you full-time and legal, license, wedding, the whole bit. I'm willing to wait, if you still aren't sure, but—"

"I'm sure, Jess, but you never mentioned marriage and I—"

He slumped in his seat and shook his head. "God, I'm so stupid. Here I am, talking about building houses and private wings and I haven't even proposed." Unbuckling his seat belt, then hers, he reached for her hand. "Lisa, I love you. Would you consider marrying a man who may need to sleep with a night-light the rest of his life?"

"Yes. Oh, yes!"

He pulled her as close as the interference of steering wheel and gearshift would allow and kissed her, his mouth betraying the hunger that had become a constant for him. Lisa responded, her body straining toward him, her lips and tongue yielding to his. Only the blast from the horn of a passing trucker reminded them that they would be wise to exercise restraint, or court arrest for being a public nuisance.

"So it's settled," Jess said, kissing away tears she hadn't realized were there.

"Jess, are you sure? How long have we known each other? Not quite a month."

"During which we've fought like cats and dogs and have seen each other at our best and our worst. I could live without you if I had to, but I'd just as soon not. I want to be your husband, Lisa, you set the terms. You can even keep your name, if you want."

Lisa's mouth curved in a smile that didn't quite reach her eyes. "What's the point? I haven't the slightest idea what my name really is. But I do," she said, kissing his chin, "like the sound of Lisa Hampton."

"Lisa Hampton. Yes." After one final nibble on her bottom lip for good measure, Jess secured their seat belts. "Let's hit it, Mrs. Hampton-to-be. The sooner we get back and see what the situation is with Mal—and Pete—the sooner we can firm up our plans."

Still dazed, Lisa closed her eyes and pinched herself. When she opened them, nothing had changed. Jess, grinning at her, was real. He loved her. What more could she want?

A conversation with his partner on Alec's car phone applied just enough pressure on Jess to convince him to stop at Security Specialists before going to the hospital. The men from the government would be leaving and it would be politic for him to put in an appearance before they departed. Lisa cajoled Jess into letting her drop him off instead of waiting in his office for what might be an indeterminate period.

"The Porsche is still at Security, isn't it?" she asked. "I'll camp out at Kitty's, and you can pick me up there when you're finished."

Jess listened and agreed to the plan, but with obvious reluctance. "Lisa, be careful," he said as he got out. "Just because Youngblood's dead doesn't mean we're in the clear."

"I'll be fine," Lisa assured him, climbing into the driver's seat. "Now, go. Lem's waiting for you."

He kissed her quickly, but was still standing in front of the building as she pulled away and headed back toward Connecticut Avenue.

Lisa almost missed Kitty, who was hurrying out, as she eased Alec's car into the slot behind the studio.

Kitty was more incoherent than usual. "Oh, Lisa, I'm so glad you're back, but I can't stay. I'm on my way down to Sara's. Something's happened to Stewart—I don't know what. The maid answered the phone and she's in hysterics. Maybe you could come with me?"

"I can't, Kitty," Lisa said, grateful to be spared the necessity of manufacturing a lie to get out of it. "Jess is picking me up shortly. We have to get to the hospital. Mal's regained consciousness."

That caught her attention. "Oh, dear. That's good news, isn't it? I guess you'd best stay here. I'm so happy about you and Jess. We'll talk." Hopping into her car, she backed out of the slot and was gone.

Lisa sat behind the wheel and thought. It was after five, so Brad would have left. As relieved as she was to have some time to herself, she was not comfortable with being in the loft alone. It would be a while before the effects of Youngblood's intrusion wore off. But there was no reason she couldn't run by and check on the house. Dutifully she called Security and left a message for Jess, indicating she'd be back in a half an hour.

Kelso Place seemed unchanged and Lisa succumbed to a bout of nostalgia as she parked in front of her house. But she had to admit that she no longer felt the yearning for home she once had. Home was wherever Jess was now. Getting out of the car, she looked up at the porch that had made her decide this was the one she wanted. She only hoped the family that eventually bought it would be as happy in it as she had been.

She strode up the front walk, pleased to see that the forsythia were in bloom and the azaleas were loaded with buds. She was digging for the keys when she heard her name. Startled, she whirled around and saw the bag lady cutting across the yard from the vacant house next door. It was a moment before she remembered the woman's name.

"Angie! Hello again. What are you doing here?"

The seamed face beamed in the twilight. "Evening, Lisa. I been waiting for you. I seen your house was empty, but I figgered you'd be comin' back by-and-by."

"You've been waiting for me? Why?"

Angie pushed her cart onto the sidewalk. "I got something here," she said, methodically unpacking the cart and depositing her belongings on the bottom step. "I seen that article about you, and I said to myself, 'Well, Angie, Lisa, she's bound to know how to get this satchel to the man it belongs to.'" Removing a layer of newspaper, she extracted a battered old briefcase and set it at Lisa's feet. "See, there's his 'nitials. J.C.M. That article about you said the man that was hurt so bad, his name was Mallory."

Astonishment paralyzed Lisa's tongue. She stared at the briefcase in amazement. "You've had it all the time?"

"Yes'm. I didn't steal it, honest." She described, in meticulous detail, how it had come into her possession. "Ain't even opened it. Course, I couldn't. It's locked."

Lisa picked it up, still incredulous. "We've been looking all over for this! Angie, thank you! I can't tell you how much this means."

Embarrassed and pleased, Angie shifted from one foot to the other. "I felt kinda bad I didn't remember you right off that day you was so nice and gave me breakfast. I don't think as fast as some, and by the time I recollected where I'd seen you before, you was gone."

"And you've been here ever since? Oh, Angie!" Lisa looked from the briefcase to the bag lady and back, anxious to share her discovery with Jess, but loathe to walk away and leave Angie to the Fates. "Come on," she said, picking up the woman's possessions and placing them in the cart. "You're coming with me."

"Where?"

The question brought Lisa up short and made her stop and think. She couldn't take Angie to Security Specialists. Jess would understand, but she doubted anyone else there would. The loft was a better idea, except that she felt an obligation to check with Kitty first and Kitty had no phone in her car. Greenhaven was her only option. They wouldn't be pleased to see the bag lady, but Lisa was willing to bet that they would handle the situation with decorum.

"I was on my way to the hospital to see Mr. Mallory. He isn't allowed many visitors, so I'm not sure they'll let you go into his room, but there's a very comfortable lounge on his floor. They have coffee and tea for visitors and you could wait for me there."

Angie turned her head to look at her sidewise. "How they gonna feel about somebody like me sitting up there big as brass? I'm clean—I mean, I washed up this morning—they got a hose connected to the back of that house there—but I'm not dressed proper."

She had a point, but Lisa was moved at Angie's show of pride in herself. Her coat was ragged and frayed, and several toes protruded through her worn moccasins. She looked what she was, a street person who had to make do with what she had. Still, she had waited almost a week to place in Lisa's hands the answer to a mystery that might have remained unsolved had she not been so persistent. For that alone, she deserved far more than a simple thank-you.

"Let's see what we can do," Lisa said. Unlocking her front door, she carried the cart into the foyer and sat Angie down on the steps. "I'll be right back."

She removed her suitcase from the trunk of the car, took it into the house and opened it. Angie was short, perhaps five-two, so they'd have to improvise. "What size shoes do you wear?" she asked.

The bag lady chewed on her bottom lip, her eyes wandering into corners. "I forget," she admitted timidly.

It really didn't matter, Lisa decided. Angie's feet were smaller than hers and that's all that counted. Extracting a pair of jeans, a knit pullover, her long red cardigan and her running shoes, she handed them to Angie and showed her the downstairs powder room. Ten minutes later, Lisa examined the transformation. The layer of castoffs Angie usually wore had masked a very thin body, so the clothes were a much better fit than either had expected. Lisa rolled the bottoms of the jeans to a more appropriate length, being careful to hide the chafed skin of the woman's swollen ankles, and nodded. "Not bad, Angie."

"I'll do?"

"You'll do just fine. Now we'd better hurry." Lisa opened the door.

"What about my cart?"

"We'll leave it and my suitcase," she said, hurrying back to shove both into a storage space under the steps. "There. They're out of sight and safe until we come back. Are you ready? Your chariot awaits."

"My char'ot," Angie repeated, following Lisa out. "I declare the nicest things have happened to me since I met up with you. That breakfast, then a whole week practically with a roof over my head, and now I'm about to go for a ride. Life ain't bad a'tall, if you fix your mind to be satisfied with the little things.''

But Lisa wasn't really listening. With the problem of Angie's attire settled, her focus was keyed on the well-worn briefcase in the back seat. Now that the moment of enlightenment was only minutes away, she wasn't certain she wanted to know what it contained. There were times when having all the answers did more harm than good. Did it really matter now why Mal had wanted to see her? Was this a case where ignorance was truly bliss?

By the time she reached Greenhaven, Lisa had almost convinced herself that she neither wanted nor needed to know the secrets the briefcase contained. If Jess wanted to satisfy his curiosity, fine, but she would ask him to keep whatever he learned to himself. It seemed a safer route. She had been through enough.

The receptionist gave Angie no more than a puzzled glance as she passed out their visitors' badges, perhaps because there was a good deal of traffic through the lobby. Aware that the bag lady wouldn't know what to do with it, Lisa pinned her own to her jacket, nodding for the elderly woman to follow suit. Angie's eyes were like bluebottle flies, darting here and there, trying to see everything. Lisa led her to the elevators at a leisurely pace, giving her time to take it all in. But on the way up, Angie's brow was wrinkled with a frown of intense concentration.

''Something wrong?'' Lisa asked her.

''No'm. Just somebody I think I seen before, I just can't recollect where. It'll come to me. This is a hospital? Sure don't look like one. Don't smell like one, neither.''

The elevator door opened and Lisa led Angie to the right, to the lounge for the use of family and friends of patients on this floor. Refreshments were laid out—coffee, tea, cookies and petit fours. Lisa filled a plate with several of each and poured a cup of coffee for her. After making certain that Angie was comfortable and could see people coming and going, she left her, saying that she would check on her soon.

"Take your time. And your young man is coming? What's he look like, so I'll know him when I see him."

Lisa described Jess, then hurried away with the briefcase. Stopping at the nurses' station, she made them aware of Angie's presence and asked that she be summoned if a problem arose. Then she requested and received what news there was of Mal's condition. She wanted to know what to expect.

Mal was not paralyzed, but his muscles had atrophied to such an extent that it would be a good while before he was ambulatory. A more troublesome problem appeared to be damage to the speech and language centers of his brain. He would have to learn to speak again. Angie was all but forgotten as Lisa approached Mal's room, her palms sweating in a display of nerves. The curtains covering his viewing window were closed. She stood outside of the door for several seconds before getting the courage to go in.

The room was less cluttered. Several mechanisms had been removed and a second visitor's chair had been added. The head of the bed was elevated and Mal lay boxed in by pillows to prevent him from slipping to either side. The contents of a pair of IV bags still dripped into his arm, but there were no wires snaking from under his gown, and the overhead monitors were silent.

He appeared to be asleep. Lisa placed the briefcase in the chair nearest the door and approached the bed. "Mal?" she said softly.

His eyes opened immediately, wide brown eyes that blazed with life. They dominated his face, imbuing his features with such dynamism that there seemed little resemblance to the comatose patient she had visited.

"Hello. I hope I didn't wake you. I'm Lisa."

There'd been no need to introduce herself. His recognition of her was obvious, a flaring of nostrils, a dilation of pupils, even before she had given her name. He began an intense scrutiny of her face, his lips parted, his breathing ragged and uneven.

Pulling the chair closer to the bed, she sat down and took his hand. It was warm, at first flaccid, in her grasp. Then his fingers curled around hers, with little or no strength in them, but Lisa was heartened that he could respond at all.

"Jess will be here soon. We just came back from Lockwood and he had to—" She stopped, seeing a change in his eyes. Uncertain how to interpret it, she tried to figure out what to say, how to say it. "Mal, I know it'll be a while before you'll be talking, but do you understand me? Not that I've said anything much, but has it made sense? Can you move your hand if it has?"

His fingers twitched around hers.

"Good. I have a lot to tell you. If you start to overload or get sleepy, close your eyes and I'll shut up. The first thing you should know is that what happened to you is my fault. I witnessed a murder involving my parents when I was a child. It looks now as if the couple who helped cover up the murder hired someone to kill me, only the killer mistook Maria for me, and you got caught in the cross fire. I'm so sorry."

He had the most eloquent eyes Lisa had ever seen, radiating bewilderment, horror, fury, forgiveness, with the clarity of the spoken word.

"I'll tell you what I've found out in the past month. Some of it will be old news to you. I saw the yearbook you left at my house, so I know you knew my mother and perhaps my father. I assume that's what you came to tell me, except that you may not know the ending. Are you ready for all this?"

He squeezed her fingers.

Lisa talked for ten minutes straight, watching various emotions parade through his eyes. She told him the story of her life with Eloise Gillette as if it had happened to someone else, keeping her tone as neutral as she could, filtering out the hurt and bitterness. To her utter astonishment, tears filled his eyes rather than hers and spilled over onto his cheeks. She wiped his face, reflecting on how much it helped to talk to him about it.

She approached the subject of her father's murder with a certain wariness. This would be fresh news for him and she could not be sure how he'd react.

"Did you know my father?" she asked. His fingers fluttered under hers. "Jess thought you might have. He's dead, Mal. My mother killed him." Mal's jaw dropped with shock. "I saw it all and until a few days ago had blocked it and the entire nine months I spent in Lockwood out of my memory."

This time it wasn't quite as easy to maintain emotional distance as she sketched the events in the Schefelds' basement. Even after bringing him up-to-date with the discovery of the body, Lisa was plagued with the persistent feeling that there was one tiny piece of the puzzle that still eluded her, something she'd forgotten. But Mal's reaction was one of such intense agitation that she could not give it the attention it deserved. His head wobbled from side to side in a parody of shaking it to indicate a negative response.

Alarmed, she got up and came around to the other side of the bed to retrieve the call button. "Do you want a nurse?" she asked.

There was no answer. He lay perfectly, frighteningly, still, but his eyes were riveted on the briefcase in the chair, previously hidden from view because she'd been sitting with it behind her back. "This is yours, isn't it?"

Yes.

Lisa was stuck. She had not changed her mind about opening it. "Mal," she said, sitting down again. "I'm in love, deeply in love, with Jess. We plan to be married." For the first time, an emotion escaped the boundaries of his eyes and his mouth twitched in a travesty of a smile. "Jess feels that whatever you have in that briefcase will explain why you wanted to see me. I have to be honest. I'm scared. I don't want to know what's in there if it will spoil what I have with Jess."

His mouth opened and emitted something between a gurgle and a groan. He scowled, his face flushing with frustration.

"Hush," she said and stroked his cheek. "Will the contents of your briefcase have any effect on my relationship with Jess? Just use your hand."

His gaze locked with hers for a long moment, his fingers limp in her palm.

"Cross your heart?" Lisa said, and he gripped her with more strength than he'd displayed before. "Well, I'll try to pick the lock, but if I can't, maybe Jess can pry it open when he gets here."

A few seconds of poking and jiggling with a nail file and the snaps flew upward. Lisa opened the briefcase. It was jammed with file folders and a small photograph album. She removed the folders, the writing on the tabs faded into oblivion. Opening the first, she placed it near his side. It held a large sheet of paper folded several times. She opened it carefully, and spread it out, feeling her eyes widen. "My dollhouse! These are the plans of my collapsible dollhouse! I was devastated when I found out it had been destroyed. How did you get it?"

He looked at her, a smile in his eyes.

Feeling silly that she had asked, she refolded it and put it away. The item on top in the second folder was a copy of the November article from the *Washington Post*.

"Jess and I guessed you'd seen this," she said, setting it aside to pick up the next item, a ten-by-thirteen envelope containing snapshots, which spilled out onto the covers.

"Mom!" Lisa whispered, her mother's face looking up at her from a dozen different photographs, some in color, a few in black-and-white. This was the mother she'd never known—smiling impishly, seductively, her eyes alight. *My* eyes, Lisa realized, hazel with the dark ring around each iris. In fact, she bore a startling resemblance to her mother as a young woman. If she was to believe the photographs, Eloise—Ellen, Lisa corrected herself silently—had been so much softer in the days before her daughter's birth.

One large photo lay facedown. She turned it over and smiled, enchanted. This was a studio portrait, the work of a professional who had used a bit of trick photography. Her mother was in profile, a classic beauty, her hair pulled back into an elaborate chignon. It was a truly lovely presentation, doubly so because the photographer had printed the profile not once, but twice, positioned so that they faced each other.

"Oh, Mal, this is beautiful! How old was she here?" Flipping it over, she read the flowing hand in the lower corner—Ellen and Ellene, 1959.

Dumbfounded, Lisa slumped back in the chair. "Mom was a *twin*? She never told me, never said one word! How could she keep something like that from me?" Filled with rising anger, she bit her lip. She could vent her spleen later. There was no point in upsetting Mal.

With a deep, calming breath, she turned her attention to the yellowing article encased in a plastic sleeve. It was dated May

2, 1964. Still wrestling with her temper, Lisa scanned the print and came perfectly erect. She started again from the beginning.

> Federal authorities report no new leads in the April 24 abduction of the daughter of J. Clifford and Ellene Mallory, residents of the Eden Gallery apartments. Three-year-old Elisabeth Anne Mallory was allegedly taken from the Wee People nursery school on Fredo Lane. F.B.I. spokesman John Casp theorizes that . . .

Lisa, immobile with shock, closed her eyes, hearing the singsong chant that had distracted her that night in the police station.

> My last name is Mallory;
> I live in Eden's Gallery . . .

Her heart racing, Lisa perused the official versions of how the feat had been accomplished as parents came to pick up their children. There were several witnesses to the fact that a woman, assumed to be the mother of the child, had departed with Elisabeth. It was not until Ellene Mallory arrived that the abduction came to light. Mrs. Mallory's identical twin, Ellen Girard, was wanted for questioning.

> Elisabeth Anne Mallory is thirty-seven inches tall, weighs thirty-one pounds. She has hazel eyes, long, dark brown hair and a distinctive port-wine stain resembling a butterfly on the nape of her neck. She may be carrying a fold-up dollhouse, constructed by her father. Anyone seeing a child matching the description is asked to . . .

Shock waves battered and buffeted her as the full picture emerged. The woman she had known as Eloise Gillette had been her mother's identical twin. Jess had said that Mal's wife had died years before—her real mother, Ellene. And Mal . . .
She opened her eyes. "*You're* my father!"

His hand quivered and his palm turned upwards in an open invitation for hers. Tears stood in his eyes again. Speechless, Lisa eased her hand into his and their fingers locked and held.

"Dad. I can't believe it! And all this time...why? How could she do such a thing?" Lisa whispered.

"Because she was a bitch." A tall blond nurse stood in the doorway, an ugly snub-nosed pistol in her hand. "So this is the man who hired the private investigator that came to get you. And I almost killed him. What irony."

Slowly Lisa came to her feet. "Eddie's wife!"

"We meet again. And it's Mrs. Sheffield to you. Sara Margaret Sheffield." Her eyes were ice-blue diamonds. "The widow of the late E. Stewart Sheffield, who killed himself this afternoon, thanks to you. The police came, asking questions about an old homicide, strictly routine, they said, and could you tell us where you lived in 1969?" She might have been reciting a poem, her voice beautifully modulated, every syllable crisply enunciated.

"It's your father's fault, you know. Eloise was the lively twin, or so she said, the one men always preferred to her sister, except for him. She hated him for that, and hated you because you were their child."

Lisa shoved aside fear for her safety. She had to get the woman out of the room. She couldn't let Sara hurt her father. She'd almost gotten him killed once. She would not let it happen again. "You hired Youngblood?" she asked.

"A mistake," she spat. "He was top gun in our neighborhood gang in the old days, and I was his girl. I knew he was going places, so I kept tabs on him, just in case. I understand he's dead now. Pity. He was supposed to be a professional. That's a laugh."

"But why?" Lisa asked, positioning herself between Sara and her father. "It was twenty years ago! I didn't even remember what happened, and wouldn't have, if you had let things alone."

"How could I know that? Besides, you were supposed to be dead. I *saw* the car go up! I watched it burn."

Lisa felt her knees begin to give way as the last piece of the puzzle dropped into place. "*You* caused the accident! Someone kept bumping us from behind until we ran off the road! It was *you*!"

"Yes! You and the slut who called herself your mother could ruin all my plans for Stewart. He was going places, whether he wanted to or not, and I wasn't going to chance either of you turning up later to divulge his one indiscretion. I was so sure you were dead until I saw that picture of you in the *Post* last Thanksgiving. The spitting image of Eloise. Showing up just when we were about to hit the top. You had to die."

"But it's all over now," Lisa said softly. "You said your husband's dead. Why make things worse for yourself?"

"What difference does it make?" she asked harshly. "What am I without Stewart? What's left for me? Nothing. You two ruined everything. I'd kill your dear old dad if I had enough bullets." She yanked Lisa away from the bed. "Come on. You're going to walk with me to the elevator. One wrong move and you're dead where you stand, along with anyone else who interferes. According to Kitty, who has kindly supplied me with anything I needed to know about you, you're the kind who'll go out of her way to see that no one gets hurt. Lovely. Now *move*!"

Lisa offered no resistance. The most important thing was to get Sara out of the room before Jess came. After that, she'd watch for a chance to do something. Sara was a good six feet tall, even in the low-heeled shoes of a nurse, but Lisa would be fighting for her life, with youth and agility on her side.

They walked slowly to the intersection of the T, past the nurses' station, the gun pressed firmly in her ribs. She saw Angie start to rise and shook her head tightly, hoping, praying that the bag lady would be smart enough to take the hint.

"You're behaving quite nicely," Sara whispered in her ear as they waited for the elevator. "Just keep it up."

The door opened. The car was empty. Sara pushed the button for the subbasement.

Angie stood by the elevator, watching the indicator pass 2, 1, B, and stop at SB. What did SB mean? Where was Lisa going? Any why'd she shake her head? Troubled, Angie sucked on her bottom lip, wondering what to do.

She hadn't liked the looks of that nurse. It was the same one she'd seen downstairs sitting in the corner, the same one she knew she'd . . . Squeezing her eyes shut, she thought as hard as she could. Where had she seen that nurse before? Wasn't at the hospital they'd put her in after the judge took Baby Girl. So where . . .

Bless Paddy, that was the same woman who had come to Lisa's house three, maybe four, times. She'd peeked in the windows and had walked all around the place, sneakylike. Angie hadn't liked her looks then and liked them even less now. She had to find out what was going on, but how?

The elevator doors opened and a tall man with dark eyes stepped off, a good-looking rascal. Lean as a bean pole, but not skinny, no sir. He had to be Lisa's friend.

"'Scuse me, mister," she said quickly. "Be you Lisa's young man?"

He stopped, surprised. "Yes, I am. And you are—"

"Just Angie, but I'm kinda worried. She went with this nurse down to SB, but she shook her head at me like I shouldn't say anything to her and she was white as a sheet. And the nurse, she's the one has been to Lisa's house peeking in her windows and I don't claim to be too smart about some things, but I declare, I got a feeling she don't mean to do Lisa any good."

Jess stared at her, trying to make sense of what she said. He was sure this was the bag lady Lisa had met, but what the hell was she doing here? It occurred to him it might be wise to ask.

"I had the gentleman's satchel, the one that's so bad hurt, and I waited at Lisa's house to give it to her and she brung me here with her, only now that nurse took her down to SB holding onto her arm and—"

He still wasn't certain what was going on, but the churning in his gut told him to find out as quickly as he could.

"Wait here," he said tersely. He left her and hurried to the nurses' station. "What's in the subbasement?" he asked the clerk.

"Oh, hello, Mr. Hampton. Isn't it wonderful about Mr. Mallory?"

"Yes. What's in the subbasement? Hurry, please, it may be important."

Perhaps catching the urgency in his voice, she said, "Sanitary engineering, the incinerator, the power plant. It's off-limits except to authorized personnel."

So the bag lady was right. Lisa had no reason to go to the subbasement. There was no time to verify the identity of the nurse, no time to work out how, if the woman was Peg Schefeld, she had wound up here. "Call security and get someone down to the subbasement immediately," he ordered. "A woman's life is in danger." Leaving the nurse gaping, Jess ignored the elevator and pelted through the door of the stairwell. He had to find Lisa.

"All I had going for me," Sara said, pulling Lisa along the long, dimly lit hall, "was a good brain and a better body. I used them to go from the tenements to that backwater college in Virginia. I used them to snare a decent husband and to get him out of education and into the political scene. He refused to run for office, so I saw to it that he became invaluable to the ones who'd already made it. Once he joined the Crandall Consortium, we'd have had the ear of the White House! Power! We were almost there! Then you showed up. Now it's all gone, because of an egotistical woman who couldn't stand the fact that a man she'd met first preferred her twin to her. I should have climbed down off the road and checked to be sure you were both dead. But I didn't. Now it's Stewart who's dead and you're going to pay for it."

Lisa didn't bother to argue. Sara was as mad in her way as Eloise had been. Thank God Jess hadn't arrived. He'd have tried to interfere and Sara would have shot him. She would not be responsible for his death. This time she was on her own.

Sara hustled her to a door near the end of the hall and pressed her ear against the frosted glass of the top half. Shoving Lisa into the room ahead of her, she hit the light switch as she followed her in and closed the door on a makeshift lounge with several sagging couches and easy chairs. Lockers lined one wall, and a bookcase crammed with ragged issues of men's magazines ran the length of a second wall. One long table was littered with the debris from someone's lunch. The hand-lettered sign beside the door in the rear wall reminded all who entered to wash their hands before leaving.

Sara waved Lisa to the corner between the bookshelf and the table and yanked open the door to be sure the bathroom was empty. Satisfied, she closed it. "There's no way out of the john, so don't waste your time thinking it will do you any good. If I hadn't been interrupted by that damned moving van, I could have taken care of you in the warehouse. And Stewart would be alive."

She sat down and glared at Lisa. "You can't imagine how much I will enjoy this. I would dearly love to watch you suffer first—say, a bullet in each knee, then—"

She stopped abruptly, listening, the gun pointed steadily at Lisa. A door had opened and closed with a slam. Footsteps ran along the hall.

"Lisa!"

Jess! Lisa covered her mouth with both hands. She could not, dared not, call out to him. She would not lure him into danger.

Sara got up, covering the distance to the door with two long strides and hit the wall switch. The lights went off, the only re- lief the pale rectangle of filtered light through the frosted glass.

"Lisa Gillette!" His footsteps continued in their direction, his shadow rippling the plane of light as he passed.

Sara's white uniform gleamed faintly in the darkness. "Don't you even breathe," she warned.

"Peg Schefeld! I know you're down here! Give it up! It's all over."

"My name is *Sara*!" the woman hissed into the darkness. "*Sara Sheffield!* How *dare* he call me that!"

Lisa heard the rage in her voice. Could she use it? "What's wrong with Peg?" she asked softly. "Are you ashamed of it, Peggy?" Dropping on all fours, she crawled under the table.

"Don't call me that! I'm Sara now!"

"Peg-gee, Peg-gee," Lisa chanted and edged toward the chair at the far end of the table. The floor was covered with a dark carpet. As long as she stayed under the table, there was less chance that Sara could see her.

"Stop it!" The pale white blur moved from the door to the center of the room. "Where are you!"

This might be the only chance she had. Lisa lunged for the woman's legs, wrapping her arms around them, and Sara toppled over her, the gun going off with a report that echoed like a cannon in the small room.

Jess, at the far end of the hall, whirled around. "Lisa!" Oh, God. The shot had come from one of the rooms he'd passed, on the right, he thought. A small-caliber gun. Not that it mattered. At close range, it killed just as effectively as a Magnum. If Lisa was hurt . . .

Stooping, he duck-walked, retracing his steps, keeping low enough so that he couldn't be seen through the translucent glass in the doors. He paused at the first, the second, the third, listening. Nothing. Nearing the fourth, he detected the sounds of a scuffle. Rising to his feet, he hugged the wall and stopped cold at the sight of the unrelieved darkness on the other side of the door.

Jess stood frozen, perspiration exploding from his pores, bathing him, chilling him. He couldn't, he simply couldn't.

A clatter, a muffled shriek. Jess's body jerked spasmodically, sweat stinging his eyes, blinding him. Lisa. If he didn't act and she died, his life wouldn't be worth living. He had to go in.

Jess scurried to the other side of the door, his heart pounding with such force that it seemed to vibrate through his whole body. Reaching for the doorknob, he turned it, yanked open the door.

"Jess! No!" Lisa screamed.

She was alive! Spurred by the sound of her voice, he dove into the room, colliding with squirming bodies wrestling in the middle of the floor. The door drifted closed, cutting off the light from the hall, but the position of the white uniform was burned onto his retina. He reached for it, grabbing a leg, which kicked out at him with surprising strength. He tried again, but she had moved.

The gun blast pounded against his eardrums, and the stench of cordite filled his nostrils. "Lisa! God, Lisa, where are you?"

"Right here. She missed me." A hand moved up his arm, touched his face. "It's okay, love," Lisa whispered. "Don't move."

She scuttled past him, and a second later light flared around him. He could breathe again. Lisa, her hair awry, a bruise blooming across her cheekbone, crouched at the door, one hand on the switch, the other lifting to point to where Sara Schefeld lay crumpled in the corner, a pool of dark red staining the nurse's cap and the carpet under her head.

"She said she couldn't shoot Mal because she hadn't brought enough bullets—one for me, one for her. She wasted the first one."

Jess started to his feet but his legs wouldn't cooperate. He lowered himself to the floor, coming to rest with his back against a sofa. Lisa dropped beside him and pulled him into her arms, feeling his body quivering like the plucked string of a guitar. She held him, smoothing his hair, her lips against his temple until the uncontrollable trembling abated.

"You did it, Jess. You came in for me."

"I almost didn't, Lisa."

"But in the end, you did, and that's what counts. Oh, I love you, Jess."

She got to her knees and kissed him gently, her hands holding his face. It was a kiss that made no demands, aroused no passion, a simple acknowledgment of how dear he was to her. For Jess, it carried every bit as much weight as any they'd exchanged in Lockwood. This was the woman for whom he had leaped into the jaws of his most virulent demon. This was the woman he loved.

His strength returning, he glanced back at Sara's body. "Where are the guards? They should be here by now. How'd you run into her anyway? And what about the bag lady?"

"It's a long story. The most important thing is that Angie brought us Mal's briefcase and I opened it. The woman I thought was my mother was my mother's twin. She kidnapped me. Jess, Mal's my father."

"What!"

"She took me to get back at him for falling in love with her twin."

Jess's gaze raked her features. "From the very first night, you reminded me of someone. Damn it, it was right under my nose all the time. The photo of his wife. Mal kept it on the dresser in his bedroom. You have your mother's eyes."

"Yes, I do. Jess, my name is Elisabeth Ann Mallory."

"Elisabeth Mallory. My God, what's next?"

"Elisabeth Mallory Hampton, that's what's next, after you've gone upstairs and asked my father for my hand."

Epilogue

... after all those years of looking for her. Of course, that was long before they started printing pictures of missing children on milk cartons.''

"Lordy, she talks a heap, don't she?" Angie said, removing Lisa's veil for her.

Lisa chuckled, knowing precisely what she meant. "She does indeed. You'd think she'd have learned something by now."

Kitty had a captive audience in Barbara Trainor now obviously pregnant, and was making the most of it, while Willborn, Mal's agent, leaned against a kitchen counter, watching Kitty with a bemused expression. "The problem was," Kitty rambled on, "Mal's private detective friend had left a message that he was on his way to Portsmouth with a strong lead, and that was the last anyone heard from him. Then Lisa's mother began to fail, and he nursed her for a year before she died. Then came Vietnam and by the time he got back, the trail was cold, as the saying goes."

"What a story," Barbara said. "But why, after Mal saw the article, didn't he just come directly to Lisa?"

"Just because she was a ringer for his late wife," Willborn explained, "was no guarantee that she was his daughter. He had to be sure. The article gave him a name and background information from which to start from this end. If he could find proof that Lisa had lived in the Portsmouth area before turning up at the orphanage in Delaware, it was almost a certainty. Even then, he couldn't be sure how she'd receive him.''

"Imagine how you'd feel," Kitty said, pouring on the dramatics, "if a strange man turned up saying you weren't who you thought you were because your mother wasn't your mother and—''

Lisa had had enough. "Kitty, why don't you check to make sure the punch bowls are filled?''

"Oh. Yes, I should. Alec could drink one by himself. Come on, sweetie.'' She bustled from her kitchen, dragging Willborn with her, and Barbara, dazed, gave a sigh of relief.

"I better go keep an eye on her," Angie said, scowling. "Alec sent her in here because she was driving him crazy. She's sweet as she can be, Kitty is, but I swear, she can frazzle a body's nerves.'' She scurried out, the skirt of her new dress billowing in the breeze.

Barbara stood. "Let me go spell Mama with the kids. Swear to God, Lisa, you have the most fascinating friends. I wouldn't have missed this for the world.''

The wedding had been a simple affair, in spite of Kitty's campaign for a full-scale, no-holds-barred production. Lisa had stuck to her guns, agreeing to use the Joyners' huge backyard for the ceremony and reception, on the condition that she had complete control of everything. She wanted only the people who mattered most to her, Jess and Mal to attend, and that included Angie, whom Kitty had all but adopted, searching for a group home that met her high standards and in which Angie was now a permanent resident.

Jess stuck his head in the back door with a smile for his new bride. "Are you coming back out or what, Mrs. Hampton? Nobody gets to eat any of that blasted cake until we cut it and make a mess trying to feed each other.''

A bubble of happiness filled Lisa's chest. "Coming, Mr. Hampton. How's Dad holding up?''

"Grinning like a Cheshire cat. Talking a little, too, to the nuns. They're having a reunion. I can't understand why it never occurred to us to check to see if he'd gone to St. Mary's.''

"It wouldn't have done any good. Sister Catherine says once they heard his story, they agreed there was a strong possibility he was my father, but felt it was his place to tell me, not theirs. They couldn't go back on their word unless Mal had died."

Lisa stepped out onto the Joyners' deck and waved to her father. She had delayed the wedding until he'd be able to walk or ride beside her down the aisle, and with that as his goal, Mal had managed it in three months, using a walker. His speech was slow and labored, but he answered the judge readily enough when asked who was giving the bride away. And, doubling as best man, had handed the ring to Jess without dropping it.

Since his move to a Virginia rehabilitation hospital, Mal had come a very long way. Being a realist, he'd accepted the invitation to live with his daughter and her husband with good grace, but was determined to be as independent as possible by the time the new house was to be ready in September. He was already struggling with the outline of his next book, the story of a man's twenty-six-year search for his abducted daughter.

Lisa and Jess cut the cake, and she put some in his mouth as delicately as she could. He returned the favor adeptly, smiling as she licked a bit of icing from a corner of her lips.

"You should have let me do that for you," he said, his eyes burning into hers. "On second thought, I guess you shouldn't have or I'd have disgraced myself and my bride."

"The honeymoon doesn't begin until we reach St. Croix," she reminded him. "Sun, ocean, sand, remember?"

"I remember," he said solemnly. "But what do you think of us making a slight detour? I admit to being awfully curious about which of the Zimmermans' twelve cabins might be the honeymoon suite?"

"Do you mean it?" Lisa's eyes glowed. "Oh, Jess, I'd love to start our honeymoon there."

Jess leaned down and kissed her. "Mrs. Hampton, you're on."

*   *   *   *   *

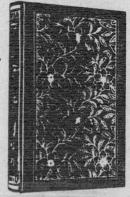

**Double your reading pleasure this fall with two
Award of Excellence titles written by two of
your favorite authors.**

Available in September

DUNCAN'S BRIDE
by Linda Howard
Silhouette Intimate Moments #349

Mail-order bride Madelyn Patterson was nothing like
what Reese Duncan expected—and everything
he needed.

Available in October

THE COWBOY'S LADY
by Debbie Macomber
Silhouette Special Edition #626

The Montana cowboy wanted a little lady at his
beck and call—the "lady" in question saw
things differently....

These titles have been selected to receive a special
laurel—the Award of Excellence. Look for the
distinctive emblem on the cover. It lets you know
there's something truly wonderful inside! DUN-1